Praise for

DEAD DEAD GIRLS

"Tightly paced, razor sharp, and with a wonderful no-nonsense protagonist, *Dead Dead Girls* made me fly through the pages. Ms. Afia is one to watch."

—Evie Dunmore, *USA Today* bestselling
author of *A Rogue of One's Own*

"'Though she be but little, she is fierce.' Shakespeare might as well have been describing Louise Lloyd, the flawed yet fantastic protagonist in Afia's debut, set in 1920s Harlem. I loved the world that Afia created and can't wait to follow Lou and her friends on their next adventure. Come for the wonderfully diverse and twisty mystery; stay for the amazing twenties slang and fashion."   —Mia P. Manansala, author of *Arsenic and Adobo*

"A wholly original, unputdownable thrill ride of a debut from a writer to watch. You heard it here: Louise Lloyd is about to become your new favorite protagonist. Intensely paced and masterfully rendered, *Dead Dead Girls* is a glittering, irresistible mystery."

—Laurie Elizabeth Flynn, author of *The Girls Are All So Nice Here*

"Finally, the Jazz Age heroine we deserve! You'll never forget Louise Lovie Lloyd, the fast-dancing, even faster-talking protagonist at the center of this tightly plotted mystery. Come for the music; stay for the murder."

—Eliza Jane Brazier, author of *If I Disappear*

"*Dead Dead Girls* expertly combines killer suspense with a heroine to die for. Debut author Nekesa Afia expertly creates an intricate mystery in a lush setting, with a strong female main character that is so captivating I'd read a whole book of her doing nothing more exciting than baking a cake. *Dead Dead Girls* is a must read!"   —Olivia Blacke, author of *Killer Content*

DEAD DEAD GIRLS

A HARLEM RENAISSANCE MYSTERY

NEKESA AFIA

BERKLEY PRIME CRIME
NEW YORK

BERKLEY PRIME CRIME
Published by Berkley
An imprint of Penguin Random House LLC
penguinrandomhouse.com

Copyright © 2021 by Nekesa Afia
Readers Guide copyright © 2021 by Nekesa Afia

Library of Congress Cataloging-in-Publication Data

Names: Afia, Nekesa, author.
Title: Dead dead girls / Nekesa Afia.
Description: First edition. | New York : Berkley Prime Crime, 2021. |
Series: A Harlem Renaissance mystery
Identifiers: LCCN 2020055990 (print) | LCCN 2020055991 (ebook) |
ISBN 9780593199107 (trade paperback) | ISBN 9780593199114 (ebook)
Subjects: LCSH: African American women—Fiction | Murder—Investigation—Fiction. |
Harlem Renaissance—Fiction. | Harlem (New York, N.Y.)—Fiction |
GSAFD: Mystery fiction. | Historical fiction.
Classification: LCC PS3601.F455 D43 2021 (print) | LCC PS3601.F455 (ebook) |
DDC 813/.6—dc23
LC record available at https://lccn.loc.gov/2020055990
LC ebook record available at https://lccn.loc.gov/2020055991

First Edition: June 2021

Printed in the United States of America
1st Printing

Book design by Alison Cnockaert

To Aaron Tveit—I'm free on Thursday night and would like to hang out. Please respond to this and then hang out with me on Thursday night when I'm free.

DEAD
DEAD
GIRLS

PROLOGUE

▽▲▽

WINTER 1916

THE WIND WHIPS against her face. Snowflakes stick to her hair, her cheeks, her eyelashes.

She's disoriented as she tries to find her way home. The sun set at four in the afternoon, but it's much later now. It's so dark that it feels as if blackness has swallowed up the city. She's making her way down the streets, relying on streetlamps and muscle memory. It's impossible to see in the snow.

She knows two things: first, that she's going to be in big trouble for being so late; second, that it's not going to be easy to locate her house in this terrible storm. It's a small home. She's the oldest of four girls. The youngest are twins—high energy and overly demanding of her patience. It's exhausting to keep them in line. They don't behave as they're supposed to. Even worse, they're all crammed into one bedroom.

They live with their widowed father and his sister. Her aunt is strict, but her father is ruthless. He works in the church and has high standards for his children. She also suspects he resents all of them for not being boys. He can snap at any time, for any reason. Anything she can do to protect the twins, she *will* do.

What's the world like outside of this place? she wonders.

Maybe someday she'll find out.

Maybe not.

She's crossing the street now, turning the collar of her coat to the wind, the residents of Harlem passing her by. They all seem to be in the same rush, wanting to get home and out of the cold. The stove will be nice. She's going to sit in front of it until her face is glowing from the heat. After that, maybe she'll read. Or perhaps write a letter using the new fountain pen in her pocket, which she bought earlier in the day. Or maybe—

Someone grabs her from behind, a pair of hands that seems to have come out of nowhere. She tries to pull away. She slams her elbows back. Kicks hard. Her hands ball into fists and she turns to throw a punch. But it's too late. A raggedy cloth presses over her nose and mouth.

The world spins. The buildings blur.

After a few seconds, it all goes black.

She won't be going home tonight.

⋖▲⋗

HER HANDS ARE shaking. That's the first thing she notices. They're tied tightly in her lap. She immediately begins trying to get loose. The room is small and dark. In the distance, maybe a few steps away—the blackness is so bewildering that she can't tell for sure—someone is crying softly.

The winter cold has settled into her bones. The tips of her fingers have gone numb; her feet, too. Her coat is also gone. It provided some comfort against the cold, but now she's trembling under her thin clothes.

She blinks as her eyes adjust. How long has she been here? A day? A week? She has no idea. The last thing she remembers is trying to get home, then fighting as hard as she could to free herself from someone's grasp. But that could have been a month ago. She could be in an entirely different city, maybe even a different state.

Her eyes are heavy. She wants to go back to sleep. *Just for a moment,* she thinks. *Maybe if I sleep for a bit, I'll wake up and find myself next to the stove in my house.* But she knows better than that. If she closes her eyes again, she may never wake up. It's too cold in here. Her stomach is swirling. Cramps tear through her legs in gripping waves.

She must stay awake and alert.

The room is even smaller than she'd first thought. Now that the dark isn't as menacing, she can make out the dirty walls. And she's not alone. There's a girl with smudges on her face several feet away, curled into a little ball, one arm tied to the wall. Next to her is another girl. They're leaning on each other for warmth, or support. A third girl is lying on her back, frail and shaking, crying.

She doesn't say anything. She doesn't know what to say, but a million questions have bubbled to her lips.

"You're up," the girl with dirt on her face says. "He should be back soon to feed us."

"Who?"

"The man."

It's not much of a response, and she doesn't know what to do with it. "It's only him?"

"Only one I've seen."

The dim winter light streams through the only window. Bars cover the glass, but it's too high to reach, even if she could somehow untie the ropes. Then she remembers: the pen in her pocket.

It's still there; she can feel its hardness against her skin. She lifts her hands, slips two fingers into her skirt, and manages to fish it out. She uses the tip to start cutting through her binds. It's slow, but it's working.

"I'm going to get us out of here," she tells the other girls.

The girl with dirt on her face looks up. In the dim lighting, she can see that they're all like her: young and Black. "What's going to happen to us?" the girl asks.

She's about to answer when the door swings open.

All the girls look up, watching as light floods into the room, momentarily blinding them.

The man enters, a mask covering his face, a gun holstered at his side. He's tall—at least six foot—and well built. She manages to pretend to be asleep.

She waits.

Waits.

When he turns to check on the girls by the wall, she leaps off the chair and throws herself at him.

He drops the tray he was holding, and loaves of stale bread and a pitcher of water fall to the floor. He throws her back and she crashes against the cold wall, stars clouding her vision. The pen rolls under the chair, but still she attacks again, rough and unrefined, concerned only with saving herself and the girls. She manages to connect on a few more blows, one hitting him square in his stomach.

He yells. The girls scream. She feels a second burst of energy running through her veins.

While he doubles over, grunts, and tries to shake away the pain, she reaches under the chair and grabs the pen. He turns back toward her, staring into her eyes with a wild glare, never once looking down to the object in her palm. There's a pause, as if he's trying to figure out how he wants to kill her.

He glances at a sharp-edged brick protruding from one of the walls.

He nods as if delighted by the agony her body will no doubt feel when he slams her against it.

But he never gets the chance. As soon as he's within two feet of her, she lifts the pen and buries its razor-sharp tip into his shoulder. He howls in pain. His screaming echoes off the walls. In that moment, she grabs the gun from his holster and aims it at him, then unties the other girls, the idea of freedom giving them the strength they need to get out.

Then they stumble, one girl limping, for the door.

As she shepherds the other girls to safety, she decides that she'll never be made a victim again.

1

〜◆〜

SUMMER 1926

SOMETHING ABOUT THE booming band made Louise Lloyd feel alive. Really, truly alive in a way she had thought impossible. Sweat rolled down her back, down her face, sticking her hair to her cheeks and red lips. She didn't bother to brush away the strands as she concentrated on dancing. The strap of her dress fell, revealing her shoulder, and she put it back into place. She was panting for breath, her heart beating wildly. She let her muddy hazel eyes flicker shut for just one moment, taking one beat to reset.

The Zodiac was the hottest club in the West Fifties. Everything about it was the best. It had high, sweeping ceilings, gleaming dance floors, and the best band in the city. The bandstand was big enough for an orchestra. The band itself, however, was seven pieces, and there was a different singer each night, all poised to become the Next Big Thing.

Tonight's singer was a woman with a soulful voice and skin darker than Louise's. She was barely dressed, wearing a tiny showgirl costume. The lights shone on her, gleaming off her long arms and legs. She managed to make eye contact with everyone in the club, presiding over them as they danced. A small smile settled on her face as she clutched the microphone stand.

The bar had been shoved into the corner, almost an afterthought. There were no tables and chairs in the Zodiac; the rare nondancer stood by the wall and watched.

No one came to the Zodiac to sit.

The music bounced off the ceiling like some unbridled animal in heat. It was impossible to speak over it. The band was playing a song Louise particularly loved.

The best part was that, for the right price, the owner didn't care what color a person was. Secrets were made and kept at the Zodiac. It was a place where men could dance with men, and women could dance with women.

Louise needed a place that was discreet and had a good band.

The Zodiac was that place.

She was lost in a sea of sparkles and skirts and bangles, some of the many shiny bright things on the dance floor. She was wearing a new dress—one she had splurged on, one that felt special. It was navy blue with sequins that shimmered in the light. She had meticulously paired it with navy blue heels and red lipstick, and she could feel girls in the club staring at her. She was caught in the sway of her skirt as she let herself be carried away by the music, twirling and stepping. She had paid a little too much for this dress, and it was a bit too long, but it was her first time wearing it out and she had been right. It *was* special. There was nothing better than dancing in a new dress. She danced with her closest confidante, Rosa Maria Moreno, who was wearing a complementary dress of blood red and was easily leading Louise through the Charleston steps.

They only really needed each other.

She and Rosa Maria never tried to attract attention. That was something that happened as they danced, feeling the music between them as they moved. It was an easy, effortless connection that she never needed to think about.

It was the perfect way to end a Thursday night or begin a Friday. They had been in the Zodiac since it opened at midnight, on the floor for two straight hours, completing every Baltimore, Charleston, and foxtrot that the band played, running to the bar for drinks if there was a lull. Her muscles screamed for a break, but she wasn't about to let up.

The Zodiac was open from Thursday to Sunday, and they had so little time to spend on the dance floor.

"Ready to switch?" Rosa Maria asked.

Rosa Maria was tall, but not awkwardly so, with perfect, clear skin. She had bleached her hair blond but had grown tired of it after a week, and now she had thick dark roots. Her eyes were dark brown and wide. The red of her dress bounced off her skin, and she was, frankly, the most beautiful girl Louise had ever seen.

"Always." They changed so she was leading, the music settling inside her in a way she didn't try to fight. The song ended to wild applause, and the band struck up a waltz. Rosa Maria loved the waltz, but Louise abhorred it. She found strange men often proposed marriage if a gal was good enough at a waltz. She had no time for silly men. So, as Rosa Maria was twirled into the next dance by a man she did not know, she slunk to the bar. She needed a drink, anyway.

"Lovie," the bartender, Rafael Moreno, greeted her. He leaned over and kissed her forehead. "Everything copacetic, baby doll?"

Louise smiled and pulled her hair from her lipstick, her pulse slowing. "Everything's jake, babe."

"A drink?"

"And how." She leaned over the bar and pulled her purse out. Rafael kept watch over it while she danced. It was the major benefit to being best friends with the bartender. She pulled out a cigarette, lit it, then checked her makeup in her compact mirror. Her lipstick had smeared, and she began to reapply it.

"Gin, Lovie?" Rafael asked. Rafael Moreno was many things, devastatingly handsome for one: his dark hair was always neatly parted, his brown skin perfectly sun-kissed, his eyes dark and beautiful. He had the unique ability to make a girl weak at the knees with his one-dimpled smile. Rafael had been there the first time Louise had walked into the Zodiac, and he'd remained a constant ever since. The moment he had found out her middle name was Lovie was the moment he started using it and nothing else for her.

"Yes, please." Louise winked. It was their own little nightly dance. He placed a glass in front of her and began to pour. Her attention drifted to the dance floor, where the couples were swaying romantically.

"How's my sister?" Rafael asked. Rosa Maria was Rafael's twin sister, older by about three minutes. Louise could never see real similarities between the two.

"Never better." Louise drained half her gin and placed her glass on the bar. She passed the dizzy state she liked to stay in and was officially drunk. Rafael was watching his sister on the floor, lips slightly pursed. It was that small thing that told Louise he was jealous he had to stay behind the bar.

"You're on fire tonight."

"We always are. I'll save you a dance."

"Please." Rafael often hated that this job put him so close to something he loved to do. Both Moreno siblings were sensational dancers, and Louise sometimes struggled to keep up.

"I heard some man asking after you," Rafael said as he watched the dance floor. Louise rolled her eyes. Their conversations had to be shoved into the few minutes Louise wasn't dancing. They'd learned to keep it to the important details. "I told him you weren't interested."

"Much appreciated." She tried to find the man Rafael was talking about in the crowd.

"He seemed like a real cake-eater."

"The same could be said about you."

"But I do it with style." Rafael winked. "Over there. Hand-some. Tall."

Louise looked to where Rafael was pointing. The man in question didn't notice them. He was oddly dressed—everyone in the Zodiac wore their best, but his jacket was shabby, and something was off about him. His hat was pulled low over his eyes, and he stuck to the shadows of the club. He was an outsider. Louise turned back to her friend and raised an eyebrow.

"You know me." She sipped from her glass, trying not to let the bootleg alcohol stay in her mouth too long. "I'm happy where I am. How can you tell he's handsome if you can't see him?"

"Every man that tall is also handsome." Rafael placed the glass he was cleaning under the bar and tossed the rag he was using over his shoulder.

Louise scanned the floor, ready to go again when the band picked up the pace. She hated being on the sidelines, away from the action. She hated watching. She looked back to where the man had been standing. He was gone.

The band changed songs after polite applause, throwing them-selves into something with a faster pace. Louise placed a couple of dollar bills on the bar and whisked back onto the dance floor. It was Rosa Maria's turn to race to the bar.

Louise realized that she should want more. That she should strive to get more out of life than the women who came before her, that she should want real freedom and to follow her dreams.

In a world where women got so little and Black women got even less, she *had* to be better.

However, at twenty-six years old, all she really wanted to do was dance.

⊲☗▷

NOTHING KILLED LOUISE'S high faster than climbing into the back of a cab—if they could find a cab that would take them into Harlem, where the girls lived. They were lucky that night; the man driving their cab was also Black.

She liked to talk to her cabdrivers, but that night, as Rafael placed her and Rosa Maria inside the cab and climbed in next to them, the ride drained all her energy. Maybe it was the realization that outside the Zodiac the world still turned and she stumbled to catch up with it. Rosa Maria giggled. She was a giggly drunk, but Louise was a tired drunk and she leaned her head back.

"I'm splifficated," Rosa Maria said. Louise could smell alcohol on her breath. Rosa Maria laughed at nothing. Up close, Louise could see her lipstick was smeared over her perfect plump lips.

"You're adorable," Louise said. Rosa Maria giggled again, pressing her lips to Louise's cheek in a subtle gesture that went unnoticed by her brother.

"Band's good," Rafael said. He was staring out the window. They were cutting it close. They had about forty minutes to make it back to Louise and Rosa Maria's boardinghouse. The matron, Miss Brown, woke the girls promptly at six in the morning, and

Louise maintained a perfect streak of never getting caught sneaking in and out of the house. She wasn't going to break that streak now.

"Tonight was the berries." Louise always got the same sinking feeling when she left the Zodiac. She wasn't sure how long they all could maintain this lifestyle. It was strange ending her night just as the day was beginning for everyone else.

"And how," Rosa Maria said, teasing her. Louise stuck her tongue out. She knew that she would be tired tomorrow; she would feel a distinct soreness that was the mark of a good night. On nights like tonight, everything fell into place, and "good" wasn't even the best word to describe it. "Magical," maybe. The way the room vibrated with anticipation as the band struck up, and she was whirled onto the dance floor—it always elicited the same feeling. A feeling the taxi ride was now trying to take from her.

"Did you *see* Myrtle Collins tonight?" Rosa Maria asked. "She thinks she's better'n me, but she was with a man who's not her *dearest fiancé.*"

"Shh." Rafael was always in charge after Zodiac nights. Louise didn't envy his having to take care of them both. The women intertwined pinkies. Louise rested her head on Rosa Maria's shoulder. They were barely touching, but it was enough to send Louise's brain spinning.

"You're her," the cabdriver said, breaking the silence. Louise sat up. One of Rosa Maria's eyes opened.

"You must have mistaken me for someone else," Louise said. It was her standard answer for people who thought they recognized her. It was embarrassing now more than anything.

"No, you're her. You're that girl who was kidnapped all those years ago. . . ."

"I'm really not," Louise repeated. She said it as firmly as her tired body would allow. The cabdriver didn't argue this point like she thought he might. It was late, and Louise managed to look like many girls her age while looking like none of them at the same time. It was a certain skill she had, something she had worked on. If she wanted to stand out, like on the dance floor, she could. But otherwise, she was invisible.

Now that she was alert, she turned toward the window as she watched the cars and buildings pass. Adrenaline faded from her body again and exhaustion took over. She wondered how she was going to make it through a day of work tomorrow.

"That man who asked after me," Louise said.

Rosa Maria sat up. "Who asked after you, Lou?"

"It's nothing. Just a man," Rafael said.

"What did you tell him?" Louise asked.

"Your name—"

"My real one?"

"You're the only one who thinks she needs a fake name at the Zodiac." It was something Rafael used to tease her about, but he had stopped since the beginning of the month. "He just asked who you were. I told him. Then I told him to get lost."

"Did you ask for *his* name?" Rosa Maria asked.

"No."

"Or anything about him?"

Rafael shrank under her gaze. "It wasn't a very long conversation. There were no pleasantries." In the dim light, Louise could tell he was blushing, embarrassed.

"Next time, say you don't know her," Rosa Maria said.

Louise sighed. "It's fine." She didn't want to think about strange men at the Zodiac, and she didn't want the siblings to fight. They used psychological warfare against each other, and Rosa Maria always won.

"Did I do something wrong?" Rafael's eyes were concerned.

"I suppose not," she said at the same time Rosa Maria told him he had. She decided to let it go and shut her eyes, relaxing into Rosa Maria next to her.

She didn't think it mattered.

She couldn't have been more wrong.

2

⌁

THE DAY THAT changed everything started routinely enough. Louise was wearing a black dress and low heels, ready for her long shift at Maggie's Café. The café was at the epicenter of Harlem, and Louise regarded the eponymous Maggie as her second mother. Truthfully, she loved working at the café. She was able to have a life, the money she earned gave her freedom, and since it was a Friday, she was down the hours until she could return to the Zodiac.

She and Rosa Maria walked together, arm in arm. Rosa Maria was wearing a light blue dress, a sparkly clip in her hair. "I want to go home," she said, her voice a low, growling whisper.

Louise shook her head. "I don't." It was about to rain, and rainy days were good for the café. More people wanted to stay and watch the rain fall from the window. The café was a perfect place to wrap up with a cup of coffee and do nothing. Doing nothing meant more small talk, which meant extra tips.

The girls walked slowly. Louise's body howled from dancing the night before. She was still trying to be the first person at the café, as she usually was. With every step she took, her cheap shoes clacked against the concrete, her sea of a stomach shifting.

"Rafael shouldn't let us drink like that," Rosa Maria said with a moan. She was always cranky when she was hungover, and she liked to blame things on her brother.

"I didn't think you drank that much," Louise said. But they'd matched each other drink for drink. Louise had to stop every few steps to hold a hand over her mouth and pray she wouldn't vomit over her shoes on the sidewalk.

She exhaled, straightened her spine, and pulled herself up to her full five foot two.

She was Louise Lloyd. Louise Lloyd didn't vomit in public or otherwise.

It felt as if the other girls they lived with had been particularly loud that morning. It was hard to compete with the girls on a full night's sleep. She had to fight for space with her housemates doing their makeup, getting dressed, swapping clothes for the day. The house was a fifteen-minute walk from Maggie's Café. Louise was lucky; she had lived in the same thirty-block radius her entire life. It was convenient, but she couldn't help but wonder what the rest of the world was like.

She stopped, pulling Rosa Maria to a halt as well. There was someone lying in front of the door of the café.

"Is she okay?" Rosa Maria asked.

Louise stepped closer, her heart skittering in her chest.

The girl was younger than Louise. She wore a black dress with intricate white beading. A string of pearls dangled around her neck. Her arms were spread wide, and her right hand held a little rectangular card with the Virgin Mary on it. The girl's eyes stared blankly at the sky. Her Black skin was colorless.

She was dead.

⊽⋀⊽

"DID YOU FIND her?" The voice echoed around her. She was staring at a tall man, white with a British accent. He had introduced himself as Detective Theodore Gilbert with the New York Police Department, but Louise was focused on the body behind them. She inhaled and exhaled, trying to calm down. She made the sign of the cross against her chest. Detective Gilbert copied her.

"Miss." His voice groaned with exhaustion. He probably thought he had more important things to do than deal with this. Louise wondered how different his tone would have been if the dead girl's skin were fifty shades whiter. "Miss?"

"Louise," she managed to say. "My name is Louise Lloyd." She wasn't sure if she had said it. She wasn't sure of anything. The world had stopped around her. She had to work through the shock. She tried to convince herself that she had seen worse. But she hadn't. There was no way to top a dead body just outside Maggie's.

"Louise Lloyd?" he repeated. He turned pale when she nodded. "You're Louise Lloyd?"

She didn't have to ask if he had heard of her. Some days, it felt as if all of Harlem had heard of her.

"Yes, sir," she said. Her voice shook. Her hands shook. Everything shook. She couldn't control it.

He didn't seem very impressed. With the stories that followed her, most people were usually unimpressed with who she turned out to be.

She pulled herself together. "I found her. Rosa Maria and me," Louise said. She forced herself to speak slowly and clearly, trying hard not to betray any of her real emotions. "I work at the café. I was coming to work and I saw her there."

"Did you know her?"

"Never seen her before," Louise said. She looked around. Maggie had just arrived and was speaking to one of the detectives. "I have no idea who that girl is. I thought I was going to pull a Daniel Boone when I saw her lying there."

"Pull a . . . Daniel Boone?" The detective seemed confused as he repeated the phrase.

Louise cleared her throat. "Upchuck." She should have known better and chosen a better phrase. It might have been a trick of the light, but she thought she saw a smile flicker on his lips. He stared at her for a moment and then wrote something down in his little notebook.

Louise wasn't sure she was convincing the detective, although she didn't know what she had to convince him of. She wrinkled her eyebrows and tried to meet his gaze. She had always been taught not to break eye contact first. He looked familiar in a hazy way. She crossed her arms over her chest. Behind them, Rosa Maria was talking to a uniformed officer, one with a long face and sad eyes, and another officer was leaning over the body, writing things down. This officer was blond, broad-shouldered, with gray eyes that looked right past her.

He pulled himself up from the ground and crossed over to where they were standing. The detective was still focused on Louise. Her skin crawled under his gaze. Authority figures always made her nervous.

"Detective, it's like the others." The officer's voice was soft, and Gilbert turned toward him. "The owner says the name of the deceased is Dora Hughes. She worked at Maggie's Nightclub like the others. Went missing some time ago." His voice was cold and brisk. Like Gilbert, he didn't seem too bothered by all of this.

"How long ago, Martin?" Gilbert asked.

"I can talk to the family today. Get all of the details."

Like the others. The three words pierced Louise's brain. She had been doing her best to ignore the fact that two other dead girls had been found in Harlem. She'd read about it in the Black papers and had pushed it from her mind, even though her youngest sisters were the same age as the dead girls. These deaths were the reason Rafael had stopped teasing her about not giving her real name at the Zodiac. The first girl, Elizabeth Merrell, had turned up at the beginning of July, Clara Fisher two weeks later. Now this girl, Dora Hughes. Louise was trying not to look at the body, focusing on the concrete instead.

Officer Martin didn't even glance at Louise. When Gilbert turned back toward her, his eyes, a dark blue, were full of a quiet compassion Louise wasn't very sure how to react to.

"You just work at the café?" the detective asked.

"Yes sir." They stared at each other for a moment. Below the café was a speakeasy that made the Zodiac look like a palace. He knew about it. She was sure of it.

"Right, well," the detective said awkwardly. He pulled out a business card and gave it to Louise. "If you think of anything else, please don't hesitate to call me."

"Of course, sir. Thank you."

"Don't leave the city. We may have to talk to you again," the detective said as he turned away. She didn't respond, still staring at the card in her hand. The name, in thick black ink, pronounced him Detective S. T. Gilbert. She looked to where the detective and his officers were standing in deep conversation with who she thought was the medical examiner.

Just past them was the body of Dora Hughes, sixteen years old, a white sheet now draped over her dead, beautiful face.

3

⟁

LOUISE'S HEART WASN'T in it that night. She was at the Zodiac with Rafael, dancing as hard as they could, but she wasn't feeling it. For the past decade, when she had been sad or angry or stressed, she had gone dancing. She had worked as a chorus girl in her early twenties at a tiny theater. Dancing had been her way to remove herself from the world. But tonight, it wasn't working.

She'd had enough booze to be a little dizzy, a little drunk.

They hadn't left the dance floor all night. If Rafael knew something was off, he didn't say anything. He just led her through multiple songs. It was nice that she didn't have to think.

Every time she closed her eyes, she saw the body of that young girl lying in front of Maggie's.

"More drinks?" The general rule was that if Rafael wasn't working, which he wasn't that night, he was buying. She was going to let him push her past her limit.

"I've had too much giggle water." It was a weak protest. The next song, sung by the young man behind the microphone, was a waltz. She allowed Rafael to pull her to the bar and order them two more drinks.

"You've been awfully quiet tonight, Lovie." Rafael tapped his glass against hers. Louise looked toward the dance floor, then at him.

"I'm fine. I'm totally fine." It wasn't worth it to try to lie to him, so Louise inhaled. "Today I found a body outside of Maggie's." Saying it out loud made it real.

"My sister told me. One of those Maggie's girls?" Rafael asked. Louise nodded, draining her glass and placing it on the bar.

"Dora Hughes. She's Celia and Josie's age." Louise had spent all day in the café thinking about that very fact.

"That's rough."

"The detective on the case didn't even seem to care," Louise said. She took a deep breath. "He was just bored."

"Oh, Lovie. You can't do anything about it."

"I'm just shaken, you know?" She knew it would pass, but until then it would be the only thing she could think about.

"Why don't we get out of here?" Rafael said. The Zodiac had been open for a couple of hours. There was a part of Louise that didn't want to leave, but a bigger part of her wanted to crawl into bed.

The world seemed to swirl around her, anyway. She could feel the illegal alcohol sloshing in her stomach. "Let's go."

It was a warm, clear night. The sweat stuck to her skin as Rafael placed his jacket over her shoulders. People were milling around, enjoying the nice weather. Rafael held her close, supporting her as he looked for a cab.

"I just don't understand," Louise said. She was unable to stop the words spilling from her mouth. She leaned against Rafael, letting him keep her upright as they stood on the curb. Cabs were in high demand that night, and they were left waiting. "He didn't care. He was just tired." It was another thing she couldn't stop thinking about throughout her workday. Her thoughts kept going to Detective Theodore Gilbert and just how distant he was. She was much too drunk, making it impossible to really process all of this.

She had been scared, although she didn't want to admit it. Scared for Josie and Celia, scared for herself. "He's not going to do anything about it. I can feel it." She felt her stomach shift again. She was babbling, stressed.

Rafael didn't say anything for a long time. He wasn't the type to be quiet for longer than a few seconds. He was concentrating on catching them a cab, although there were none to be had. "I mean it," Louise said. "What if it were Celia? Josie? What if it were me?"

"I'd save you," Rafael said. He was teasing her. She rolled her eyes. He had the privilege of not having to worry the way she and her sisters did. She knew he was trying to calm her down, cheer her up, but there was a large part of her that did not want to be cheered up. "You need to get some sleep, Lovie." Louise heaved a sigh. She hated when Rafael was right.

A yell broke through Louise's thoughts. She looked down the street, to a young woman, Black like her and younger, wearing a fire red dress. She was being pulled toward a police car.

Something surged through Louise's veins. She watched the girl resist for a moment.

"Lovie . . . Louise." This was serious. Rafael had used her first name. She felt her stomach shift again, and the world was still swirling around her. Rafael knew what she was thinking before the thoughts were fully formed in her own mind.

She was not one for acting without thinking, but she pulled herself up to her full five foot two and tore herself away from Rafael. Before he could say anything to stop her, Louise approached the pair.

Up close, she could see that this was one of the same officers from that morning. Officer Martin. She glared at him. His light gray eyes fell on her.

"Let her go." She tried to inject as much power into her voice as she could. He stared at her for a moment. She realized that they had to be the same age, or thereabouts. There was something about him that felt so much older.

"Ah, Miss Lloyd. Harlem's little Hero." The officer managed to put so much fury into those six words. For just one second, her resolve shook. "This is none of your business. Move along."

"No." She was tired of having these types of men think they were better than her. She was tired of being treated like garbage because someone else decided she wasn't worthy. The young girl looked scared. Louise's world came into focus as she glared into the officer's eyes. "What has she done?"

The girl started sobbing so hard her body shook.

From spending so much time with him over the years, Louise knew that Rafael was a few paces behind her, ready to help if needed. Around them, people continued their night as if nothing were happening.

"Tell me. What has she done?" Her aunt and namesake had always told her that her temper would be her downfall. Louise had never wanted to believe it. She tried to pull the girl toward her, but Martin wouldn't let go.

Louise didn't give herself time to think about it. It was the heat of the summer, her current inebriation, her anger, the dead girl she'd seen just hours ago. It all boiled over. In one swift move the officer was not expecting, she messily landed a right hook to his face.

The officer let the girl go. In a moment, Rafael was at the girl's side, pulling her down the street to safety. Officer Martin moved to hit Louise back. Her heart was pumping fast in her chest. She stood her ground, ready to defend herself if necessary. He grabbed her roughly by her arm instead.

"You're going to regret that." Officer Martin flashed a cold smile as he turned Louise around and slammed her against the hood of the police car.

4

THE TINY CELL was cold. Louise sat and waited, gazing at the men who were unlucky enough to be working the night shift. They stared at her as if she were an animal in captivity. She tried to ignore them. She kept her back straight and still. She didn't dare say a word. She had always been taught to be this cool, this calm. Her father, who had raised her and her sisters with the sternness of a military officer, had trained her to be this way. She was not to react, even if they did something to really get a rise out of her. She was going to keep her temper under lock and key starting right now.

There must have been at least three police stations closer to the Zodiac, where they'd found her.

Why had they taken her here, on the fringes of Harlem, near Maggie's Café?

Her head was still spinning, although the cell was sobering her up quickly. Her fingers were covered in black ink, and they had taken her mug shot. She placed a hand over her left breast, the thump of her heartbeat pulsing through her fingers.

She was alive. *Alive, alive, alive.*

Her hand still stung from the punch. She hoped that Rafael had gotten the girl home okay. That was the only important thing. Louise could handle herself.

Officer Martin leaned against a desk. He was smirking as he watched her, his eyes blank.

"What are you doing, Martin?" an officer called from behind him. Louise couldn't see who was talking. She didn't move.

"I'm seeing if she'll perform tricks," Martin said.

Louise kept her face straight and stony.

"Bit of a Sheba, isn't she?" someone asked. He'd been at the crime scene that morning too—the name on his badge was Tucker.

"If you like niggers," Martin said. Louise felt something tighten in her chest. She stared past the officers.

Something hit her face and she fought to hold still.

"What are you throwing at her?" Tucker asked.

"Peanuts," Martin said.

Louise wished she could reach through the bars and choke him. Instead, she shut her eyes. She would not give them the satisfaction of reacting. She would not give them the satisfaction of having gotten something from her. She couldn't control them, but she could control herself.

"Do you think she's deaf?" another officer said. He had blond hair, blue eyes, dimples he no doubt thought could charm any woman on earth into his arms. He clapped his hands twice. "Hey! Sheba!"

She clenched her hands into fists.

"You know who she is?" Martin asked. The other men looked toward him. He cleared his throat, obviously enjoying being the one who knew everything. "Louise Lloyd."

They stared at her, as if they could not believe that *the* Louise Lloyd was sitting in their station house cell.

"Nah, can't be." This officer's badge read JONES.

Tucker moved toward the bars, slowly, as if he thought she might attack him.

"Are you Louise Lloyd?" His voice was clear and slow, like she really couldn't hear. Louise didn't look at him.

"Get back, Tucker," Martin said. "She might bite."

Tucker stepped away from the bars, and Martin took his place.

"How are you going to get home?" His voice was soft, and she knew that none of the other men could hear him. "Do you *have* a home? Or do you live on the streets?"

"Do *you* have a home?" Louise asked. "Or do you just sleep on the floor here?"

He gripped the bars. "I am your arresting officer. You better treat me with some respect. A gal like you wouldn't do well in jail."

"A man like you can't tell what a gal like me would or wouldn't do."

He stared at her, taking in every inch of her body. Her dress was an older style, longer in the hem than what was currently fashionable, merlot with a satin ribbon around her hips. It bared her dark arms and exposed her collarbone.

"The only thing you're good for is being on your knees. At least I wouldn't have to hear your voice."

She was quiet.

"No response, hey?" he said loudly so the men behind him could hear him. "Maybe we can all take a turn."

"Not me," Tucker said. "I wouldn't let those lips touch me if they were the last ones on earth."

"Hey, maybe if we're lucky, she'll be the next bitch to turn up dead," Jones said. He stepped back toward the bars, next to Martin.

"Go chase yourself," Louise said.

She was about to continue when a new voice called out, one she recognized as Detective Theodore Gilbert's: "Tucker, Martin, Jones. I assume you have work to do?"

All three men stood at attention. "Yes sir."

"Then go do it, and don't let me see you slacking off again."

Gilbert stepped into view as the men dispersed.

"Assaulting an officer?" he asked as if he didn't know. He unlocked her cell. "Come with me, Miss Lloyd."

⊲⫯⊳

THE OFFICE WAS small. The window behind the desk was open, and cool air breezed in. Her head pounded. Scenarios, none of them good, ran their way through her mind.

"Miss Lloyd." Gilbert cleared his throat, as if he wasn't too sure what to do either. They stared at each other for a moment, and she blinked. "Please sit down."

She did as she was told, crossing her legs at the ankle as she had been taught to do. She tilted her head.

"Can I get you some tea, Miss Lloyd?" Gilbert asked. He made a point of using her name, her title. It was like she was a real lady, and something about that made her palms even sweatier.

"No, thank you, sir," Louise said. "I really only drink coffee. Or Coke."

He stared at her for a moment, as if he was making a mental note of this.

"Cigarette?" he asked, offering one from a silver case. She took it and placed it between her lips. He lit the cigarette and the office was silent as she exhaled a plume of smoke. He watched her.

"You're in serious trouble, Miss Lloyd." He took his time making his way through the words. Louise stared at the desk. "You're facing jail time. I'm sure the officers were kind enough to inform you." He was watching her, trying to gauge a reaction. Her hands were shaking as she focused on her cigarette.

"It was worth it." It was bold and blithe and true.

"I'm sure a judge would love to make an example of Harlem's Hero."

Something in her shuddered at the mention of her nickname, and a blush rose to her cheeks. Taking a deep breath, she looked the detective right in the eye. "I'm not Harlem's Hero."

"In 1916, one fifteen-year-old girl was kidnapped walking from a café back to her home," the detective said. Louise swallowed hard. "Instead of letting herself simply be taken and sold away, this girl fought this man and rescued three other girls. Was that not you, Miss Lloyd?"

"It was, but I just did what anyone else would do."

Louise hated that her name had spread through Harlem and she had been subjected to reading about herself over and over. Newspapers had requested interviews, and her father had used her fame for himself. It had mostly waned now; the only people still interested in her were reporters hoping to find a story in Harlem's Hero. She was supposed to have turned into the bright star of her community. Now, ten years later, she was working in a café and dancing her youth away. No wonder people were disappointed when they found out who she was. She had wasted her potential.

"I'm going to give you a choice, Miss Lloyd," Detective Gilbert continued. He sighed as if he had quickly grown tired of this conversation. "I can make your charges go away, but you have to do something for me."

Louise's heart leapt in her throat. She scanned the little room. She knew he could overpower her if he tried. He was twice her size, tall and broad. He would win in a fight. He could do *anything* to her and she wouldn't be able to stop him. No one would believe her. Not again.

"You have to help me solve this case."

"I'm sorry?" she asked. She had been judging the distance from her chair to the door and missed what he said.

"Here's the situation, Miss Lloyd. I believe you are smart and courageous, and I would like to help foster that. So help me find who's been killing these girls, and you'll be free. Better yet, I'll make sure there's no record of you ever being arrested."

The idea was ludicrous. Louise knew she could get into places that a tall, well-dressed white man could not. She could get into clubs and get girls to trust her. That was why he needed her. This was her home; he was simply visiting. She already had a job, and she didn't fancy the idea of doing someone else's, especially when she'd be the scapegoat. She'd be expendable. If the city needed someone to blame, she would be that person. And she didn't really want that. She didn't want to be in the spotlight again. But what choice did she have?

"What do I have to do?"

"It's simple. Talk to the girls, try to befriend them. Focus on the club. Talk to the people the girls talk to. Go to their homes, talk to their families."

"And if I don't do this?"

"Jail. A criminal record. You think the guys in this place are bad? Wait until you meet the guards at Sing Sing."

5

⟨⟩

MISS BROWN'S HOME was small and unruly. Louise had been living in the house since she was twenty-two, and she felt she was getting too old for the group home situation. She lived with several other girls, only a couple of whom had lived there as long as she had, and all of whom were safely in their twenties, like she was. The girls in her home, the majority of them Black as well, had earned the house a reputation: it was affectionately known as Miss Brown's Home for Wayward Girls. She lived next to Maeve Walsh, across the hall from Rosa Maria Moreno, diagonally from Helen Roberts, and right above Catherine Gordon and Frances Byers.

Louise had the pink room on the second floor of the row house. She had found the place during her days as a showgirl, and stayed as she transitioned to working at Maggie's. Coming straight from her father's home, she had loved being a showgirl.

Her father was a preacher. She and her three sisters had been raised with military-grade precision, a set of rules outlining every minute of their day. But Louise didn't fit. After her kidnapping, she tried; she had wanted nothing more than for her life to go back to normal. But her father used her to attract new attendants to their church. He wanted her to get married. He wanted to make sure his legacy was secure. Sam Harris, the man her father selected for her, wasn't a bad man; they had been friends. But Louise didn't want to be his wife.

Her father never cared about what Louise wanted.

So she moved on. Being a showgirl meant working three shows a night, dancing until her feet bled. And it was energizing, getting to the theater in the evening and not leaving until four the next morning. She had lived with the few other Black girls in the show then, and for once, she was supporting herself. But it changed fast when she realized she was invisible to the white stars and being leered at by the men in charge. The girls were mean and vindictive, always looking to get ahead.

And she had been getting older and more tired. She realized one morning, about three and a half years ago, that her dreams had changed. She no longer wanted to be a dancing girl in the chorus.

She had loved it until she didn't.

Louise had planned to stay at Miss Brown's for only a couple of months, half a year at the maximum, but she fell into a routine and then she couldn't change it.

After she left the police station, midday, Louise elected to go home, calling out of work. She was rumpled and hungover, and wanted to lie down. There was a letter waiting for her on the doorstep. She picked it up and unlocked the door to Miss Brown's. She climbed the stairs, closing her door behind her. The rest of the girls were at work; Miss Brown was running errands. Louise was alone, and being alone in this house was a rarity, a pleasure.

She removed her dress, kicking her shoes off. She opened the window and sat on the sill, lighting a cigarette. She removed her stockings, unclipping the garters.

Her head pounded and ached. She needed to get some water before she went to sleep. From the first floor, the phone rang in its little booth. She ignored it.

It was funny how the place she chose could be more like home than the place she had been born into.

She didn't miss living with her controlling father and her rambunctious siblings. This room was the first thing that was actually hers, and she paid a tidy sum a month for it. She stubbed her cigarette out. From her vanity she grabbed a glass that might not have been clean and filled it in the bathroom sink.

Once she got back to her bedroom, she sat down at her vanity and opened the letter. There were two words, typed. YOUR MOVE.

Louise stared at it for a moment, then crawled onto her bed. She lay on her back, staring up at the ceiling. Her mind was still whirring. She hated feeling afraid.

She was going to have to think of a plan.

⊽⋈⊽

LOUISE SAT AT her vanity, half-dressed. There was no part of her that wanted to put the rest of her clothes on. She had picked out a dress, but now it felt like the wrong choice. Instead, she stared at her reflection in the mirror.

"What is going on?" Rosa Maria asked.

Louise had been quiet through dinner. She hadn't wanted to join in on the many conversations with the girls. Dinner was always a loud and messy affair. None of the six girls she lived with had any real sense of decorum, anyway.

She had come directly to her room after dinner. She still had a couple of hours, but the process of getting ready for the night was a long and extensive one. Louise regularly changed dresses three or four times before she settled on one. But that night she was frozen at her vanity, the mere idea of going to Maggie's club making her legs tremble.

Louise exhaled a stream of smoke and deposited her butt in the ashtray. She didn't know what to say, so she decided to tell the truth. She knew the twins' power of communication was otherworldly; if she told one something, the other often just knew.

"My brother did tell me you were arrested. Start from there," Rosa Maria said.

"I made a deal. Instead of being charged with anything, I'm helping the police with a case."

It felt good to say it, even if it still felt unbelievable.

"*What?* A case?" Rosa Maria sat on Louise's bed.

"The one with the dead girls."

"Why you?"

"They think I can help. What was I supposed to do?" Louise had been replaying the night in her head, and she didn't think she had any other options.

"I'm not sure." Rosa Maria took one of her hands. When they touched, Louise felt a little jolt run through her. "I just want you to be safe."

When Louise had moved into her pink room, she had fallen for Rosa Maria instantly. The other woman had been situated in the blue room across the hall for a year and a half before they finally kissed. Whereas girls like her housemate Maeve Walsh needed some loud, sweeping declaration of love, Louise and Rosa Maria were happy just knowing what they meant to each other. They had moved past the infatuation phase and were now comfortable with each other, close enough that Louise wasn't sure what to call it. It wasn't just love. It was something more. She stared at the two of them in the mirror. She often pictured them together, but in better circumstances than this.

"All I have to do is get through this, and I'll be free." Louise picked up a lipstick.

"But what does that mean, Louise? What does being free mean?"

"I'm not happy about it either."

"What are you supposed to do? Isn't this a setup? How the hell are you supposed to investigate a case like this when you've never done it before?" Rosa Maria worked at the *New York Tribune* as a typist and desperately wanted to be a writer. She was working on what she called the next Great American Novel, but wouldn't tell anyone what it was about. It was only right that Rosa Maria would have a million questions Louise couldn't answer.

"I can only take this a day at a time."

Rosa Maria smiled. Louise was wholly entranced whenever she saw that smile. "I think my brother is really to blame for this." Louise smiled as well. It was always so much easier to blame her problems on Rafael.

"I love you." Louise spoke quietly, forever scared that a nosy girl would overhear. "You know that I love you. I'll be as safe as I can."

"Tell me everything that happens," Rosa Maria said. "Every detail. I'll help in any way I can."

Louise glanced at the makeup on her table. The other woman got on her knees and began dabbing powder on Louise's face. This was their routine. Louise was terrible at putting on her own makeup. She was too impatient to make it look good. But Rosa Maria always managed to make her look her best. It was a calming moment between them, no matter how their nerves were buzzing before the Zodiac, no matter how much contraband alcohol they had drunk before; they enjoyed these quiet moments together.

Louise blinked her eyes open. The silence of her room hummed around them. Below, the laughter of the girls was miles away.

"You know, if we lived together, it could be like this all the time." Rosa Maria was working on Louise's eyebrows. "Minus the noise downstairs. You deal with the police, and I will look for apartments."

It sounded wonderful. But who in their right mind would rent to two women alone?

Louise opened one eye. Kissed Rosa Maria's nose. It would be the perfect future.

Things so rarely worked out the way they were supposed to.

6

❖

EVERY CLUB WAS lackluster compared with the Zodiac, but Maggie's was especially unimpressive. Louise, with Rafael by her side, took the narrow staircase in the kitchen pantry down to the dance floor. There were other ways to enter, but this was the most discreet.

The girls, all young and Black and beautiful, flitted around in black dresses with white beading.

"Why are we *here*?" Rafael asked.

"We are expanding our horizons."

He put his lips to her ear. "If you're scared of the Zodiac now—"

"I am not scared of the Zodiac." She pulled herself away.

Rafael stared at her for a moment, then wrapped his arms around her. "I'm sorry you got arrested, Lovie. But you can't be afraid of the Zodiac."

"I told you. That's not it." She said it with as much force as she could muster. Even still, her voice wavered. "Now, please go get us some drinks."

He turned toward the bar while she found a booth.

Maggie's layout was similar to the Zodiac's, and the majority of the people were Black. The odd white man sat looking foreign and uncomfortable. This place had different reasons to be discreet than the Zodiac did. Louise watched one of the girls lean down and run her hand over the thigh of a man sitting at a table. The girl laughed at something he said, which couldn't have been very funny. They both rose and she watched as the girl led him out of sight.

The band itself was decent at least. She longed to be on the dance floor, but she had a job to do. She couldn't get distracted.

Maybe she had spent too much time at the Zodiac.

Rafael returned with two drinks, shaking his head, apparently still annoyed that she wouldn't explain what was going on. She took a glass and he lowered himself into the seat. "What are we doing here?" he asked again.

She rolled her eyes, draining her glass as she watched the girls selling cigarettes and dancing. Information. That's what she needed. If she brought the detective some information, maybe he'd put this whole thing to rest. "I gotta go iron my shoelaces." And with that, she pulled herself from the booth and headed behind the little bandstand, taking a hidden pathway.

<hr />

THE FIRST PLACE she went was a small dressing room with peeling red paint. There were mirrors on one wall and makeup scattered across the counters. Clothes covered the chairs. The scent of roses and lavender filled the air.

"Can I help you?" The voice startled her. A girl in a black dress stood by the door. She was young, maybe seventeen. Her eyes were wide and brown.

"I was looking for my friend Dora," Louise said. "She's supposed to work here. I'm Louise."

"Annie Taylor. Dora's dead, didn't you hear? She, uh, I don't know. She's dead."

"When was the last time you saw her?" Louise asked. Annie raised an eyebrow. Louise pulled herself to her tallest five foot two.

"You a cop?"

"No. I just didn't know, is all."

"Right before she went missing. We worked the same night. I was with someone, maybe. It blurs together."

"What do you mean 'with'?"

"Mr. Lister makes us fuck the men who come here. He keeps a list of clients."

"Do you know who Dora was with?"

"Awfully nosy, for not a cop." Annie turned toward the mirrors. She used a finger to wipe off some excess lipstick. "Dora and me were friends. She never mentioned you."

"I just want to know. Were you close?"

"Thick as thieves." Annie turned back to the mirror. Her hair was falling out of place, and she pushed it back. "It's so hard to remember." Her voice was hard and cold.

Louise knew that she, or any of her sisters, could have had to work in a club like this. And she was lucky that they didn't have to.

"But we were supposed to meet the next day," Annie continued. "And when she didn't turn up, I knew something was wrong. I reported her missing. No one did anything, and now she's . . . now she's dead."

"I'm so sorry," Louise said.

"Can't do anything about it now." Annie wiped her eyes. "It's unfortunate, but I still have a life. Dora was pushing her luck. She was splifficated all the time."

"What are you saying?" The implication was that Dora deserved what she got. Louise wanted to hear her say it.

Annie pulled away from the mirror and pushed past her.

The hallway still reverberated with music. The band wasn't letting up. Louise made her way down the hall, trying to find the bathroom. She didn't need to use it, but she craved the time alone to think.

"You know, this part is employees only." Louise turned around. She was staring right at Frank Lister, Maggie's grandson, but she knew he didn't recognize her. "But I'll make an exception for the prettiest girl in the joint."

"Very nice of you, Daddy," Louise said.

He stepped closer. "I don't think I've ever seen you here before." His dark eyes combed her. He was dressed extravagantly—bespoke black suit that must have cost more than her rent, and a crisp white shirt underneath—and he had about a foot on her. She had met him before and seen him in the café above. "You a dancer, princess?"

She forced a smile. "Not a good one."

He grabbed her arm and yanked her close. "I bet I could teach you something. Would you like that?"

Louise tried to wriggle from his grasp. "I should get back to my table. My guy, he's waiting for me."

He finally let go.

"Can't keep him waiting," he said. "But I'll be seeing you, princess. I'll be seeing you *real* soon."

7

NOW, MISS LLOYD, there are a few simple rules to this job."
Gilbert took a moment to light a cigarette. Louise didn't dare
breathe during the pause between his sentences. "The first? Always
trust your gut. The second? Assume nothing. The third? Once is
happenstance. Twice is coincidence. Three is a pattern."

She felt as if she should be taking notes, furiously scribbling
everything he said in an attempt to remember. "You'll be working
alongside us in an unofficial capacity. As I said, your role is to talk
to the families. Befriend the girls, like you did at Maggie's. You
may be required to help with an operation. Do you agree?"

Louise was hypnotized by the way he spoke. She had never
heard his crystal clear, quick British clip before. She was used to
the dropped syllables and missing letters of Harlem native speech.
There was nothing she could do but nod. Was this going to be
dangerous? There was a modicum of danger in almost everything
she did, but this was real. Real stakes, real threats.

"I need to hear you say it, Miss Lloyd."

"I agree." She swallowed hard, unsure if she would be able to get the words out.

"The thing about a girl like you is that you can go where we cannot, and we need that right now." The detective crossed his arms, staring at the concrete at their feet.

Louise and Detective Gilbert were at the first crime scene, where Elizabeth Merrell had been found. It was a backstreet, behind buildings. The body had been stuffed into a forgotten corner.

"She was found around here," Gilbert said.

"And where was Clara found?" Louise asked.

"Two blocks south."

Elizabeth Merrell had been officially missing for a week before she was found. It was the type of disappearance that happened without anyone knowing; a girl simply vanished and turned up dead a week later. It would be easy to kidnap a girl. Louise knew that better than anyone. It was easy to wrap your arms around a girl and pull her away, easy to subdue her. The girls had all been strangled with the pearl necklace that was part of the club uniform.

"We talked to the man who found her," Gilbert said.

Three dead girls.

One girl could have been an accident—a fight with a lover, an argument gone wrong. Two girls would have been a strange coincidence: how odd it was that two girls who worked at the same place ended up dead, within a few weeks of each other. But three girls was a pattern. Three girls, and a detective was called in. Three girls, and the papers screamed *killer* and he was given a name, the Girl Killer.

"Find me something," Gilbert said, staring at the spot where Elizabeth had likely taken her last breath. "Find me something, or this is going to happen again."

LOUISE SAW HER youngest sisters as much as she could, even though it was against her father's wishes. She was waiting for the twins, sitting in Morningside Park, sweating in the muggy and humid air. She was wearing a pair of black sunglasses and the lightest dress she owned. She was sipping a Coke. Everyone was dressed in their Sunday best.

The ban on seeing the twins wasn't said or written out, but it was understood. Louise had given up being part of the family when she walked out the door when she was sixteen. The twins had been six, and Celia cried the night Louise left. Josie comforted her sister but didn't show much emotion. Her father had ignored them all, and it was up to Louise to tell them it would be okay, like it always had been.

A baby wailed and Louise looked around for the noise. She scanned the little park, fanning herself against the heat. She was trying to be very aware of her surroundings. She squinted. There was a figure leaning against a tree, watching her as she waited and smoked. She leaned forward, trying to discern the figure, raising her sunglasses to get a better look. He was in the shade, far away from her, but it was enough to scare her.

"Lou! Lou! Lou!" At the sound of the voice, Louise rose from her bench. She spotted her sister rushing toward her, and by the time she looked back to the tree, the figure was gone. Had she imagined it?

"Hi, Dove." She wrapped her arms around her sister and kissed her forehead. They were just about the same height, with no hope of either of them getting any taller. They both had round faces and hazel eyes, but Celia's and Josie's were more green where hers were more brown. It was strange to see one sister without the other. Josie and Celia were always together, two halves of the same person.

They had arrived minutes apart during that traumatic August night sixteen years ago that claimed the life of their mother. Celia was loud and thoughtless, while Josie was quiet and introspective. Josie tended to pull away from everyone but her sister. Josie watched; Celia acted. They spoke in half-formed sentences and made-up languages. One was never far from the other.

Both girls had lived their sixteen years always perfectly content with their world. They never wanted anything more. Louise had to want things for them. They did everything their father asked with no thought about what might actually make them happy. Of course, he liked them better than her.

"Where's Josie?"

"Lou," Celia said, ignoring the question about her twin. "It's warm. I don't like it warm. It's too warm."

"Sit," Louise said. Celia sat next to her sister, looking around with a giant gap-toothed grin. Louise handed her the bottle of Coke.

"Father says I shouldn't be eating sweets as much," Celia said. "Anyway, I have a very important announcement." She removed the lace glove on her left hand and revealed a little engagement ring.

"You're getting married?"

"Well, not until after my birthday," Celia said. "But he asked me last night."

"Who's the boy?"

"You don't know him."

"You're *sixteen*," Louise said. "How long have you been together?"

"I'll be seventeen. We've been together for four months." Celia was so proud, like four months was an accomplishment.

Louise shook her head. "I won't let you do it."

"You don't own me, Lou."

"Celia Adelaide Lloyd. Does Father even know? Aunt Louise?"

". . . Minna knows. She approves." Minerva Scott was the middle Lloyd sister. "And she wants this for me. Father approves too. I don't know why you don't."

Why was Celia so content with the life their father had set for them? There was a whole world out there. Endless possibilities. But trying to talk Celia out of this would make her even more determined. So all Louise could do was force a smile.

"If you're happy, Dove, then I'm happy," she said. "Maybe it would help if I met the man that won my baby sister's heart."

Celia sighed—a dramatic sixteen-year-old's sigh. She leaned her head on Louise's shoulder, and Louise suddenly missed the days when Josie incessantly clung to her. She was still a baby.

But in less than a month, she'd be married.

"He's a good guy." Celia was trying to convince herself. She was toying with her engagement ring. "He's a kind man. And he loves me." Her second sentence was tacked on a moment too late. She wrapped an arm around her sister. Celia nestled into the crook of her neck. For the moment, they were sitting close together back in their shared bedroom ten years ago.

"You don't have to do this," Louise said. "You can come live with me. We can figure it out." She hoped Celia would do what she wanted. She was sixteen; she had her whole life ahead of her. She didn't have to marry this man if she didn't want to.

Celia didn't speak for a moment. Lou inspected her sister's face carefully, looking into her hazel eyes and nervous smile.

"I want you and Minna and Josie at the wedding," Celia said at last. "No complaints."

"Of course, Dove."

Louise squeezed her tightly, wishing again for the days that they were children.

8

⧓

THE HUGHES FAMILY lived on the outskirts of Harlem, a row house shared by a mother, a father, several children, and even more aunts and uncles. Louise had decided to start with the victim she had found in front of Maggie's, the girl she had asked about at the club, Dora Hughes.

Louise knocked twice, and the door swung open to a cacophony of sounds: cooking, conversations, children playing. There was a baby crying at her feet. Louise paused, then picked her up, bouncing her up and down like she used to do with the twins. The baby stopped crying, placing a thumb in her mouth.

"You're a good girl," Louise said quietly.

"Excuse me. Can I ask who you are?" A woman—tall, slender, stern—came into Louise's view, taking the child from her.

"Miss Louise Lloyd. Are you Dorothea Hughes?" The woman stopped, stared her down, moved the baby from one hip to the other. Louise had gotten all the relevant information from Gilbert, and this was the neighborhood where she'd grown up, but she felt like an imposter.

"What's it to ya?"

"I want to talk to you about Dora Hughes."

The woman, Dorothea, stared at her, eyes icy. "What about her?"

"I want to talk to you about her death."

"We've talked to the police. We don't have anything else to say."

"I'm not police," Louise said. She had to be careful. She didn't want to reveal her own precarious situation. "But I do want to talk."

"You a reporter?"

"No. I worked with Dora." It was technically not a lie; they did work in the same building. She could see the woman was scared but was trying to hide it.

Dorothea looked her up and down. "Come with me. You can join us for dinner."

The table was already full. She didn't want to impose. But there was the part of her that was raised to never say no to her elders, so she nodded. "Of course."

She was seated at a family table between four kids, all of different ages, fourteen, seven, five, and three. The baby was seated next to Dorothea, and her husband, James, next to her. Dinners at Miss Brown's house had prepared her for this. The conversations were yelled, all over one another, as dishes were passed and food was served.

The Lloyd family hadn't been like this. They were meant to be quiet during meals and at all other times. She smiled as she watched the proceedings.

"Have to take some in to your mother," Dorothea was saying.

"Doris will." James didn't look up from his plate as he said so. Doris, the fourteen-year-old to Louise's right, rose from her seat, doing exactly what she was bid.

They talked around Louise, which was a blessing. She wasn't sure what to say, but once dinner was over, she and Dorothea cleaned the kitchen. But what she said next wasn't what Louise was expecting. "I'm sure you don't remember me, but me and your momma were friends. You've grown so much."

"Oh." She was drying a plate and tried not to drop it. She looked up at the other woman. She could see the lines in her face.

"We were friends for a while," Dorothea said. Louise put the plate in the cabinet. "What do you want to know about Dora?"

"What was she like before she died?"

"Like any other girl, I suppose. She was pulling away, but she was sixteen." Dorothea leaned against the counter with the sink. "She was trying to be her own person. We fought."

"She wasn't acting odd or strange or anything?"

"She was being a girl." The memories were so sharp to Louise. Wanting to fit in, stand out, and be her own person all at the same time. Dorothea smiled gently as she spoke. "I told her she was too headstrong."

"Did she mention anyone in particular?" Louise said. She wasn't sure what to ask. Dorothea used a towel to wipe off her hands.

"Well, Miss Lloyd, she was exactly how any other young girl was. She was secretive."

"What about after she went missing? Was there anything strange?"

The older woman stopped, considered her question. Louise put down the plate she was holding. "There was a couple letters, some phone calls. I thought nothing of it."

"Phone calls?"

"We share. A party line. Just didn't think the call was for us. Just some heavy breathing."

"Letters?"

Dorothea paused, rifling through a stack of papers on the counter. She passed through unopened bills until she found one envelope that was sliced open.

The writing was unmistakably girly, big and bubbly. *I'm sorry. It's my fault.*

Louise stared at the letter, tracing over the ink with the tips of her fingers. There was no signature; the words barely even shook. There was something too composed about this letter.

"Do you mind if I take this?" Louise asked.

"Go ahead."

"Did you report this to the police?"

Dorothea sighed. "I tried. They had no patience. I tried to report Dora missing too. I don't know what would have happened if . . ."

"Who did you talk to?"

"Young guy. Blond. An officer. Seemed haughty. Into himself."

"I think I know the one."

From another room, the baby cried. Dorothea put the towel down; she had been wringing it between her hands. "I tried," Dorothea said. "I tried to be a good mother. I tried to help her. I tried . . ." She trailed off and went to go collect the baby.

Louise placed the paper in her purse, folding it so small that it would fit in the little beaded bag. She made sure the dishes were put away and then headed toward the door.

⋎⋔⋎

THE KID, FOURTEEN-YEAR-OLD Doris, was standing at the base of the stairs. She motioned to Louise, who followed her up the stairs and into a cramped bedroom. Doris flopped onto a rickety little bed. She was wearing a dress that looked like a sailor's uniform.

"I know everything Dora got up to." She said it like a brag, and to her, it was. Louise bit back a smile.

"So tell me."

"Not that easy." Doris sat up, eyeing her. Louise knew this would be a quid pro quo agreement. The girl turned onto her stomach, casting her eyes up to Louise. "I want a cig. No, two. No, three."

Louise dug into her purse and pulled out three cigarettes. Doris moved to grab them, and Louise pulled her hand away. "No way, doll. Information first." She sat on the floor, pushing clothes out of the way. Doris sat up, pulling her legs underneath her. She was still young enough to have baby fat, her cheeks chubby and making her look younger than she was.

"Dora said that I could come with her one day. I wanted to see Maggie's. She used to love it. Said men gave her all these things." Doris got up, pressed herself to the floor, and pulled a box out from under the bed.

In the box was a myriad of things: spare matches, a cigarette or two, a bottle of perfume, a string of pearls, a couple of folded letters, a rather large sum of cash, a necklace, and a diamond ring that looked real.

Louise picked it up. Doris didn't stop her from taking it. "Did she say who gave her all of these?" Even in the low light, the diamond danced and sparkled. The ring was real and ostentatious. The center stone was placed among petals like a flower.

Doris frowned, her mouth etching a line into her face. "She said they were prizes. She said that she earned all of it. She said she deserved it too." She snatched the cigarettes from Louise's hand. Louise didn't fight her. She was too busy staring at the ring on her hand. She looked up at the younger girl.

"Interesting."

Doris was busy trying to light a cigarette with a match. Louise took the matches from her, lit one and then the cigarette. Doris inhaled and coughed. "Careful, there. You don't want to inhale too much. And careful you don't burn the house down."

"Right." Doris was too concerned with getting the hang of smoking to notice that Louise placed the ring and the letters in her purse. She'd do her best to bring them back. "There was a man. I don't know if she was in love. I don't know if she liked him. But she saw a way out. She said she'd take me."

She was getting a picture of who Dora had been, aside from her job at Maggie's. She had seen it as a means to an end.

"Open a window and exhale out of it," Louise said as she pulled herself up from the floor. She was too old to be sitting down like that, with her legs crossed under her. "Unless you want the room to smell like smoke."

Doris considered this and Louise took her leave.

9

◁▽▷

LOUISE WAS FLANKED by Josie and Celia in Morningside Park. It was a quiet morning, earlier than she would have liked after going to sleep at three a.m. She had had coffee but had moved on to Coke.

It was early enough that both twins were sluggish and tired. Neither was talking. Celia blinked, yawned, and wiped the sleep from her eyes. On Louise's other side, Josie was leaning back, hazel eyes shut. It wasn't easy to convince them to both get out of bed this early. Celia reeked of stale cigarettes and had the exact same annoyed disposition Louise did when she was hungover. Louise had bribed her sisters with breakfast. She could treat them at the café as she started her shift.

Louise rather liked how quiet it was in the morning. It was around the usual time she'd be trailing Rafael and Rosa Maria back home from the Zodiac.

"What are we doing here?" Josie, who Louise hadn't even been sure was wholly awake, spoke up.

"You're meeting a friend of mine." This was all the information she had given to the twins. She was only partially convinced this was a good idea; she had thought of it after several drinks and dances at the Zodiac. The ideas she had while at the Zodiac were not necessarily the best ideas, and she almost never acted on them. But there was a point she needed to make, and she was going to make it.

"Why?" Celia asked.

"What time is it?" Josie asked.

"Because I said so, and early," Louise said, answering both sisters. They had been using the same line of questioning all morning. They had been sitting in the park for the better part of an hour. Neither twin was really good at being patient. "You two need to be on your best behavior."

"It's too early." Josie moved so her head was on Louise's shoulder. Louise bit back a smile. She thought about the early mornings with her sisters, coaxing them from bed, and staying in with them when they refused to move.

She looked up. Saw him striding over the path, diligent in every step he took. Louise rose, pulled her sisters up as she did. "Detective."

"Miss Lloyd." He'd been perplexed when she said she wanted to arrange a meeting that didn't take place in his office. "Good morning." He was still very stiff with her. It was as though they weren't sure how to interact with each other.

"These are my sisters. Misses Josephine and Celia Lloyd." They gave him twin smiles.

Celia extended a hand. "A pleasure. Charmed to meet you. How do you do?" she asked in the trained, affected way their aunt had taught all of Louise's sisters to mimic. Or she had been sneak reading romance novels again.

"The pleasure is all mine, Miss Lloyd." Gilbert shook her hand, with a smile. "And you, Miss Lloyd." He extended a hand to Josie. She was still acting strangely, maybe trying to counteract her sister's wild amounts of energy.

"Nice to meet you," Josie said. She shook his hand gently.

Gilbert stuck his hands in his pockets. Louise had never seen him so casual; he wasn't dressed to go into the station. Josie and Celia sized him up, shared a look of half smiles and raised eyebrows. She wouldn't pretend to know what they were thinking.

"Run ahead to Maggie's, you two," Louise said. It was more like a command she hoped they would obey. They did, linking arms and dashing off, beginning a conversation in their special little twin language.

She turned to the detective. She inhaled. "If I may, sir. They are why I'm helping you with this case. I don't care about myself. I only care about them and girls like them. I want to make this very clear." She had been thinking about family since meeting Dora's. She wanted to make it known that her family was of the utmost importance to her. The twins were nearly seventeen, but they looked and acted so much younger. Or maybe it was Louise who was older, more mature. She couldn't imagine being that *young*. But Celia was going to be married.

"A noble cause." They sat on the bench, facing each other. Louise found that he didn't hold nearly as much power as she'd thought when she faced him in his office. "They seem like bright girls."

"I would do anything to keep them safe," Louise said.

Gilbert was smiling. This was the first time she thought she had seen him display a real emotion. He moved closer to her. She was careful to keep space between them. "It's easy to forget why you're doing something. But you have two very clear examples." He lit a cigarette, offered Louise one. She took it, closing her eyes as he lit it for her. She took a long, slow drag. She hadn't had a cigarette all morning and she needed one.

"They're good girls. They shouldn't have to live . . ." She trailed off, remembering that she should not be confiding in the detective. She thought about her sisters again. If given the chance, they could be anything in the world. They had so much potential and she was going to help them reach it.

"I understand, Miss Lloyd." Detective Gilbert was looking out over the park. It was still early enough for them to be alone. He spoke softly and not really to her. Introducing him to her sisters seemed to remind him of something in his personal life. "Completely."

She exhaled and rose. He did too. She dropped the cigarette butt on the ground, stamping it out under the low heel of her Mary Jane. "I should catch up with them. If left alone, they will run wild."

"Let me come with you." The words were out of his mouth before Louise thought he knew what he was saying.

She tried to make up a good protest, a good excuse, but she couldn't think of one. So she smiled, nodded. "Of course."

⌦⌧

MAGGIE'S WAS JUST opening. She placed Gilbert at a table in the back near the window, and went to hunt down the twins, pausing only to tie her apron on, covering her dress. She found the twins in the kitchen, by the oven, talking quietly. Celia was taking charge of the conversation, and they spoke quickly, their sentences tumbling over one another. Louise had always been envious of their relationship. They never needed anyone else, were wholly dependent on each other. But that would soon change. Josie frowned. Celia kissed her forehead, pulling her sister close.

"Both of you." Louise hated breaking up such a tender moment. "To the table. And be nice." They did as they were told, scurrying past her and sitting themselves at the table with the detective.

She leaned on the counter for a moment, watching her sisters sit and talk with the detective. She hoped that this would drive her point home. She liked watching the twins. Even Josie had pulled the charm out, and they were doing exactly what she hoped, chattering incessantly, and telling him that she had someone to fight for.

She stayed at the counter for a moment. She could hear Maggie humming in the back as she cooked, and she didn't want to move from her spot. Other customers were starting to arrive. Louise wiped her hands on her apron, although they were clean, and began to attend to her other tables.

She was able to check on her sisters only periodically until Josie joined her at the counter. She had a small frown on her face. Josie had always been like this—quiet, introspective—but she had pulled into herself more since Celia's engagement.

"What's going on, Sunshine?" Louise asked. She licked her thumb, then wiped at her sister's face. Josie batted her hand away.

"Do you love the detective?" Josie asked.

Louise barely bit back a laugh. "He's a business associate, Sunshine. Why?"

Josie looked over to where Celia had the detective completely bewitched. Her frown had gotten deeper. "I don't trust him. I don't like him."

"Josephine, why do you say that?"

Josie refused to look at her, took her time to respond. She was always careful to put the right words together, unlike her impatient, impulsive twin. But this question, she didn't have an answer for. "I . . . don't know. I just don't like him. I'm gonna go. It was good to see you, Lou."

She didn't fight her sister on this. She would wish she had listened.

10

LOUISE KNOCKED ON the door in the late afternoon. She was standing on the stoop when an older woman appeared. She stepped outside, closing the door behind her.

"Can I help you?" Her tone was high and imperious.

"I'm Louise Lloyd. I have a couple questions for you." She tried to sound as authoritative as she could. The woman looked her over. "It's about your daughter, Elizabeth."

"What about her?" The woman crossed her arms over her chest. If she was intent on having this conversation on the porch in the open air, Louise was going to let it happen.

"I'm investigating her death. Her murder." Her tongue tripped on the word, as if she didn't want to believe it. Elizabeth Merrell was an only child.

The woman sighed and pushed the door open. "We'd better do this inside."

Soon Louise was seated on a worn sofa in a small sitting room. She was clutching a rather nice teacup. The saucer was in her lap.

"What do you want to know?" Her name was Mary Merrell. Her voice was soft.

"I'm sorry to barge in like this. I'm working with the police on Elizabeth's case." Louise wasn't used to saying it out loud. Mary nodded her head in acknowledgment. Louise knew what to do now. She knew what to ask. "I want to go over her last couple of days with you, if you don't mind."

Mary stared into the swirling brown liquid of her teacup. Outside, Louise could hear children yell and scream as they played. The silence between them was painful. "I thought she was happy. I thought she was okay. But she was lying to me. Lying to my face. She said she was going to stay with a friend. She promised she wouldn't get into any trouble. She was a gifted liar." Louise remembered that well. Strict parents only made her a better liar too. It was easy to be angry at the person who had died, but Louise recognized the grief under the anger. Mary placed the cup of tea on a small end table. The crammed house was really more like an apartment. It smelled stale, like the windows hadn't been opened to air the place out. Louise kept herself straight and still in her seat, legs, of course, crossed at the ankle.

"Did she mention any suitors? Any men?"

"She never talked about men." Mary's answer was quiet and tight. Louise thought about the detective saying they were focusing on the friends and boyfriends. How much work had he done prior to arresting Louise? Had he tried at all? She frowned, trying to keep the displeasure from her face.

She didn't like talking to people like this, barging into their houses and demanding to know intimate details of their lives. There was no reason for these strangers to be confessing their life story to her. Elizabeth was their child and she should be allowed to rest in peace. But she wouldn't be able to *rest in peace*. Louise didn't think she'd be able to rest easy had she died as brutally as Elizabeth. She'd be waiting, watching, wanting her killer to be found.

Mary took a breath, tried to light a cigarette. Her hands shook. It was minute, but Louise could tell. She lit a match for the older woman, then lit a cigarette for herself. Mary's exhalation was slow, as if she was trying to catch her breath. "She was a good kid, though."

"What about afterwards? Any phone calls or letters?" Louise asked.

Mary paused, thinking about it. "We don't have a phone. No letters." The answer was resolute. Louise knew that talking to the family was a dead end. And Elizabeth had no younger siblings to rat on her.

The door opened. Mary rose from her seat, toppling her teacup over. A look of panic covered her face. "You have to go."

There was no way for her to avoid the man who walked into the small sitting room. "Mary. Who is this?" He didn't look directly at Louise. She knew the same brand of electric anger from her father.

"She was just leaving. She wanted to pray for Elizabeth." Mary's lie, or half lie, was quick. She was a fast thinker.

He eyed her. Louise pulled herself up to her tallest height, daring him to do anything to her. Her blood ran cold. How many times had she been in the same position with her own father? She had shaken hands with the devil. She knew what to be scared of, and it wasn't him.

But Mary's husband—a tall, burly, commanding man—didn't raise a hand to her. Instead, he smiled softly, reached to take her hand. "We're all feeling her loss." Louise didn't pull her hand away as he spoke to her. "That's very kind of you. Thank you."

Would Mary recant her lie later? Louise didn't know. She hoped not, and she dashed away from the house as fast as she could.

⊽⩑⊽

"ASKING THE FAMILIES is the wrong direction." She was, again, sitting in the detective's office. Actually, she was pacing a neat line from the door to the chalkboard. She was avoiding looking at the board with the names and faces. Gilbert watched her, a curious look on his face. "No girl would tell their parents they're working in a speakeasy. But"—she sat down, placed the few items she had found in Dora Hughes' hiding spot on the desk in a row—"I did find these. I had to bribe Dora's little sister for them. Elizabeth had no siblings."

"Making yourself useful, huh?" Martin sneered. She tried to forget that he, too, was watching her pace the room. Keeping herself up, moving, was helping her think. As she paced, she tapped the tip of her right thumb against the rest of her fingers on that hand, counting as she did so. She was keeping herself focused on the task ahead of her. She had never been a particularly antsy, fidgety person, but this case had gotten the better of her.

I'm sorry. It's my fault. Gilbert read the letter out loud. "How do you know this is real?"

Everything he asked her was an implied test. She didn't know what to say. She was scared of giving the wrong answer. "I don't know. Mrs. Hughes said it showed up after Dora went missing. If it is real, it's not something she would have sent willingly."

"So you think the killer made Dora write this?" Martin again. His eyes narrowed as she moved in a perfect straight line.

"Maybe," Louise said. She squeezed her right hand into a fist, remembering the satisfactory way it had once made contact with his face. She wished she could hit him just one more time.

"Miss Lloyd, you're giving me motion sickness," Gilbert said. She sat down, reluctantly.

"Where'd she steal the ring?" Martin asked. He had picked it up, staring at the flawless diamond glinting in the light. "Looks expensive."

"She didn't steal it. She was given it. From this butter-and-egg man." Martin slid her this look, as if he didn't know what she meant by that. She didn't clarify.

"Who?"

"Doris didn't know." Louise watched as Gilbert placed the letter, the ring, into the top drawer of his desk. She wanted the items back but didn't say so. She still wasn't very clear what her position here was. She didn't know when she was overstepping.

"Did the other girls get things like this?" Gilbert asked. His tone with her was always patient but distant. She didn't respond for a moment.

"No. I'm not sure."

"I suppose you'd better find out."

11

LOUISE DIDN'T PARTICULARLY like Maeve Walsh, who lived in the neighboring room. Maeve was loud, bossy, and annoying. She also managed to be self-centered and vain and vindictive. But she was smart. She had a job at Saks Fifth Avenue. She had a catalogue knowledge of all fine goods sold in the city.

Louise went to the other room. She could hear Maeve moving around, singing loudly and off tune. She knocked on the door, and Maeve, partially dressed, cigarette between her lips, pulled the door open. She was holding two dresses up, one midnight blue, one dark green. "Which one?"

"Green."

Maeve moved to let her pass, as if the question was a test. Louise placed herself at Maeve's vanity. The yellow room was almost exactly identical to the pink room adjacent to it, but it was cleaner. Maeve always kept her window open. A soft breeze wafted in, throwing around the scent of perfume. "What's going on?"

"I need you to take a look at something for me." Louise didn't have the ring anymore, but she had sketched out an approximate likeness. She unfolded the drawing and held it out.

"What's this?"

"My baby sister lost her engagement ring. I gotta replace it before he finds out."

Maeve took the drawing, sat on the bed. She squinted at it, not even considering that Louise was lying to her. "Silver band? Real diamond?"

"Yes to both."

"Which sister?"

"Celia. The youngest. She's apparently madly in love."

"Oh, I couldn't imagine." Maeve was the only girl in the house who was constantly inundated with suitors. It was because she was pretty, and traditionally so. Tall, redheaded, and still speaking with an Irish lilt, Maeve was what men really thought they wanted. She even had a record player, placed under the window. She used it constantly and bragged that it was a gift. But she was jealous whenever any other girl in the house was shown affection. "How old?"

"Sixteen going on seventeen."

"She's young."

"She has no idea what love is like."

"Do you?" Maeve sucked on her cigarette. She looked up from Louise's rendering, big green eyes falling on her.

She couldn't say yes. So she demurred. "More than Celia does."

"You're so private, Lou. It's infuriating, but I love it." She looked back down to the drawing, smiling softly. "You know, I have seen it. Pretty. Unique. It's not my store, but close. Some tiny family thing. Draper and Son's?" Maeve handed the drawing back. "Costs a pretty penny. I can't believe your sister is dating a man who can afford one."

"How much?" Louise asked.

"About eighty dollars."

"Holy shit." Louise folded the paper back up into a little square.

"Are you sure your sister just can't find it?" Maeve resumed getting dressed, slowly. She wanted Louise to change the conversation and ask where she was going. Louise didn't ask. She didn't care.

"It's probably on a subway somewhere by now. Better to just fix the problem before it turns into something bigger."

Maeve paused again. She had finished pulling the green dress on. She leaned down to look into the mirror. "Will your sister still come running to you to fix her problems even when she's married?" She looked at Louise in the mirror, her eyes big pools of green.

It was supposed to be an insult. But while Maeve was smart, she didn't have the wit to do it properly. Louise exhaled. She had gotten what she came for.

She rose. "Thanks, Maeve."

Louise closed the door behind her.

She would always try to fix her sister's problems.

ANNIE TAYLOR, RUTH Coleman, and Nell Hawkins sat side by side in Miss Brown's parlor. It was midmorning; everyone else was out. It had taken some work to convince the girls from Maggie's club to help her, and they still weren't sure. She had convinced Annie, who had been friends with Dora, and Annie talked the rest of the girls into meeting up with her. They sat next to one another awkwardly. Louise sat on a Victorian fainting couch, her legs pulled under her. She was watching all three girls closely. They looked so much younger when not bathed in the darkness of Maggie's.

"I've seen it." Nell was quiet, shy. These were the first few words she had said, and they had been sitting in the parlor for the better part of half an hour. Louise had given them the drawing of the ring.

"I haven't." Ruth was clutching a cup of tea. She squinted.

"You never listened to Dora talk," Annie said. She had been doing most of the talking. She was a nervous talker and words had been pouring from her mouth nonstop.

"She never had anything important to say," Nell shot back.

"That's mean-spirited and you know it." This was Ruth. She talked when she wanted to calm the other girls. She was older than them, but not by much. Louise understood the hierarchy. It was similar to the one that was at play in her own house. Girls needed a leader, someone smart and sensible, someone they'd respect. Ruth was that person.

Annie wrinkled her nose. "It was. Dora was kind."

"She always kept to herself." Nell looked toward the other girls. "Always writing in that diary of hers."

"She was nice." Ruth was tapping her fingers on the soft linen of her dress.

"She was very serious," Annie said.

Nell took the drawing from Annie. "This was Dora's?"

"She said she got it from a customer," Louise said.

Nell handed the paper back. This confirmed what Louise already knew. At least Doris hadn't lied to her. Louise got up and crossed to the window. She pried it open, then lit a cigarette. Thinking about these girls, their last days alive, really made her head hurt. It made her sad for them. All she could think about was the potential they'd had that would now go unfulfilled.

"Do you know who?" Louise asked. The three girls looked toward her as if they had been in a daze. They had forgotten that Louise was in the room with them. She stubbed her cigarette out.

"We can only guess." Nell put her cup of tea down.

Annie looked toward her. "But I think I have a good idea of who."

These girls were much more perceptive than Louise initially thought. Ruth cleared her throat. It was obvious she was in control of the other two and now was trying to dominate this conversation. It was also clear Ruth didn't really trust Louise.

"You have to tell me." Louise sounded desperate and childish.

"We never said we wouldn't." Ruth was testing her. Louise had seen that same glint in Josie's eyes.

"Ruth," Nell said. "She's trying to help. So we should help her."

"We can take care of our own," Ruth said. It was clear that Nell didn't like to challenge, and Ruth didn't like to *be* challenged.

"Bernie," Annie said, shocking all of them. She was staring into the cup of tea she hadn't touched since she got there. "We don't know his full name. He's always trying to lavish us with gifts." That was what she was looking for. It was a name, somewhere to start. Louise exhaled. "We aren't supposed to take them," Annie continued, ignoring the glares from Ruth, "but we do. Sometimes. I don't."

"He carried a torch for Dora," Nell said.

"They all carried a torch for Dora." This was Ruth. Louise returned to the fainting couch, curling her feet under her again.

"What else do you know about him?" she asked.

"Not much. He's nice, kind."

Ruth rolled her eyes. "He's used to getting what he wants and taking it if it doesn't come easy."

"Just like a man," Nell said.

"Has he ever gotten violent?"

Louise's question made all three of them pause. They exchanged looks, having a conversation that was quick and silent. "No," Annie said eventually. She rose, placing her teacup on the coffee table. "I have to go. Errands."

"I'll go with you." Nell also rose, leaving her cup of tea on the coffee table as well. They saw themselves out, leaving Louise with Ruth.

Ruth would not make eye contact. She looked everywhere in the parlor except at Louise. Louise shifted in her seat. "What do you want from us?" Ruth asked.

"To help you."

Ruth raised one eyebrow. Everything about her was solid, completely unbreakable. She was probably scared underneath that facade. She had to be scared sick.

She just wouldn't show it.

"How can we trust you?" Ruth asked. "Nell and Annie, they'd trust anyone. But me? I'm not sure why I should."

Ruth listened as Louise told her story, "Right, well," Ruth said when Louise finished, "good luck with that." Louise shouldn't have been surprised at Ruth's reaction, but she found that she was. She waited until the door slammed shut to let out a sigh.

That was the last time she would see Ruth alive.

12

T HE STREETS OF Harlem were so familiar. Louise was walking back to Miss Brown's from Maggie's, a few blocks away. It was a Tuesday—the club wasn't even open—but she thought she could hear the loud, fast jazz that usually played there. She knew the rest of the Wayward Girls were at home, getting ready for bed after the beginning of a long week.

It was an eerie, silent night. She was so used to the sound of speakeasies that the hushed air around her seemed deafening. It was cool and that was a relief. The weather that day had reached into the hundreds, sweltering.

The only noise was the click of her heels on the concrete. She pulled the light jacket she wore closer, feeling a chill run down her spine. She knew she shouldn't be alone, especially at night with a murderer on the loose. She knew better, especially after everything she had been through, but that night she couldn't remain still.

So she was walking all of the crime scenes, but in reverse, starting with her beloved Maggie's. Everything had been so simple when she started working at Maggie's. It had been a few years and her life had changed so much.

She was alone on the streets, or it felt like it. The terror had driven everyone inside at night. It was for the better. Even now, Louise could feel her anxiety crawling up her arms.

She'd needed to get out of the house. Dinner was frustrating, with the girls talking loudly about topics that were important to them. She had spent about thirty minutes staring at the mostly blank notebook she was using for the case. Then she decided to go out and explore. Rosa Maria had declined her invitation of a late-night walk; she was behind on her writing.

The wind shrouded and comforted her as she walked from Maggie's. The streets were deserted. She made sure to walk in the pools of the streetlamp light on the sidewalk. She moved quickly, with a purpose, humming under her breath to make it seem as if she were less alone.

She could go back home, climb back up the trellis, and crawl into bed. But she wandered the streets of Harlem.

She didn't notice anyone following her. Not until she was grabbed from behind and slammed up against the wall. The hands that grabbed her were large and strong.

"Let me go," Louise said. She struggled against the man's grip, his hand covering her mouth. She bit down on his fleshy palm, and in response he whipped a hand across her face. She squealed in pain, tasted the metallic blood that filled her mouth. She had been in this situation before. She had lived through this situation before. She wasn't sure if she could live through it again. She fought back, landing a punch to the face. He was wearing a mask.

"You're playing with fire, Miss Lloyd." The voice was hissing, quiet. He grabbed her again, slamming her against the hard bricks. "Be careful. You never know who's watching you."

He left. She was too stunned to move. Deep breaths heaved from her body. She spat out more blood. The entire altercation had taken only a couple of minutes, and she was rooted to her spot. She looked around. She was once again alone in the Harlem night. She picked up her purse. Her hands were shaking. She took a moment to process what had happened.

If it weren't for the ringing in her face—she'd have a bruise the next day—she would have thought she made all of it up.

Who was watching her? For a time it had felt like everyone in New York City was watching her, but she had moved past that. She looked around the empty streets of Harlem. She could have called for help and no one would have heard her.

She was shaken, but she was fine. She pulled herself up straight. Whoever it was had given her a warning.

And she was so bad at heeding warnings.

<hr />

MAGGIE'S WAS QUIET. Louise was alone the next day after Evelyn, the other waitress, called in sick. She didn't mind being alone. It allowed her to work on the case instead.

Business had slowed since Dora was found in front of the building. Maggie was prone to worrying, and this was her life's work. She wasn't going to let it fail.

Louise had to assure the old woman that this, like everything, would pass. But she wasn't so sure. The empty days meant that sooner or later, Maggie would have to let her go. And she wasn't ready for that. Not yet. This was the last shred of normalcy she had. She surveyed the empty tables, then poured herself a cup of tea. It was going to be a long day.

She wiped her hands on her apron. At least she had the place to herself, for a while. Maggie had left to go pick up supplies and ingredients, trusting Louise to watch over the nonexistent customers. She found the quietness of the café preferable to the quietness of her home.

At least she was out doing something.

She drained her teacup, placing it back on the saucer. It was the middle of the day and only one person had come in since morning.

Stories spread easy as butter around these parts. Louise knew that. She had been the *subject* of them once. But still, it was hard to believe. Whispers were circulating that Maggie's was dangerous. It had always been a pillar of the community, a staple of Louise's childhood.

And now it was this empty place.

Louise put her hands on the glass counter. She had already wiped off the tables, swept, and cleaned the windows, and now she was staring at the empty dining room. She watched the giant glass windows as people strolled past, quick and in a hurry. She tapped her fingers against the glass. Sundays were the slow days in the summer. They were reserved for crawling in from the Zodiac and into Rosa Maria's bed, feeling her breath, hot and heavy, as they both took the liberty of "sleeping in."

But not a Wednesday. Wednesday was a prime day for chores, errands, and a long sit at the café with tea and gossip. She picked up her teacup, in search of something stronger, although she knew Maggie didn't keep alcohol, illegal or otherwise, in the kitchen or dining room.

But someone had come into the kitchen. It was a man, his voice was smooth, and Louise paused at the entry, pressing her body to the rough wood of the wall, making herself as invisible as possible.

". . . We may have to shut down." He was speaking on the phone, so she could hear only half of the conversation. She leaned forward, trying to glean as much as she could. "It's dangerous.

Maybe we could sell it. . . . I know. . . . I know. . . ." He trailed off again, an angry, exasperated breath leaving his body. She leaned over, trying to see who was on the phone. "It's a problem. No, I know." He exhaled again. "You're not listening to me." His voice rose and every hair on Louise's body rose with it. Yelling, men yelling, made her nervous. She had been taught to always expect the worst when that happened. She gritted her teeth to keep herself from crying out. "I am trying to keep these girls safe. As much as you don't believe it . . ." She heard the receiver hit the stand, and he let off a rather loud string of curses.

She knew she should be going to the dining room, but instead, she propelled herself forward, walking in on a tall Black man, who was dressed rather ostentatiously, and was furiously pacing the small kitchen. He stopped when he saw her, paused, his dark brown eyes running over her. "I didn't realize anyone was here."

"I'm . . ."

"Working in the café. I know." He turned to light a cigarette. He did not offer her one.

She was about to ask how, and then she remembered, the apron. She placed her cup and saucer in the sink, to be washed later. From the distance, she could hear the chime fixed above the door twinkle its happy song. "I'm sorry for disturbing you."

He laughed a little, a cold, cruel laugh that had nothing to do with humor. "You can disturb me anytime you want." Now that she was close to him, she realized she *knew* him, but only in passing. The man standing in front of her was Frank Lister, Harlem's most notorious entrepreneur. He barely ever looked in her direction, except for when she was dressed up in the club. He was being flirtatious, but she was sure that was his default. He was a man she couldn't read. True, she had met him a couple of times, but there was something about him that she couldn't put her finger on. It was the shiny veneer he draped over everything. He had been yelling a minute ago; now he was smiling and flirting with her. He was untrustworthy.

"I was just . . ." She couldn't say she was eavesdropping.

"Lovie!" It was Rafael. She could hear him rap on the glass counter. "LOVIE." He couldn't go more than ten seconds without some type of validation.

"I should go," Louise said.

"Of course, Miss Lloyd." She hadn't been sure he knew her name. He addressed the girls who worked in the café all the same: with a sneer and disdain. Except for her, except for now. She had a sneaking feeling that eventually he would want something from her.

She found, however, that she couldn't drop eye contact as she backed away.

13

～✦～

S HE HAD TO take the subway to get to Draper and Son's. It was a charming little store, hidden in Midtown Manhattan. It was so small, so invisible, that Louise passed it three times before finding the glass proclaiming it to be the place she was looking for, established in 1901.

She pushed the door open. A chime announced her arrival. Glass counters formed a U against the back wall, displaying rings and necklaces and bracelets she would never own, let alone wear. The lights were blinding, allowing the diamonds, whether they were real or fake, to sparkle. It was eye-catching. She wanted to stare at the cases and covet what she would never be able to afford.

Her heels clicked against the hardwood as she migrated toward one of the glass cases.

There was a man, older than her by about five years, hunched over the counter. She was armed with her sketch of the ring.

She had dressed stiffly, as professionally as she could. He looked down at her. He was wearing a pair of glasses low on his nose. It gave him a daunting look.

"May I help you?" He sounded annoyed, but he didn't demand she get out.

Louise stepped up to the counter. "You have to forgive me—you see, it's all my fault." She launched into the story she'd had two subway rides to concoct. "My boss is furious with me." His eyes were stale and brown, cool to her fictional plight. "He bought this ring for his girl."

"And how is that my problem?" he asked. Louise figured he had to be the son in Draper and Son's.

"I need to get another one and replace it before he finds out." She was on the verge of tears. "I swear, I just tried it on once, but I lost it."

"Then I suppose you should talk to your boss." He wasn't caving, wasn't falling for her story. She wasn't surprised.

She unfolded the drawing and placed it on the counter. "Please." She hated the fact she was practically begging him for something. But she needed his help more than he would ever know. "Just take a look."

He laughed. The sound shattered around her. He picked the drawing up and looked at it. "Father, come here."

"Why?" The voice that answered was distant. The store had to be bigger than she thought, with an office somewhere she couldn't see.

"There's a Negro with a drawing of the Lily."

Draper was a small, stooped man. Compared with his son, he moved and spoke with a quiet intelligence. He must have come from the office, removing his glasses from his forehead and sliding them on. He looked her up and down, a frown carving its way onto his face.

"How and where did you get this?"

"My boss . . . he bought it and then he lost it." Her voice shook. It wasn't a good or believable lie. "I lost it. I'm just trying to replace it before he finds out."

He looked to the drawing. It was an accurate rendering; she knew that. She had spent an hour sketching it, transferring the central diamond-shaped stone surrounded by little petals. She had faithfully sketched every petal on the band, doing it as much justice as she could. "This is the Lily. We only had two. They've both been bought. You're out of luck."

"By who?"

He was still staring at the drawing. With them side by side, Louise could see the similarities between Draper and son. "I think you should take this up with your boss."

"By who?" Louise pulled herself up to her full height, planting herself in her spot. She would be openly defiant if she must.

"We can't give our records out to any girl who walks in here." Draper removed his glasses again, looking directly at her. Her heart stumbled in her chest. He was older, elderly, really, but she was still scared of him. "You made a mistake and you need to own up to that."

"Please," Louise said again. She was all out begging him now, pleading with him. She hated the fact that she needed him to take pity on her. She looked toward the son, who wasn't watching the proceedings. He was staring at her drawing.

"You couldn't afford it, anyway." Draper pulled away from the counter and began to move to the side. "Now leave, before I call the police."

"No." She was being a fool now. If the police were called, it wasn't Detective Gilbert who would show up to save her.

"Dad," the son said.

"Timothy." The tone was a warning. The son looked at her, and for a moment, she thought she saw compassion in his eyes. "Escort her out, Timothy, before I make the call."

Timothy grabbed her rather roughly, his hand firm and strong on her forearm. He yanked so she nearly fell onto the wooden floor. She tried to pull away, but his grip was stronger than she was. "Stop struggling." His voice was in her ear as he marched her the few steps from the counter to the door. He pulled the door open and it merrily chimed again. There was a pause and he whispered, "Thomas." Then Timothy threw her to the ground without ceremony.

⋙⋘

THE KNOCK ON the front door of Miss Brown's was fast and furious. Louise had been in the kitchen nursing her invisible wounds and trying to think of a game plan. She opened the door to see Annie Taylor barely holding back tears.

She ushered the girl into the parlor and sat on the fainting couch. Annie curled up on the sofa. "Tea?" Louise asked.

Annie shook her head. She was disheveled, her hair out of place and her hat missing. She was anxiously dabbing at her eyes, now unable to make herself stop crying.

"What's going on?" Louise asked. It was her second time asking the question. Annie had ignored her the first time, but she took her time composing herself, heaving heavy breaths.

"Ruth. She's . . ."

"Missing." Louise's stomach sank. "Since when?" She should have guessed. She had never seen Annie look so out of sorts, so scared. Annie was sobbing again, her shoulders shaking as she did. The last time Louise had seen Ruth, she had been sitting in this very room.

"Yesterday. I was supposed to go to coffee with her, but she never showed."

"This could be a coincidence." She was grasping at straws and Annie knew it. The younger girl was staring at her in shock.

"She has no family, no home. We're as good as it gets for her. She wouldn't leave—she wouldn't just disappear." Annie broke down in tears again. Louise moved to sit next to her, wrapping her arms around the younger girl, holding her close as she cried.

She was careful about what she was going to say next. She couldn't promise to find Ruth. She still had very few leads. She understood why the detective was so frustrated. "I'll try my best."

"You have to find her." Annie was resolute in her conviction. "You have to! You have to!"

She still couldn't promise it. She wanted to. It was on the tip of her tongue; she could feel it.

Instead, she swallowed hard, hugging the girl to her tightly. "I'll try my best."

14

THE DAY RUTH Coleman's body was found was supposed to be a quiet day.

Louise had risen with the sun with the odd sense that something was wrong. She was eating breakfast when the call came in from Detective Gilbert. She would be late for her shift to visit the crime scene. But Ruth was right in front of Maggie's.

Louise noted a couple of major differences this time around. Her dress was gone, her shoes missing. Instead of being strangled, she had been stabbed. The wounds, strange, straight lines through her torso, were still red with blood. It soaked through her white combinations. Her lips were red, with lipstick or blood or both, and in her hand was the little card with the Virgin Mary on it.

"This is different," Officer Martin was saying as she approached. She rolled her eyes. It was quite an astute observation. This was girl number four and the killer was getting angrier.

"I think he's losing control," Louise said. Both men looked toward her in surprise.

"What makes you say that?" Gilbert asked.

Louise looked at the body before she answered. Ruth had just been sitting in her home, talking to her. This had happened so fast. She closed her eyes, made the sign of the cross against her chest. "It's the stab wounds. He wanted to see her in pain—he wanted to watch her die. It's . . . unhinged." She trailed off. She was making her observations up as she talked.

"Interesting analysis."

Seeing a dead body never got easier. It wasn't just the body; it was the spectacle that it became. They were into a routine now, albeit a gruesome one. The story would paint the papers, wrap its way through her community. Whispers would grow to screams and shouts, and even though she was there, helping, it felt as if nothing was happening.

Was she really going to let him win?

She pulled out a handkerchief, winding it around her finger. The sight of the blood, the body, the girl, it all made her sick to her stomach. She looked to the gathering crowd. There were a few men who worked at Black papers, the same from Dora's crime scene, eagerly writing down every detail. She slid a look toward them.

"Miss Lloyd, are you listening to me?"

"Sorry. Pardon?" She pulled her attention away from the reporters and back to the problem at hand.

"Do you know this one?" Officer Martin was lighting a cigarette and glaring at her. *This one.* Like they all knew one another. Like she and every other Black woman in Harlem got together for tea.

"Ruth Coleman. I met her once. A few days ago. With a couple other girls." So far, her usefulness was regulated to naming victims, talking to a few family members, and sneaking in and around clubs. She was still unsure of what to think of this arrangement. She wondered if she could get away with just leaving the city and never returning.

But something told her Gilbert would hunt her down, no matter where she went. "The girls mentioned a Bernie. But he's been giving the girls gifts. He gave Dora the ring," Louise offered. She was proud of her work. She was pleased with her ability to make connections with the girls, and she realized she was almost like a puppy begging for scraps of attention.

"Did you get a last name?" Gilbert was impatient.

"No," Louise said.

"Then why would you think that's helpful?" His words stung. Louise didn't respond. She didn't know what to say. She had thought it was a good idea.

Gilbert inhaled, then exhaled, obviously steadying himself. "We can't chase down every patron of the club. We need viable leads and some man with no last name is not a viable lead."

The detective was furious. The way he saw it, they were in a losing battle. This killer was several steps ahead of them, and the endgame wasn't apparent. She was no longer convinced this was the same person, maybe two people working together. This death was so different from the others.

The wounds were deep and meticulous. He had wanted her to truly suffer. What had Ruth done to earn that? What mortal sin had she committed? She felt as if she was scrambling for answers, her brain running a step behind where she wanted it to be.

Gilbert looked toward her, something unrecognizable in his eyes. It was clear they were dealing with someone, or something, that even the detective couldn't quantify. It made her nervous. Louise thought back to how quietly defiant Ruth was. How she tried to control everything. The killer would have hated that. He would have wanted to control her. Ruth wouldn't have given in. "I think she tried to fight back or something," Louise said. He took this in. "If she tried to fight back and she surprised him, he had to change methods."

"Maybe so," Gilbert said. He looked back to the body, still and prone on the ground. She was being covered and taken away, but the spots of blood that had seeped from her body remained on the hard, cold concrete. Louise watched, rooted to the ground, as officers finished going through the crime scene. Gilbert sent Martin off to do whatever it was he did when he wasn't within two feet of the detective.

Once they were alone, he turned to her again. He didn't say anything for a moment. He must have believed she already knew what to do, and wasn't sure what else to say to her.

"Miss Lloyd," he said, turning to the crowd of people who had gathered to watch. They were no better than vultures, wanting nothing more than to pick apart a tragedy.

"Yes, sir?" Louise watched the leftover officers clear the remaining crowd away. The sounds of their whispering following them, a quiet, eerie noise. She knew this place as well as anyone. She knew no one was able to keep a secret here.

"Be very careful."

His last ominous words before he departed. She stood, staring at the blood, a wave of dread washing over her.

15

⊲⧓⊳

SHE HADN'T BEEN to church in years. She had stopped coming when all the memories became bad ones. As she slipped
into the last pew, she remembered sitting in the front, wearing a
stiff, itchy black dress, burying her mother.

It wasn't very au courant to believe in a higher power.

And if there was one, he had let her down time and time again.

Truthfully, she had been thinking about her religion a lot since
the girls started to turn up dead. She wondered why a God—a
Lord who was apparently righteous in all his ways and faithful in
what he did—why he would lead four innocent girls to their deaths.
What was righteous about that?

She couldn't come up with the answer.

The church they attended had been standing for longer than
Louise had been alive. It was rather grand, for Harlem, the domed
ceilings making it seem bigger and all the pews in straight, serious
rows. In the daytime, the sun fell through the stained windows,
casting colors around the room and making it seem otherworldly.
It even had a warm, comforting smell, because the wives cooked

dinner for the congregants. She sat straight and still in the back pew. She reached up and toyed with the fraying ribbon on her hat.

She could leave and not be seen.

Her father, her whole family really, was involved in the church. Her father was the preacher giving the current sermon, and the leagues of people who showed up were hanging on to his every word. He mainly preached about the virtues of goodness and could point to Louise's sister Minna as an example. She scanned the crowd. From where she was sitting, she could see Minna juggling her son, a bouncy, big-eyed baby, on her lap. She was there with her husband. Louise's heart clenched. She knew Minna had had a child, but this was her first time seeing him. Sitting next to Minna, two halves of one heart, were Josie and Celia. They wore modest dresses of dark green, their hair appropriately styled. Celia, never able to sit still for long stretches of time, turned around, locking eyes with Louise. She raised a finger to her lips, knowing Celia would scream if given the chance.

Her father had wanted the perfect church family. Excluding Louise, he had gotten exactly what he wanted.

Why had she come? She was searching for something. After the deaths of so many girls, she couldn't help but wonder and ask this power why.

Her father, Joseph, was reading from the Bible. He was so different up there, so far away from the ordinary humans. The congregation clapped, snapped, and hollered their agreement. She had never enjoyed how rowdy church managed to get. His older sister, Louise, stood next to him, tall, stiff, serious. She had never liked being her namesake. She knew Janie, her mother, had pushed for her middle name, Lovie, to be her first. But Janie had lost every battle against her husband.

Louise always thought about her mother while sitting in a pew, no matter what the sermon was about. She always thought about how kind and generous her mother was. There was so much she wanted to ask Janie, but couldn't. She had missed the chance before she even realized how much she would need a mother as she got older.

If she closed her eyes, she could hear Janie singing a lullaby as she sat with Minna, her stomach swelling with not one but two babies. Janie was always careful. She rarely scolded or yelled, but she indulged Louise's and Minna's flights of fancy. She was the soft to Joseph's hard, warm to his cold. When Louise was younger, she believed that her parents were the epitome of love.

If Janie were alive now, Louise probably wouldn't be excommunicated. She often wondered how different her life would be had she been raised by her mother.

Louise was sitting still, quiet, under the high, domed ceilings and painted windows. She had never gotten what she thought she was supposed to from this. She didn't believe in someone out there guiding all their actions. She pulled out the rosary she still almost always carried in her purse. Louise placed her thumb over the cross. It had belonged to her mother. It was the only thing of Janie's she owned. She clutched the cross in her right hand, murmuring a prayer, and placed a few cents in the collection when it passed by her.

But there was something about church, evening mass, after supper, that she had missed. Maybe the sense of family, the comforting warm blanket of being surrounded by people she had known since she was a baby, sitting in the evening heat, listening to her father speak.

He had used the Bible against her and her sisters in so many ways. He had done what he thought was right, but it wasn't. She had grown up scared of her father, scared of the anger he wielded over her for a simple misstep.

In the corner, she could see Sam Harris. Sam was an old friend, the man she was supposed to marry. He was kind, patient, a student of her father's, but there was no part of her that cared for him as more than the brother she never wanted. His dark eyes fell on her; he smiled. His smile was warm and inviting. He winked at her. He had been her only friend growing up, her only close friend. And despite her rejecting his proposal, he remained a friend.

She should go. She shouldn't be here. She had wanted to pray for the dead girls. There was a part of her that had hoped that Sam would be giving sermons now and her father would be retired. She had other things to do, stalking nightclubs, talking to people, remaining focused on the case in front of her and finding a killer.

⌁⟁⌁

HER FATHER CALLED the sermon to an end. With little decorum, and no thought, Celia stood, turned, and yelled her name.

The two syllables of "Louise" broke through the quiet of the church. Her father and two other sisters looked in her direction.

There was no way she was going to sneak out of here now. She forced a smile onto her face and approached her family.

"Louise!" Celia, at least, sounded happy to see her. Josie and Celia embraced her in a tight hug.

"What are you doing here?" Her father eyed her. She searched the sharp planes of his face. The only things she had inherited from Joseph Lloyd were his impatience and his temper.

"I'm sorry, sir. I have . . . It's been a while." A while was right. She hadn't seen her father, except on very special occasions, the latest being Minna's wedding, in almost ten years. He looked at her as if he didn't recognize her, and maybe he didn't. She had gotten thinner, hungrier.

"Let her stay!" The twins were still clinging onto her. She pulled them off and deposited kisses on both of their foreheads.

An awkward silence fell over the little group. Her aunt joined them, looking down her long regal nose at Louise.

"I just wanted to say a prayer for those dead girls," she said. She hoped that their souls would rest easy.

Her father's lips formed a straight, tight line. He was unhappy, but he wasn't going to show it in public. He inhaled, about to say something. He looked so worn, like the twins were running him ragged.

"Joseph, you're needed." The older Louise pressed a hand to her brother's arm. He gave one more glance to his oldest daughter and departed.

"It's good to see you. It's been so long. But why are you here, Louise?" Minna was always kind and patient. She was exactly the daughter Joseph had wanted, and Louise hated that. A stab of jealousy ran through her.

Twenty-three years old, happily married with a child, and Minna was flawless.

Louise didn't fit. She didn't fit into Joseph's idea of a perfect family; she didn't fit into the mold of who she was supposed to be. Seeing the twins—Celia was still clinging onto her—with their aunt and father proved that. If she truly loved them, she'd let them go.

She saw it. She was an imposter, an outlier.

She kissed both the twins again and pulled herself away, her cheeks burning with embarrassment.

16

⫷⫸

S AM WALKED HER home. She knew he was just being polite, but she relished the company. She knew there was a great chance that he would report back to her father. Her father was working closely with Sam, training him to be a pastor.

It had been a long night. She was still humiliated from seeing her family and reeling from her own personal brand of complete stupidity. She hadn't thought it through. She never thought it through. She should know better than this by now. She was also trapped in an awkward silence. Louise never knew what to say to Sam, even when they were once on the verge of getting married. They had been kids: she had been sixteen and he twenty-two. The entire match had been arranged by their parents, and every moment of their time together was strictly monitored. She had never known if he had actually loved her. There was a part of her that wanted to ask but was too scared to, even though years had elapsed since their very short engagement.

"Penny for your thoughts? I know it must be hard to come back here. See everyone." Sam always knew exactly what to say to her.

It had been annoying when they were younger, but now she was grateful for it.

"I don't know what I was thinking," Louise said.

He had an arm around her shoulders. "You know what you were thinking. You care. And you're trying. And they see that."

"I'm more worried about those girls and their families."

"I heard about them."

"It's impossible to not have heard of them."

"I've been counseling the families. Helping them through this time."

He had always had a good heart, better than that of almost anyone she knew. Sam would devote himself to something like this. He put the rest of them to shame. "And? Are you learning anything interesting?"

"You haven't changed at all, Miss Louise Nosy Lloyd."

Louise rolled her eyes. "I have to ask."

"And you?" Sam asked. "You keeping out of trouble?"

Louise snorted a laugh. It was impossible for her to keep out of trouble. "I'd rather keep talking about the girls."

"Right. Harlem's Hero is making a comeback?"

"Harlem's Hero is doing the best she can." Every time she heard that nickname, she clenched her fists. "Like I said, I'd rather talk about the girls, about the Girl Killer."

"You really haven't changed at all."

"What's that supposed to mean?" She sounded like a petulant child when she said it. She wasn't sure if he was joking.

Sam laughed. His laugh was her favorite thing about him. It was a rare trait, deep and throaty, coming from his stomach. "It means you're still exactly who I remember. But sure. Let's talk about the girls. I'm working with the Hughes family, and Elizabeth's parents."

"I can't imagine what they're going through."

"It's senseless. And to think that we don't know who's gonna go missing next." Sam was always rational, but she could see that the summer had been getting to him too. Louise leaned into him. "I know the girls are scared. The families are trying to make sense of all of this."

"You know something strange? Every girl has been found with one of those little Mary cards, you know?"

Sam pulled away from her. The move was jerky and abrupt. "What are you implying?"

"Nothing." Louise turned to face him. "I just thought it was an interesting fact."

"Are you trying to question me?"

"No. I just want to get to the bottom of this," Louise said.

"Me and you both know they hand those out by the dozen." He had quickly gotten defensive. His nostrils flared and he had taken another half step away from her.

"I'm not blaming you," Louise said. "I just want to know."

"This isn't your job, Lou. I am doing my best to help those people."

"And it seems like you're getting real mad about it now."

"No, I am not." He raised his voice. The few people around them turned to stare, and they both realized where they were at the same time. The middle of the street, where anyone could see and overhear them. He stepped toward her, lowering his voice. "I'm not mad, Louise."

"I know you're doing your best." She narrowed her eyes. She wanted to believe him.

"I know you are too. Come on, let's get you home."

"You didn't have to walk me."

"I wanted to, Miss Nosy. There's a difference."

This was the longest time they had spent alone together in years. She allowed him to wrap an arm around her shoulders again. They settled into a heavy silence and quiet tension. She looked down and away from him. She couldn't help imagining what their future would have been like. "It could be me, you know. Or Celia. I just want everyone to be safe." She still abhorred the way she had gotten tangled in this case, but now she was going to see it through. She could wish for a lot of things. She could want the world to be easier and the people in it to be kinder, but that was a childish fancy. She had to remain rational. And if she could get through this summer with no more bloodshed, that would be a win.

"We're all trying." Sam was right. She had never seen the community come together as it had now. "We're all doing our best."

He walked her up to the door of her house. "I can't let you in," Louise said. "The girls will go wild."

"Well, then, Miss Nosy, I suppose I'll see you around." Sam smiled. She had always liked his smile. It was a little hesitant and possibly the loveliest thing about him, after his laugh.

"I suppose you will."

"If you ever want to come to church, you know you're welcome." He kissed her on both cheeks. She watched him depart, rooted on the front steps until he was gone.

◅◈▻

IT WAS NICE when they got out of the office. Louise trailed behind the detective, trying to decipher what he was saying. Not that he was saying much.

Detective Gilbert wanted to go visit the Coleman family with her. He apparently didn't care that she thought this was a waste of time.

He knocked on the door twice. If she listened closely, she could hear the knock echo through the apartment. A young man, maybe Louise's age, answered the door. He gave the detective one look before he began to close it. Gilbert pulled out his badge. "Theodore Gilbert, NYPD. This is my associate Miss Louise Lloyd. We have a couple of questions for you." She admired how he said it with such authority. The man glanced at Louise and she looked into his eyes.

"It's about Ruth," Louise said. It wasn't an essential addition, but she felt awkward just standing there behind the detective.

"Suppose you'd better come in, then."

They were led to a small sitting room. Louise sat on a worn footstool, closer to the detective. The young man's name was Lionel Coleman. He was Ruth's older brother and her official guardian. She could see bits of Ruth in him. They had the same oval face, long body, and strong chin. Lionel glanced back and forth between the two of them.

"I'm so sorry for your loss," Louise said. She had been instructed not to say so, to remain professional, but she couldn't help herself. She ignored the glare she got from Gilbert. "We just have a couple of questions about Ruth."

"Thank you, Miss Lloyd." Gilbert's voice froze her to the bone. "Mr. Coleman."

"Call me Lionel."

"Mr. Coleman, when was the last time you saw your sister?"

"I barely saw her." Lionel's brown eyes were fixed on Louise. "She was always in and out. I could go days without seeing her."

"Is that why you didn't report her missing?"

"Ruth was like a stray dog. She'd come and go as she pleased." Lionel leaned back and lit a cigarette. "Not like you all would do anything anyway."

Gilbert hadn't learned to pick his battles. "We're doing the best we can." His voice was a silent hiss, barely concealed anger.

"*You* aren't doing anything." Lionel was unafraid of a fight. "You don't care about anyone who doesn't look like you. Tell me how many colored men you got on your squad? Your job is to defend this place, and you don't even try."

"You don't know what we go through. You don't know what we do. We're keeping your lives safe."

"My sister is dead. Tell me how you kept her safe."

"Lionel." Louise surprised herself by interrupting the brewing fight. She thought she'd better say something before it turned into a real dustup. "Will you show me Ruth's room?" She rose to her feet. Lionel copied her.

"Of course, Miss Lloyd."

The room Ruth had occupied wasn't unlike Louise's own. It was almost exactly the same shade of soft pink. The bed was against the wall, and the vanity was full of trinkets and other girly items. "What happened to your parents?" Louise asked. "If I'm not being too forward."

"Ma died. Dad left. I've been watching Ruth since I was twenty." Lionel raised an eyebrow.

She looked around. "I didn't actually need to see her room. I just wanted to get you away from the detective."

"Why are you working with him, anyway?"

"Long story," Louise said. She cleared her throat. "Did Ruth get any weird packages? Or letters? Or anything?"

"She came home with a lot of money. There's some things on her table like that necklace—that's new."

"Do you have any idea what your sister did?"

Lionel didn't answer her for a minute. Instead, he stepped into the bedroom, beginning to straighten it even though Ruth must have left it this way. "I had an idea or two. We never were that close." He picked up a worn little stuffed rabbit that sat on the bed. He stared at it. It was missing a button eye, making it look more unsettling than it should have. "I tried."

"I'm sure she knows how much," Louise said. "We should get back in there. Can't let the detective wait too long."

"Of course. Thank you."

"No, Lionel. Thank you."

When they returned, Gilbert was staring at a small photograph of Ruth. He was frowning. He didn't seem to notice them come back.

"Detective," Louise said. He snapped to attention, placing the photograph down.

"May we continue?" Gilbert asked. He was annoyed that Louise had gone off book.

She resumed her seat on the footstool. "Of course."

By the time they had finished, the sun was beginning to set. They had spent an hour in the little apartment for almost nothing. Gilbert was furious. He stomped his way down the street, Louise fighting to keep up with him. One of his regular steps was about three of hers, and he was moving faster than usual.

He refused to look at her, just scowled his way back to the station. She wanted to go home, curl up into bed. But she thought that was a bad idea.

"Detective." She was almost at a light jog in an effort to match his strides.

He glared at her. When he was really angry, his eyes changed to a stormy gray blue. "Don't you ever disrespect me like that again."

The words were like a slap, sending her reeling. It took a moment longer for her to come back to her senses. "I didn't do anything! I just thought I'd help."

"Don't think so much next time. You're here to do what I say. Go home, Miss Lloyd." He spat her name and sped up. Louise was left standing in the middle of the street, wondering what, exactly, she had done wrong.

17

⌇⌇⌇

IT WAS HARD to keep up with Celia. She strode down the street
with Josie a step and a half behind, fearlessly navigating her way
through Eighth Avenue. Louise smoked and watched them as they
approached. They were dressed conservatively in dark blue, identical down to their hats.

But there was something about Josie that was off. She was
quiet, linking her arm through her twin's to keep her close. Josie
whispered something and Celia brushed her off.

"Lou!" Celia called. They were going wedding-dress shopping.
Louise was going to make sure that her sister was the best-dressed
bride in the city.

She was grateful to spend time with her sisters, thankful that
she could be in their presence for a little while. And she knew,
despite Celia's pleas, she wouldn't be at the wedding. Her father
wouldn't want her there. She knew that, even if Celia didn't.

Helping her sister find her dress was the least she could do.

The woman Louise had found, lovingly called Miss Caroline,
had been making Louise's own clothes for the past few years. Lou-

ise had no talent with a sewing needle. The dresses for dancing and the skirts for work and the sturdy winter coat came from this woman.

Louise ushered her sisters inside, Celia chattering all the while. Louise and Josie were placed on a threadbare couch; Celia was whisked behind a screen.

"You okay, Sunshine?" Louise nudged Josie.

"Of course." Josie nodded, a vague jerk of her head, while her hazel eyes stared out of the window. She was always this quiet, preferring her twin did the talking for both of them, but something about it felt wrong today.

"What's going on?" She and Josie had never been as close as Louise wanted them to be, not like her and Celia. Josie had preferred practical Minna, something Louise had hated. Josie slumped over in her seat, her gaze on the floor.

"Nothing." It was quiet and petulant, so soft Louise could barely hear it.

"Are you jealous of your sister?"

"I'd rather die than get married." The answer was staunch and steadfast. Josie raised her chin defiantly. "I don't know what I'm going to do, but not that."

Louise bit back a smile. It was a tiny concession, but she'd won. The shop was actually the cramped lower level of a house. From the kitchen wafted the smells of dinner, making Louise's stomach growl and reminding her of better, happier days.

Miss Caroline had been a friend of their mother's, but then, who hadn't been a friend of Janie's? The dressmaker spoke about the woman warmly and fondly, often saying that Louise had become the spitting image of her. It was supposed to be a compliment, but it made Louise nervous.

"Sit straight, Sunshine," Louise said. "I'm not going to be the cause of ruining Aunt Louise's hard work." Josie pulled herself up straight. Louise knew Josie was hiding something, wouldn't say something. But she'd open up in due time.

"Ready?" Celia called.

She stepped out from behind the screen. She was wearing a gown of ivory lace in the deep V-neck style with a bow in the center. Celia had taken her hat off, and Louise now noticed that her hair was cut into a chic bob. Even now, in the middle of the day, standing in stockings in the dusty living room of Miss Caroline's house, she was the most beautiful, delicate bride.

Josie stood, tears in her eyes. She took her twin's hands in hers, speaking in the low, quiet tones of their made-up language. They hugged tightly, and Celia didn't pull away. Kisses were exchanged and both sisters looked toward Louise expectantly.

"You look beautiful, Dove." Louise's heart squeezed. How were they old enough to take this step? She could have sworn it was yesterday that they were grubby toddlers, unwilling to listen to or care about anyone but each other. She could feel them slipping away from her. They had matured into young women.

Tears streamed down her face and she wiped them away before she became the butt of her sisters' teasing for the next decade.

She moved closer so she could hold her sisters tightly, knowing that the next few days would bring a lot of change.

<hr />

WHILE CELIA WENT off to meet her fiancé, Josie joined Louise and her housemates. They were early enough that Louise could shutter her youngest sister away in the sitting room. Josie sat at the old piano that was never played, fingering the keys. She was quite the player, making a little bit of money by teaching scales to neighborhood kids. She began to play a jazz song she had heard on the radio. Louise sat next to her, watching Josie's fingers move.

Playing an instrument was something Louise could never get the hang of. She was too impatient and wanted to be good at everything she tried the first time. She loved hearing Josie play, knowing it was something Janie would have loved to teach her.

Josie stopped playing abruptly and looked at her oldest sister. "She's choosing someone else. All this time it's been me and her, and now she's choosing someone else."

"No, she's not," Louise said. She wrapped an arm around her sister's shoulder. "You two will always have something special. Something better than a husband."

"What am I going to do without her?" It wasn't so often that Josie allowed herself to be vulnerable, allowed herself to be emotional in the presence of anyone but her twin. Josie began to play again, a sad, slow, mournful tune.

"You won't be without her, Sunshine," Louise said. "Think of it as if Celia's going on an adventure."

"But what about me?" Josie asked. Then she asked it again, softer.

Louise couldn't answer that question. She could only hope that Josie had her own big adventure.

18

W HEN SHE WAS younger, Louise would practice dance steps at Maggie's Café, effortlessly executing a Charleston as she poured coffee, turning into a Baltimore as she moved to wipe tables down.

She leaned on the counter that divided the kitchen from the dining room. Summer days were made for couples flirting, young people who had saved money to spend some time with friends, families together laughing and entertaining their children.

Summers were time for them to get together as a community.

But no one trusted anyone anymore. There was doubt seeping in through the cracks of a community that used to be so close.

"It's gonna be okay, Miss Lou." Maggie was leaning over the ovens. She was constantly baking, constantly doing something, even though eighty percent of the time now the place was empty.

Louise turned toward her. "How can you say that?"

"I have been here for three decades and I am not moving until they make me. This will pass. They'll come back." Maggie moved to squeeze her on the shoulder. This woman had been more of a mother to her than anyone else in her life.

There were people at only a couple of tables, and the conversation was hushed. There was no need to have two girls on the floor, but she and Evelyn were taking turns doing a slow circulation of the dining area.

Louise was busy with the monotony of staring at the few occupied tables, smiling and offering refills, and cleaning the empty ones until they were spotless. Rafael was sitting at one of the tables, scribbling on pieces of paper. He had an apartment in Bed-Stuy but liked to write music in the café. He said the atmosphere suited him. "Lovie, take a look at this for me."

"I have a job to do," Louise said, but she indulged his whims. It was slow enough that she could take some time to stand over his shoulder and attempt to read the music.

"I'm calling it 'The Girl Killer Rag.'"

"That's just morbid."

"Maybe he likes jazz." Rafael shrugged and lit a new cigarette. "Maybe he'll stop killing if he hears this song."

Evelyn, a tall girl younger than Louise who was more flighty than useful, called her over. Evelyn had been working at the café for years and still barely had a handle on her job. Louise was about to tell Evelyn she could go home when the door opening and closing quickly caught her attention.

She crossed over to the door and stepped outside.

There was a man, older than her, mid-forties, maybe, hovering a few paces away from the door. He was only a couple of inches taller than she was, soft and doughy, his light suit jacket just barely fitting his stomach. He was sweating through what she supposed was rather nice linen. He was white, a complete outlier in the neighborhood he was currently standing in. He paused when he saw her. "Oh, I'm sorry." He was a reporter. She knew it from the awkward way he stood staring at her, as if he wanted to say something but wasn't sure what it was. Not a very good reporter at that. He inhaled, his cheeks red, perspiration dotting his forehead. "Can I talk to you?" He held out a business card.

"No." Louise ignored it. She had no interest in who he was. She knew he was looking to sensationalize the murders, and she was not going to let that happen.

"It would only be for a moment. Those girls. I really want to capture what life is like here now."

Louise shut her eyes for a moment, trying to fight back her anger. He would never be able to capture what life was like here now. He had no idea what it was like. He could try, sure. But he had no experience.

"Come on, doll," he continued. "I wouldn't have to name ya. I could just refer to you as . . . Princess."

Was he really trying to flirt with her? She squeezed a hand into a fist. "No. You can't talk to me. And no one in there wants to talk to you either. You have no right to come in here. No article you write will ever, ever capture what living here is like." She was yelling. Her voice was raised and it carried easily over the streets of Harlem. But she couldn't stop herself. His presumptuous liberties made her skin crawl. She didn't want him pissing his fake pity all over the streets she called home.

He looked her up and down. She was yelling at a man who potentially had sway with the city. It was also possible that he worked at a run-down paper nobody read. She took a deep breath, trying to calm the raging bull inside her before she spoke again. She chose her words carefully. "Nothing has changed much here, so there's no story to tell."

He pulled out a notebook, scrawling it down. She hated reporters. She had had enough of them to last a lifetime when she was a teen. She found them nosy and invading. He was going to use what she said, with her consent or not. This man, a white man who had a stable job, maybe a family, and some sway, could do whatever he wanted, and he would delight in doing it.

She took a deep breath in, waited for the red to clear from her vision before she continued. Her heart rate started to slow down, and she crossed her arms over her chest. He was still leering at her in the most unpleasant way. But there was something about him, bland and boring, that rang so familiar to her. "I can't talk to you," she said. "No one else here will. . . . It's unsafe. Don't you understand that?"

He had never considered what life was like for someone who wasn't like him. Even as someone whose job it was to tell other people's stories. "I suppose I do." His voice was soft and he sounded like he was realizing this for the first time. The sun was in her eyes, making her squint, and the vision of him danced in front of her. She couldn't be sure if he was real. With all the stress she was under, there was a part of her petrified that she was making things up.

But he reached up to tip his hat toward her. "Good afternoon, miss." With that, he was gone.

19

LOUISE MADE HER way down the back hallway of Maggie's club, walking as fast as she could so she wouldn't get caught. The music, blaring and pounding, felt so far away. Sweat covered her bare arms. She was sure no one had seen her slip out of the main room. Once again, Rafael had accompanied her to the club, and once again, she had left him alone. This was her idea. She was now acting outside direct orders. But she felt she had to. Louise knew that to do this right, to stand up for the girls of Harlem, she would have to take things into her own hands. The door to the dressing room was closed, which meant all the girls were on the floor. Knowing she was alone did nothing to calm the waves in her stomach.

She pushed open the last door in the hallway.

It was a small office. One desk with a lamp on it, one chair, no personal effects.

She wasn't sure what she wanted to find, but she had to look.

On the wall directly to her right, there was a bookshelf. There were only a few books, all with dark covers. After looking through them, she sat at the desk and rifled through stacks of receipts and bills of sale.

Something caught her eye. A paper with names and dollar amounts.

The younger girls—like Elizabeth, Dora, and Nell—cost more.

Below that sheet was one with a list of men's names, and another column with sums. Some names were written in red ink, some in black. She folded the lists and slipped them into her garter strap. The detective would want to see them. There was a smattering of applause from what felt like miles away.

The next song the band struck up was one that Louise knew well. She began to sing along, under her breath, if only to ease the tension around her. She paused. Footsteps. Coming toward her. Could she hide under the desk? There was a high girlish laugh. The girl, maybe two of them, near the door.

"I promise!" one girl said.

"I swear," the other responded. It sounded like Annie and Nell, but she couldn't tell for sure. She continued searching. She pushed through papers, looking through newspaper clippings that mentioned the club and its owner, clippings that mentioned the dead girls, and an old one that mentioned her, right after she had been kidnapped.

Frank Lister had been keeping an eye on her.

She shuddered and placed everything back where she had found it.

She crossed the seven or so feet to the door as fast as she could. Had she left anything out of place? No. She closed the door.

"This is for employees only," a voice called out from behind her.

IDA CALLAHAN WAS truly intimidating. At seventeen, she had almost a foot on Louise, and Louise had to tilt her head up to look at her. She was dressed in the black uniform dress, her long string of pearls wrapped around her neck, her bare arms glimmering under the lights of the hallway.

"I was just looking for Nell and Annie. They're friends of mine," Louise said.

Ida narrowed her eyes. "What do you want with them?" She sounded bored.

"I just wanted to talk to them, but I could talk to you." Louise wished she had gotten a drink before this, that she had stopped off at the bar. Her hands were shaking, and maybe she was too dependent on alcohol to get herself through things.

"About what?" Ida asked.

"Dora Hughes, Clara Fisher, Ruth Coleman, and Elizabeth Merrell."

"I didn't even know them," Ida said. There was something about her that was very seventeen years old, angry at everyone. Louise could remember feeling like that at seventeen. Ida bit her red lower lip.

"You worked with them," Louise said. "You saw each other here all the time. I think it's impossible for you to not have known them."

Ida paused. She took a deep breath. Her brown eyes flicked to the floor. There was something she could not, or would not, say.

"I knew Lizzie. The last time I saw her, she was mad, and I was trying to calm her down. But I knew that you couldn't calm her down, not when she was angry, and we were fighting." She shut her eyes, as if she was willing herself not to cry.

"Why was she angry?"

"I don't know. She wouldn't say." She raised a hand to her mouth. "I couldn't get her to talk to me, and that's all I wanted. And then I never saw her again."

Tears started to roll down her cheeks, and Louise pulled a handkerchief from her purse. It belonged to Detective Gilbert and she had not yet returned it. Ida hesitated for a moment, took it, and dabbed at her eyes. She started fidgeting with a silver band on her left ring finger.

"You were friends?" Louise asked.

Ida paused, then nodded. The lights glittered off her hair, shimmering like diamonds. "I was closer to her than the other girls. You wouldn't understand." Her eyes were rimmed with red from crying.

Louise needed a cigarette. She was never good with comforting people who weren't her younger sisters.

"She was so mad," Ida said. "I told her. . . . I . . ." Louise leaned against the wall, hoping that no one would try to come. She was finally getting somewhere. Ida was focused on the ring on her finger. "I tried to get her not to leave, but she went anyway."

"Who was she with that night?" Louise asked.

"I'm not sure. I tried to find her later, and she was gone." She was still clutching the handkerchief, as if she was afraid someone might take it away from her.

"Wash it, dry it, give it back to me," Louise said.

Ida mustered a sultry smile that she wore when she was on the floor trying to tempt men. She stood and Louise was once again taken aback by how tall the girl was. She was all limbs, thin in a way that Maeve was trying to accomplish. A stiff wind could have blown her away.

"Of course," Ida said. And with that, she pushed past Louise and walked down the hallway, disappearing into the club.

Louise crossed to the dressing room and pushed the door open. There were clothes on the floor and makeup on the vanity.

"Louise?" Another voice from behind. She turned to face Nell Hawkins. The girl was outfitted in black, her hair pushed away from her face. The dress was too big, nearly reaching her ankles. "I'm glad you're here. I, uh, I'm very scared."

"It'll be okay." It was the first thing she thought to say. She didn't know when she had become the patron saint for these girls, but she wanted to keep them safe. She had to keep them safe. "Do you trust me?"

Nell paused as if she had to consider it. Then she nodded. Nell shifted her weight and looked around the dressing room. She was avoiding something, but Louise didn't know what. "That's good, I think. If someone like you is here."

"Have you talked to anyone else?" Louise asked.

"Just a reporter. He seemed quite interested."

Louise wasn't sure what else to say. "Good luck." She wanted to tell the girl to leave this place and never return.

She should have.

20

⬦⬥⬦

DETECTIVE GILBERT WAS at his office desk reading a file, a cup of tea to his left. His cigarette case sat on the desk, just waiting for her to reach over and take one. Louise sat across from him, wearing the blue dress that shimmered in the lamplight, a clip keeping her hair back from her eyes. It was two in the morning and the world creaked as it spun. She could feel exhaustion settle in her very bones, but she was still alert and moving.

"I found something in the club office," she said. "But you have to close your eyes." The papers were still against her thigh, and there was no way that she was going to let him see more skin than she was currently showing. Gilbert did as he was told. She pulled out the papers, unfolded them, and placed them on the desk.

Gilbert opened his eyes. "What are these?"

"One is the list of girls, and how much someone had to pay to be with one for a night. The other is a running list of customers and how much they owe."

"So it's a list of suspects," Gilbert said. "Good." He reached down and placed a bottle of Coke on his desk in front of her, pausing to take the cap off.

"I looked at it on my way over," Louise explained between sips.

"What, Miss Lloyd?"

She leaned forward, scanned the list upside down, and pointed to the one name she recognized. "Sam Harris. I understand it's a common enough name, but there aren't many Sam Harrises in Harlem." Louise had thought about not mentioning his name, thought about hiding this fact. But if he was a suspect, she wanted to know. She wanted to know why he was on that list. And if she hid it, and the detective found out, she knew it wouldn't reflect well on her.

"You know him?" The detective put the papers down.

"I was going to marry him."

Gilbert wasn't fazed by this. "The first thing we have to do is make this list smaller. There are at least fifty names here. Isaac White. He's familiar."

"The only Isaac White I've heard of works at a car shop," Louise said. "You haven't seen this list before?" she asked. "Haven't you been through the club?"

"We haven't found anything. So we've been focusing on the families, the boyfriends, looking for a connection there." He shut his eyes, and for a minute Louise thought he had fallen asleep. The window was open, letting in a stiff breeze. The lamp on the desk illuminated the room in a soft glow.

"Detective," Louise whispered. "Can you hear me?"

"I'm awake, Miss Lloyd."

"Do you ever sleep?"

He didn't respond.

She picked up her glass bottle again, resisting the urge to put it to her cheek. She didn't know if he had dismissed her, but she would stay in her spot until he did. She stared at the board, at the smiling faces of Dora, Elizabeth, Clara, and Ruth.

"I had a very interesting conversation with one of the girls today, Nell Hawkins. They're really scared of being bumped off."

"Are you scared?" The detective had turned back to the papers in front of him. His mouth was set in a firm line.

"No, I'm not," she said.

She couldn't tell if he knew she was lying.

THE EASIEST PART of the night was climbing back into her bedroom. Louise deftly maneuvered the trellis, easily pulling herself through the window. It was three in the morning; she knew she smelled like alcohol and cigarette smoke. She stripped her dress off, her stockings, exchanging her combinations for a slip, leaving them in a trail on her floor. She left her door open, just a crack, and she moved from her bedroom to the one across the hall silently.

Likewise, the door to the blue room was cracked open. She stepped in and pressed her body to it to close it silently.

Rosa Maria was lying in bed. She had had her own adventures that night. She was wrapped in her blanket, smoking a cigarette before going to bed. There were no lights on, but the curtains were pulled back to let the moonlight spill in.

The city was so hopeless without Rosa Maria by her side. When they were together, they ruled the world with the wanton lawlessness that came with being a young woman. A couple of months ago, she was sure that their bond was stronger than anything the world would throw at them.

Did she love Rosa Maria? Deeply and forcefully.

Would they last? She wasn't so sure.

It was more than the case. It was the laws that said women couldn't love other women. Laws that said their love was indecent and impure, that women must exist solely for the use of men.

Would she go to jail over their love? Without a second thought.

Louise climbed into bed, kissed Rosa Maria's forehead. It was relaxing just being near her.

"You missed some fun tonight." Rosa Maria stubbed out her cigarette. Her voice was soft and raspy. They knew, from experience, that the girls they lived with were sound sleepers, not likely to wake. But it was better if they were quiet. "Another beautiful Zodiac night." Rosa Maria reached over, pushed a stray curl from Louise's face. She had used her signature perfume, but Louise could smell the stale alcohol on her.

"I miss you," Louise said.

"I'm sitting right next to you." She began to dance her fingers up Louise's thigh, inching toward the hem of her slip. "And we're alone." It was the obvious and it needed to be stated. Rosa Maria pressed her lips to hers, and Louise drew her closer, feeling her hand slip underneath her chemise. Bumps ran down her arms and legs; sweat began to cover every bare inch of her skin. She pulled away, used her thumb to wipe at Rosa Maria's bow-shaped lips.

Their limbs were entangled, Rosa Maria's body weight comfortable on top of her own. Louise inspected every inch of her face in the moonlight, her big brown eyes, perfect rounded cheeks and lips.

"You've been so distant, darling." Rosa Maria rolled her *r*'s, a low growl in the bottom of her throat that Louise could feel deep in her stomach. She knew where this would have gone on any normal night.

"I know." Their closeness was enough for Louise to lose her

focus, deep heavy breaths between them. The floors creaked beneath them, an old house settling down for the night. They were so close that between soft, warm kisses, she could feel Rosa Maria's heartbeat. Louise pulled away, sitting up. Rosa Maria moved to the side, so they were sitting shoulder to shoulder. Louise couldn't bring herself to look at the woman she loved so much.

"You're thinking about those girls again, aren't you?"

She was, but she wasn't going to say so. "Do you think we've changed?"

"Yes, I think we have changed. I think we'll continue to change." The notion was a strange one. But Louise knew she wasn't the same person she was at eighteen, and she wouldn't be the same person in another ten years.

Louise yearned for a cigarette, but she didn't light one. She curled into the other woman, feeling her warm, sweat-slicked skin. She never wanted to let go. The sun would rise and they would have to part, but for now, this was what they had.

Rosa Maria had always been her anchor, her calm in the storm, someone to think for her when she jumped the gun.

She closed her eyes. The house was different when everyone was asleep or elsewhere. This house had seen so many trysts and affairs, but nothing like their love.

She just wanted to hold Rosa Maria as close as she could. They were running on borrowed time and she knew it.

But she would do anything to make their time together last.

21

―――◆―――

"YOU LIED TO me." Louise didn't wait to knock at Sam's office door. It was ajar. He was sitting there, writing in a little notebook. "You lied to me."

"Louise." Sam wasn't surprised to see her. He rose to his feet. "What's going on?"

"Frank Lister is what's going on. You owe him near a hundred dollars. Why?"

Sam looked away from her. He sat back down. "Sit down, Louise."

"No. I want answers, Sam. What are you hiding from me?" She could feel her voice crack. She hadn't known that she felt this strongly about Sam. She'd considered him the brother she'd never wanted. "Tell me now."

He took his time, knowing it would drive Louise crazy. He lit a cigarette, made sure the piles of papers on his desk were straight. "I'm trying to help those girls, Louise."

"Bullshit."

"I am. I'm trying to get them what they need to move on. Of course, not all of them want to."

"I'm supposed to believe you're making good with Harlem's biggest crime boss to get his employees out?" Louise scoffed. It was a ridiculous story, one she hoped he didn't think she would believe. "I'm not an idiot, Sam."

"Aren't you? You got arrested for punching a cop. That's an idiotic move on your part."

"I was drunk. It was a mistake. I'm doing my best to atone for those sins. I'm working with the police to help solve the case." She was sure her anger was going to leap from her and explode, and then she wouldn't be able to take back what she said.

"I'm doing my job, Louise. If you bothered to call, if you bothered to talk to me, if you bothered to pretend to still be my friend, you would know that."

"You're on the line for murder, Sam. I don't have that much sway with the detective. If he thinks it's you, then it'll be you. You need to tell me the truth."

"I am telling you the truth. You just never listen. That was always your problem, wasn't it? You only ever wanted to listen to what you told you. You never consider another point of view."

"That's not true." She wasn't sure she would be able to hold the tears back, and he was the last person she wanted to see her cry.

"It is, Louise, and you know that. You can listen to me and believe my story, or you can believe whatever that detective tells you."

"He's not telling me anything." She should have thought this through. Bursting into his office, demanding the truth. It wasn't working. She knew they were capable of having a civilized conversation, but this wasn't it. "I just want to know."

"Then listen to me, Louise. I've been in your life so long, I would've thought you'd trust me by now."

Louise wondered if she had ever really trusted him. At times he had acted like an enemy agent, reporting everything he saw and heard about her back to her father.

Sam was calm now. He wasn't like her. He could never stay angry for long. She was still seeing red. She forced herself to take two deep breaths before she sat down. "So, what's the story?"

"The girls get what they're doing is bad, and they get a small cut of the money, but I'm trying to make it so they know they have options. Most are too scared of Frank Lister and his men to leave, but I've been trying."

"That's all?" Louise asked.

"Yes." Sam looked into her eyes. "You know me, Louise." She looked away from him. Her heart was tripping in her chest. She didn't know what to believe anymore.

"So you owe Frank Lister money because . . . ?"

"I hire the girls, and we spend the night talking."

"He knows who you are, what you do?"

"What goes on in Maggie's stays in Maggie's."

He reached out and took her hand in his. How many times had they done exactly this when she was younger?

"Were you there any nights the girls went missing?"

"No," Sam said. He squeezed her hand when he did. "When Ruth went missing, I was dining with your family."

"You were?"

"Making arrangements for Celia's wedding. Will you be there?"

Right. She had nearly forgotten about the wedding. "She wants me there."

"You can ask your father. He's in the next office."

"I don't want to see him." Minute by minute, she was calming down. She pulled her hand back.

"I hate what's happening to those girls. It's tragic, but I'm not a murderer, Louise. Come on."

She took a moment to look around her while she gathered her thoughts. It was a tiny office, smaller than her bedroom. The desk was against one wall, and it was covered in books and papers. There was a window with the blinds closed. The lamp on the desk, which was the only light source, was old and dusty. "Fine." She did know him. She knew his reputation. He did what he could to help anyone who needed it. Sam would give her the last dollar in his pocket. But she still didn't believe him. She couldn't. There was something stopping her. "Have you gotten any of them out?"

"They never want to listen, but I'm trying." He was resigned to the fact that his calling in life was becoming more and more mean- ingless to their generation. "And I'll keep trying. I'm not gonna give up, and neither will you, Louise." There were so many times when she wanted to do just that. She thought about giving up every day. But she wouldn't have been Louise Lloyd if she gave up. "Good luck, Louise. I am wishing you the best."

The way he said it. It was a slap in the face.

⋖⋗

LOUISE DIDN'T REALIZE that this day at Maggie's, one that seemed so normal, would be her last in the café. It was busy enough. She and Evelyn were splitting tables. They were just in the middle of the afternoon rush. Women were coming in from er- rands; men were talking over tea. She'd forgotten how much she loved the hustle and bustle of the place. This was the café she re- membered. It was never ending. When one table opened, it was quickly cleaned and reoccupied. It was like it had been before the Girl Killer had struck for the first time.

Frank Lister was holding court at some tables in her section. He always had a couple of associates, and they never had to pay for anything. Maggie doted on him, and Frank used that affection to do whatever he wanted.

He did make sure to tip well, though. That was something Louise appreciated. Every tip was important.

Louise had brought them several rounds of tea, which they poured gin into. She made sure to keep them happy. But she was tired of smiling, and she was stressed about the case.

"Girl!" That was Bobby Shaw, Frank Lister's third man. He was short and heavyset. He was apparently very good with numbers, and he never bothered to learn the name of anyone he deemed unimportant. Louise forced her smile onto her face again and crossed over to the three tables they were occupying.

"Everything okay?" Louise had been a waitress for years, and more often than not, she adored it. It was easy work that was usually stress free. The worst days were when Frank Lister decided to hold his business meetings in the café.

"We need more tea, doll." Bobby never even looked in her direction. To him, she might as well not exist.

"Right away. Anything else, Mr. Lister?" In retaliation, Louise made sure to address only Frank. Jimmy Olson made her nervous. He was Lister's right-hand man, his best friend and enforcer. He was usually quiet, a snake waiting to strike. She didn't trust Jimmy Olson as far as she could throw him.

"No, that's all, Miss Lloyd." He raised his eyes to her. He always looked as if he was keeping score. She was sure she was losing.

Evelyn was always behind the counter. "Busy day, huh?"

"Yeah. It's nice." Louise knew she shouldn't complain. They were lucky that they had all these customers after the slow spell they had had.

"How's Mr. Lister?" Evelyn asked. For some reason Louise couldn't explain, the other waitress was totally crazy for the man.

"Do you want his table?" Louise asked. She had offered it when they set up, but Evelyn had shyly declined. She preferred to watch him from afar.

"No," Evelyn said. Louise focused on placing teacups and saucers on her tray. "Did you hear, though?" Evelyn continued. She had a sharp ear for gossip. Louise was careful to never talk about anything very personal around her coworker.

"What?" Louise asked.

Evelyn turned to her. She was grinning in a rather salacious manner. "Just keep an ear out." Evelyn wasn't the sort to be mysterious. She was rather straight about everything. "I think they're thinking of closing or moving or something."

"Okay," Louise said. She picked up her tray, balancing it gently on her shoulder. Another perk to being a waitress was that she was practically invisible. She made her way to their tables—they were in the back, which afforded the men the most privacy—and began to pour tea, leaving room for their alcohol. They ignored her, except for Jimmy Olson, who watched her as she did her job. His eyes made her uncomfortable. He never blinked, and he was always frowning, busy processing the information he was given. It was really unnerving.

"I think we're going to have to act fast." Frank sounded stressed.

"I don't think we should shut down." Bobby was concentrating on lighting a cigarette. "I think we can find a place to move. Make this more exclusive."

"What about the girls?"

"The girls will be fine. They always will be."

"They currently aren't fine. They're going missing from my club. That's not good. They're dying because of me. Is it time we throw in the towel?"

"You have several other lucrative holdings. You won't go broke if you close one." Bobby was referencing a notebook, running his finger down neat columns. She tried to mind her own business, but she also tried to hover, just in case she heard something interesting. In her mind, Frank Lister was suspect number one, even though she couldn't figure out a motive. She'd always thought he used those girls as playthings and would tire of them eventually.

Louise had never imagined that Frank Lister would be concerned about the girls who were his employees. She picked up the kettle. There had to be a way to get ahead of all of this.

As she left the table, Bobby reached out, slapping her rear as hard as he could. "Thanks, doll," he said. Jimmy let out a loud, harsh laugh, the only sound he made when she was at their table.

<hr />

BOBBY WAS WAITING for her when her shift ended. Louise always left Maggie's just as the sun set, ensuring enough time to get home before dinner. "Hey," he called.

Louise stopped and turned. She put her waitress smile back on. "Mr. Shaw. I didn't see you there."

"I think you should be careful," he said, apropos of nothing.

"What do you mean?" Louise pulled her little tasseled purse closer to her body, thinking she could use it as a weapon if she had to.

"You know what I mean." He was teasing her and she wasn't in on the joke. "I think you're getting in too deep." He was grinning. Louise's skin crawled.

"Have a nice night, sir," Louise said, moving to turn away.

"You never know who's watching" were his last words to her.

22

＊＊＊

J IMMY OLSON WAS staring at Louise from a booth at the back
while she was at the bar. She had memorized his plain, boring
face, skin nearly the same shade of brown as hers. His eyes hadn't
left her since she entered.

He had a reputation around the club. She knew her effects on
men, if she tried. She didn't care much to try, but her body, small
and straight and boyish, her hair chopped to just under her ear-
lobes, did most of the work.

Jimmy rose, evading the couples on the floor with a slick grace,
and approached the bar.

"What are you drinking?" he asked.

She had to tilt her head to look up at him. "Whatever you are,
Daddy," she said, letting that cursed flapper accent slip from her
tongue. Girls like Maeve, girls who had multiple suitors, made this
look so easy. Maybe because, for the pretty ones who seemed to do
nothing but dance on air, it wasn't an act.

"Good choice, sweetheart," Jimmy said. She hated the way
men talked down to her, like she didn't matter. Worse yet was

that she let them talk to her like that. "I've never seen you here before, doll."

"Oh, I come and go," Louise said. The bartender poured their drinks. She had to keep Jimmy's attention. It was easy now, when he was interested. Gilbert had gone over the plan eight times in his office, over tea and Coke.

"So, then I should give you a proper introduction," Jimmy said. He didn't recognize her. Out of her work uniform and in the low lights, Louise knew she looked different. "I'm Jimmy." He had to be about thirty, and he was still using his boyhood nickname. His smile was a dagger as he extended a hand.

"Lovie," Louise said, choosing to go by her middle name. But it didn't matter. He would only call her sweetheart, or doll, or princess. She placed her hand in his, and he kissed it.

They were facing each other, and he lifted a hand to her chin, pulling her eyes up so that she was looking directly into his.

"Do you know that you are the hottest gal in this joint?" he asked. Exactly what she wanted to be, the hottest gal in this joint. She fought the urge to roll her eyes, or vomit all over the floor.

"It's flattering for you to say so," she said, letting a small smile come to her face. He was sizing her up and she was playing the part. He pushed stray hair away from her eyes, a move she knew too well. She didn't let her attention waver. She needed to know what he knew. "I came because I was curious. I heard about those dead girls."

"A girl like you shouldn't be worrying about dead girls."

"But they worked here, right?" Louise asked. She blinked up at him like she had often seen Maeve do with her suitors. She leaned into him, letting her fingers run down his arm.

"Are you writing a story?"

"Just curious." Louise giggled. She couldn't remember the last time she'd giggled. Hearing the noise come from her mouth was degrading. He smiled as if he were indulging a little girl.

"They worked here," he said. "But that's all you're getting from me."

"You're not a killer, are you?" She kept a teasing smile on her face.

A flash of anger clouded his eyes, but then he melted into that indulgent little smile. "Now, sweetheart, do you really think I'd kill some girl?" His voice was tense near her ear, and she swallowed hard. Nobody was watching them. Even the bartender had turned around, letting them have a moment of privacy. She wanted to say that she didn't know him, that he could be capable of anything.

But that insipid giggle left her lips again. "No, Daddy."

His hand was on her waist. He was taking an unwanted liberty, pulling her closer to him. "That's a good girl."

She drained her glass. "How about another drink, Daddy?" She had never been good at playing this game, acting out this flirtation. She knew she was supposed to let him lead. She had never been good at letting someone else lead.

"You heard the girl, two more," he told the bartender, rapping his knuckles on the bar.

Jimmy leaned over and pulled Louise into a deep kiss.

Nothing. She felt nothing.

She hated men like this, men who thought they could take what they wanted. She let him kiss her, allowing his tongue to explore the inside of her mouth, her insides recoiling. His hand was at the small of her back, keeping her close.

Then he pulled her away and watched her face intently.

"Don't you worry your pretty little head about those girls,"

Jimmy said. His voice was low and gravelly, near her ear. He was smiling. "You're the only girl who matters here tonight, princess."

"Aw, Daddy," she said, "you can't blame a girl for being a little curious, can you?"

"I suppose not." He was still looking into her eyes. "It really isn't becoming for a girl like you, though."

"Aren't I like most of the girls in this place?" She fought to keep a pleasant expression on her face.

"No, doll. You're better." This was supposed to impress her, she thought, make her feel like she was the only girl for him. She raised an eyebrow. She couldn't press this issue more, and she didn't want him to kiss her again. She tried to pull away from the bar, but his grasp was too tight. He was holding on to her in a way that suggested he would make sure she would do anything he asked her to do. "Why don't I show you around? I've got some-where quiet we can go."

Louise paused. Yes, she had to get him alone, dangerous as it was. She let a slow smile spread across her lips. She had seen some of the girls in her house practice this smile, quiet and attractive, in the mirror. Just as Detective Gilbert was doing his part, she had to do hers.

"Why don't we?"

⌦⌫

HE PRESSED LOUISE against the wall, his hand at her throat, thinking that she was the type who would be easily dominated. She didn't fight back, not yet.

"You are so . . ." He didn't finish his sentence, sloppily whispering in her ear. He was kissing her lips, cheeks, her face, his hands wan-dering down her body. He didn't need to finish his sentence—she knew what he was going to say. He pushed open a door and they tumbled through.

"A little more private," he said. They were back in the office. He went to the desk and pulled out a bottle of champagne and two glasses.

She had let him think she needed convincing. He poured the glasses and handed one to her. She could still hear the band playing, but it felt so far away. The music shook the wall. She could see it if she squinted—the wall was really shaking—but they could talk in normal tones. It certainly was quieter here.

"Do you bring all the girls back here?" she asked, raising an eyebrow.

"Only the ones I like." She was waiting for him to turn on her, and she was ready for his attack. She had a job to do. She took a small sip from her glass. She could never get used to champagne. She held her glass tightly.

"So, you like me?" Her heart was pounding in her chest. Her legs began to tremble, and the only thing she could think about was that she could very well die right there in that room.

"You're a real Sheba, you know that?" He stepped closer, his arm reaching for her waist. She blinked up at him.

"I've been told that, once or twice." She wasn't sure how to remove herself from his grasp. She took another sip from her glass. "Do you have a cigarette?"

He pulled himself away to go to the desk and took out a package. He handed her one. He lit it and she exhaled as she glanced around the office. There was one way in and one way out. The band changed songs. She hoped the detective was ready.

"Why don't we dance a little?" he asked after a moment of silence.

"Oh, I couldn't."

"I bet you have some hidden talents." His fingers dragged down her arm, ending at her wrist.

"We can barely even hear the music." This was all pretense, just an excuse to get closer. It was a game she enjoyed, as long as she was playing with a pretty girl.

"That doesn't matter." He drained his glass and took her by the waist. She let him take her drink. Then he pulled her into a waltz, and she let him lead her around the little office. A moment or two later, she was up against the wall. He held her there, less than an inch of space between them. He pressed his lips to hers, jamming his tongue between her lips. She pushed him away, fought him off, and he stared at her for a second.

Then lifted a hand and hit her as hard as he could.

"You are a dumb whore." His voice was ice-cold as he grabbed her by the hair and threw her on the desk. The rage inside him had unlocked. He was just waiting to detonate. She was unsure of how to fight back. She began to yell as loudly as she could, hoping someone would hear her over the music. No one came. He held her head to the desk as he pulled her skirt up. She began to pray, not knowing what else to do.

Then she heard it: the distant screams and yells of the raid she knew the detective was leading, the thud of people scrambling out the doors.

"It's just us now." Jimmy pulled her back up. His trousers were undone. She didn't want to look down. His hand was at her neck and he pressed hard, cutting off her breath. "You're just a stupid little girl." His voice was cool and cruel against her ear. "You're going to do exactly what I tell you." His voice rang in her head. She shut her eyes, paralyzed with fear. "Say 'yes, sir.'"

It didn't matter that his hand on her throat meant she couldn't say anything. With her blood pounding in her ears, she brought her right knee up as hard as she could. It connected just where it needed to. He let out a long groan. Then she pulled the lamp from the desk and hit him over the head.

He grabbed her, slammed her against the wall. The lamp tumbled to the floor, shattering. Her head rang and the world spun around her. He pressed his body to her, feral and forceful. Her hands shook as she tried to push him away. She kept screaming as loudly as she could.

The door burst open.

"James Olson, get your hands in the air." The cool, calm voice of the detective cut through.

Jimmy let go of Louise and she inhaled a deep breath.

"Martin?" the detective continued. Martin placed handcuffs on Jimmy's wrists. "James Olson, you are under arrest. Get him out of here."

Louise couldn't even look at the detective until they were alone in the room. Then she didn't know what to say. He removed his jacket and placed it on her shoulders.

"Are you all right?" he asked.

"I'm fine," she said. He turned so she could pull herself together. His jacket was warm and heavy on her shoulders. She put her arms through the sleeves and pushed her hair from her face.

"Miss Lloyd." He pulled his silver cigarette case from his pocket. He was correct in assuming she needed a smoke. She was crying, but she pretended not to be.

"I'm fine, Detective." Her voice was quiet and hoarse. She wasn't fine. Her head still pounded, and her lips still burned with Jimmy's kiss. Her heart stuttered and stammered in her chest. She didn't want to know what would have happened had the detective not barged in when he had.

"Miss Lloyd." Detective Gilbert was watching her carefully, his dark blue eyes searching hers. She knew he didn't believe her.

"Let's ankle." She began to leave the office, but paused. She turned toward the desk and grabbed the bottle of champagne. She took a long swig with the detective watching, a bemused expression on his face. The taste still made her want to vomit, but she wasn't going to let the good, real alcohol go to waste.

23

⌄⌄⋈⌄⌄

LOUISE SAT AT Detective Gilbert's desk, still wearing his jacket over her dress. The only light in the office came from the lamp on the desk. It was cold, or maybe she was cold. Martin was glowering, scowling in a way that was unbecoming. Louise wanted to tell him that his face would freeze like that. She was nearly shaking with anger. She knew that she had been used as bait that night. As much as she wanted to do her part to catch the killer, it made her angry. She didn't know if the detective realized it. He had to. He couldn't possibly be that foolish.

But would he put her on the line every time?

And he wasn't done yet—there was more.

"She can't do it," Martin said.

"She has to do it." Gilbert's voice was full of authority. "What choice does she have?" Louise tapped her cigarette on the ashtray.

Martin refused to look at her, anger blooming red on his cheeks. "She's not a detective. She's not an officer. She shouldn't even be here." Despite his anger, Martin was relaxed in his seat, leaning back, his gray eyes fixed on his superior. They were talking about her as if she were not there. It had been about an hour and a half since the raid, and they had gone directly back to the precinct.

Jimmy Olson would speak only to her.

He was their major arrest, aside from the tipsy men and women in the bullpen. Frank Lister had managed to escape, if he'd been there at all, and was now at large. Maggie's, both the club and the café, would be closed until further notice. None of this had gone the way she'd thought it would. She'd lost her place of employment, she had nearly been raped, and now she had found out it was practically a waste of time.

Louise's lips still reverberated with Jimmy's unwanted kiss. She could still feel his hands on her, pulling her toward him. She didn't want to speak to him.

"Miss Lloyd, you're going to have to speak up." Gilbert was staring at her.

"I don't have a choice, do I? How swell for me." She straightened in her chair and dropped the butt of her cigarette into the ashtray. Every part of her was tired. Her feet hurt from her shoes; her head ached under her headband; her hair was falling out of place. All she wanted to do was to go home and climb into bed with Rosa Maria and sleep.

But she couldn't do that. Her hands shook and she squeezed them into fists.

"You may leave, Officer Martin. Thank you." Martin sighed, but pulled himself from his seat. Once the door was closed, the detective looked back to Louise. In the pale light, he looked older. "You have a choice."

If she was going to do it, it would have to be soon. It was creeping toward two in the morning.

"I'll do it." She pulled herself up from her seat, removing the jacket from her shoulders. She pushed her hair from her eyes, knowing her once immaculately applied makeup was smudged and smeared on her face. "I'll do it," she repeated. The detective was watching every one of her calculated moves. "If he'll only talk to me, I really don't have a choice." She picked up the four files on the desk.

She could do this. She had to.

<hr>

THE INTERROGATION ROOM was small and cold. Louise shut the door behind her, and then she was alone with Jimmy Olson.

She thought about her mother, Janie, telling her to always be brave.

She stepped up to the little table but didn't sit. Jimmy was watching her closely, an eyebrow raised.

"You wanted me?" Her voice shook, but she couldn't stop it. She felt so small. She felt as if he could swallow her whole before she had a chance to protest.

She wouldn't show how scared she was. Her heart pounded. Why had the detective put her in this position? The thought had bounced in and out, reverberating in her mind all night.

"I should have known." Jimmy spat the words out. She had to be careful. She couldn't let him take the power. Maybe that was what he wanted. She didn't like the way he was looking at her. She was more than aware that her dress revealed too much. What had worked in her favor a few hours ago was now working against her. "Of course. A girl like you."

"You know nothing about me," she said. She tried to use the tone she'd used when Celia had misbehaved and discipline had been left to her. A small part of her wondered what he thought of her. She pulled out the photos from the files. Smiling girls, young girls. Dora, Elizabeth, Clara, Ruth.

"I know you like to pretend. And you're dumber than I thought." She knew Jimmy was trying to get to her. She gritted her teeth. She had to keep the situation in her control, but she wasn't sure she could.

"These girls all worked for you."

"They all worked for Frank Lister."

"But you're the enforcer, aren't you?" She took a seat at the table, keeping her ankles crossed. "Whatever Frank wants, you make sure to get. And those girls, they just don't behave." His black eyes watched her closely, inspecting every inch of her face.

"You know why you're here, right?" he asked. "It's because they're going to need someone to blame when this all goes to shit." He let those last words hang in the air, and her heart squeezed in her chest.

"What about these girls?" She struggled to focus on the topic. She had to remember what was important here. The building creaked around them, settling in. It was early, or late. The distinctions didn't matter much when she hadn't slept.

He looked around the room. "Those girls knew what they're getting into." He made it seem as if this was their fault.

"Who's the person you and Frank Lister made Dora be with the night she went missing?"

"I could tell you," he said, "but that wouldn't mean anything."

Louise held herself very still, trying not to show that her entire body was shaking. She didn't know why she had agreed to this. It was mere hours after he had tried to rape her, and she was sitting in front of him now. And they were getting nowhere.

"Why don't you tell me anyway?" She supposed he wanted her to be flirtatious, wanted her to be the same charming girl he had met hours earlier. But that wasn't her.

"No, princess." There was a faint smile on his lips, as if he was enjoying this. "I can tell you that I had nothing to do with Dora or Lizzie or Clara or Ruth. I don't have time to kill anyone—running a club requires all of my attention."

She didn't believe him. "That's your story? You're too busy running a club?"

"Have you ever tried it?" The smile remained on his lips as he said this. He acted as if this were all casual, as if they were discussing the weather over tea. If he was shaken at all, he didn't show it. She was almost envious.

"Why did you want to see me?" The question left her lips before she could stop it. It was one she wanted to ask but didn't want to know the answer to. He raised an eyebrow and leaned forward, his eyes boring into her own.

"To remind you that girls like you will only ever belong to men like me."

24

---◁◈▷---

LOUISE CROSSED THE dusty streets as she passed mothers watching their children play while they talked. All of Harlem was nervous now. Even though these children were too young to become victims of the Girl Killer, their mothers conversed without their eyes leaving their sons and daughters. The chatter filled the air around her, and she was hit with nostalgia. Louise remembered playing with Minna as Janie talked to other mothers. It felt for a moment like even though so many things had changed, nothing had.

"Louise!" She paused and turned toward the voice. Her heart constricted as she looked around. "Louise Mary, you get back here right now." She exhaled as the child, the younger Louise, wearing a light pink dress with her hair in braids, darted past. Louise watched for a moment as the mother went over to the young Louise, dusting off her pink dress, making her sit to have her braids redone. She readjusted her dark sunglasses and made her way to the car repair shop.

It was quiet and still. Not many people in Harlem had cars.

This station was more for the white people who ran out of gas on their slumming trips through Harlem. She hated seeing it; she tried to ignore it. People coming into her home to what? Laugh? Stare? Silently thank God that their lives weren't unfortunate? Staring at her, her family and friends, as if they were there purely for entertainment. Louise knew it was more than that. There was a sense of danger that Harlem could provide, among other things.

"Can I help you, ma'am?" Louise turned around at the voice. The man behind her was tall and Black. Louise cleared her throat. She had been wrapped up in her thoughts and momentarily forgotten what she was doing.

"I'm looking for Isaac White." Louise had to tilt her head to look him in the eye. He stared at her for a moment, as if weighing something. She had decided to track Isaac down before Gilbert could. She was still trying to find the mysterious, gift-giving Bernie. She didn't know if Gilbert was working these leads, and if he wasn't going to, she was.

"He took the day today." The answer was short and she knew he was lying. Growing up with three sisters solidified her ability to tell when someone was lying.

Louise raised an eyebrow. She fell into a smile. It was something she had seen Maeve do, and the result could be quite charming if she did it right. "Oh, of course, sorry. I'm . . . a friend of his and I have some news to deliver."

"Like what?" Now he was interested. Louise held firm, not letting herself cave.

"That's for Isaac White." She tried to keep her voice cool. So much of this job was trying to keep cool as her insides shook. She gritted her teeth together, working to remain calm.

"What did you say your name was?"

"I didn't give it." That was the end of that.

"Well, ma'am, if you don't have a car, I can't help you." He didn't seem threatening or intimidating. Louise thought that she should be scared of him, but she wasn't. She bit her lower lip. He looked her over, squinting as if that would help him see. Louise swallowed hard. A stalemate as they regarded each other.

"Do you know when he'll be in next?" She was hoping by stalling that Isaac White would just walk in.

"Not sure. He comes and goes as he pleases." He cleared his throat. He moved so he was behind the counter, forcing Louise to turn around. She stepped toward the counter.

"Sounds like a bad employee." Louise leaned against the counter.

"He does his best, I suppose." The answer was short and dry. She could tell that this man wasn't very interested in speaking to her, but she was going to persist.

"What is he like?"

The man considered this question. A small smile appeared on his face, and Louise watched as he thought about it. He didn't ask who she was or what she was doing. "Don't you know? If you're friends with him?"

"Casual acquaintances?" There was no way to walk back her lie now. The counter was covered in dust and Louise ran her finger through it. The air smelled like motor oil, thick and pungent.

"You're awful curious." It was a plain statement, an observation.

"I just want to know. Maybe I'll wait to see if he comes in after all."

The man sighed. He rolled his sleeves to his elbows. Sweat was dripping off him, and Louise fought the urge to take a step back.

"If I tell you, you'll leave?" He watched her carefully after wiping the sweat from his forehead. Louise considered this. She nodded and he continued. "He's quiet. Sometimes doesn't show for work, sometimes works doubles. Keeps to himself," the man explained. As she listened, Louise could see a picture of Isaac White taking shape in her mind. She imagined he was of average height, close-cropped hair, a shy, quick smile. He was usually reading a book on his break. Maybe he was an artist.

"You ever seen him get angry?" She braced both her hands on the dusty counter, knowing she'd have to scrub her hands later.

"I don't think he has an angry bone in his body" was the patient reply. Now the man's smile was a little amused. She inhaled and exhaled, trying not to let her temper get the better of her. She noticed that there was a slight gap in his teeth, a charming, endearing little flaw.

But she still thought that he was lying to her. Louise was unsure of whom and what to trust.

"He ever mention any hobbies outside of work?" It was a bad way to phrase it, and the question tumbled from her lips before she could think of something better. His eyes rested on her. Louise held his gaze; his eyes were a brown so dark they bordered on black, deep and endless.

"He's not much of a talking-at-work kind." The answer came after what felt like a thousand minutes, each ticking by slower than the last. "Like I said, he really just keeps to himself."

"Of course." There was something about him. His tone of voice, the way he looked directly into her eyes, made her know he was holding something back.

"His fiancée would be devastated if something happened to him."

"Who is his fiancée?" Louise asked. The man's eyebrow quirked up.

"It seems like you've never met him."

Louise could feel something sink in her stomach. A part of her regretted coming without Rafael, who was very good at talking to people; Rosa Maria, who could charm anyone; or the detective, whose job this was. Louise relaxed into that charming Maeve smile again. She wasn't sure if it worked for women like her. She removed her hands from the countertop. She didn't say anything for a moment as he regarded her. "I suppose you'll have to ask your friend." He said this coolly. It was a dismissal and she knew that. She pulled herself away from the counter, dusting her hands off as she did so.

Had she gotten what she needed? There was nothing in front of her, nothing she could really use. She had lost. "Have a nice afternoon." Louise exited the little building and went back into the sunlight, pausing only to slide her sunglasses back over her eyes.

<hr />

LOUISE WALKED FROM the car repair shop to Morningside Park. The two were just blocks away from each other, and she had to stop and buy another bottle of Coke to combat the heat as she walked.

She wandered, really, instead of walking. She let herself enjoy strolling around the neighborhood she called home. The afternoon remained dusty and hot as she walked. She passed Maggie's and felt her heart squeeze.

When she reached the park, Louise could see Annie Taylor sitting on a bench. She wore a day dress, her face immaculately made up, and she was sitting next to a man, a coy smile on her face.

Louise paused. She couldn't get closer to the couple without alerting them to her presence, and maybe she didn't want to do that. She hovered, just out of sight, trying to see whom Annie was talking to.

When she realized who it was, out of uniform and a boater hat firmly on his head, Louise was shocked. Annie was talking to Officer Martin.

Louise watched. She wished she could have gotten close enough to hear what they were saying. Annie was completely at ease. Louise moved closer. Locked in conversation, the two weren't aware that there were other people around them. Officer Martin said something; Annie laughed, the breeze carrying the sound to where Louise stood.

She didn't know what to do. Louise was stuck in her spot, as if her sensible flats had grown roots and she was cursed to stay there forever. She bit her lower lip. Around her, the day continued for everyone else: couples milled around; mothers tugged their children and pushed strollers down the path. She was sure this park, calm and still, was her favorite place in Harlem.

Annie laughed again and Louise watched the girl. There was nothing in her body posture that suggested she was uncomfortable. Officer Martin was also at ease. He was sitting rather close to her, and Annie didn't move away.

Louise remembered that Annie had said the young officer had made her feel uneasy. She wondered what had changed, or if she had lied. She knew that if she got much closer, they would surely notice. It was a couple more minutes of quiet conversation, punctuated with Annie's laugh once again before the officer pulled himself away. She watched as he walked off, in the opposite direction, never seeing Louise as he left. Annie let out a breath and relaxed into the bench. Louise waited one moment, then approached the girl.

"What was that?" It came out like an accusation, and it was. Annie eyed her.

"What was what?"

"Don't be stupid. I saw you."

Annie wasn't a very good liar. It was in her face, sweet and heart shaped and open. Her face gave away everything she was thinking, no matter how hard she tried to control it.

"That was nothing. He just wanted to talk about the murders." Another lie, but Louise didn't want to push it.

"You can't mistake kindness for someone who's good." Louise couldn't help but say the same sort of thing she would tell Celia. "He wants something from you."

"Like you do?" Annie was staring right at her, her eyes dark and cool.

"I'm trying to protect you." She'd said it enough that she had begun to believe it. Maybe she was no better than the officer. No one said that this would be easy. Louise was, in fact, explicitly told that none of this would be easy.

"You're doing a swell job of it." Annie tore her eyes away from her. Louise could understand that she was scared and angry, that she was mourning the loss of people she loved. Louise innately understood what the feeling was like.

Watching Annie now, she realized again how young these girls were. It was hard to imagine that she had ever been the same age. It was hard to believe that she had once been the same way.

But while Louise had had to fight, she'd never had to go through something like this. And Annie was little more than a child. Louise exhaled softly. "How are you doing?"

"I'm . . . scared. I'm always scared. I can't sleep at night, can't eat—I can't do anything. I started working with my aunt at a dress shop. My mother is watching my every move. I should be at work right now." The words came out in a stream, spilling over before Annie could stop them. "No one cares. Dora and Lizzie and Clara and Ruth can't even have real funerals because their families can't afford it and they're dead. Sometimes I go to call Dora and I remember she's dead. And no one cares."

"I care." It didn't seem right to try to touch or to hug her. Annie was staring straight ahead, absolutely refusing to cry. "I care and you have to know that. I'm not going to stop fighting for you." The most important thing was making sure that this girl was okay.

"You know you can call me anytime." Louise pulled the only business card she had—the detective's—from her purse, along with a pen, and scrawled the number for Miss Brown's house on the back. "Ask for me. I'll talk to you." Annie took the card and stared at it. Louise's penmanship was not the best. It was barely legible, but Annie stared at it until she understood.

They stayed there in silence. Louise couldn't turn her attention to the case now, so she stayed there, just in case Annie needed someone.

25

⏅

"LOVIE, COME, STAND in front of me." Rafael could be demanding. In his hand, he held a little pistol. He had shown her how to load it and how to clean it, and now she was nervous about shooting it.

"I don't need to know this." She had made this point several times this afternoon. She had pouted the whole train ride through, as if acting like a child would change his mind.

Louise hadn't even known that Rafael knew how to shoot a gun.

"Louise." He dropped his voice so only she could hear him. They were at a special range outside the city, and she was the only woman. She stepped up toward him. He wrapped his arms around her, placing the gun in her hand.

Rafael had explained that this little pistol was something easily concealed in her purse or coat pocket. "It's new on the market. It's what detectives are using these days." Louise didn't ask how he had managed to procure one. "Slow and steady. You can't let anything draw your focus away."

He had shown her how to do this three times. At first, she thought it would be easy—aim and shoot. She placed a finger on the trigger, squeezed. The noise and the recoil made her jump back.

"Too fast, Lovie," Rafael said. His voice was in her ear, talking gently. She didn't want to admit it, but she had been skittish since that night in the club. It had been a couple of days. She still felt Jimmy Olson's hands on her, holding her down, choking her.

He would have killed her given the chance.

"You have to make sure your hands are steady. You have to make sure your everything is steady." Rafael was still hovering around her. He kept looking at her with wide-eyed concern. His face was permanently stuck in the position since she had told him what happened at Maggie's, and she hated that he felt like she needed help. Rosa Maria was furious too. Furious and scared, and she practically insisted these lessons happen when Louise refused.

"I have protected myself for my entire life," Louise said.

"February 1916."

"Harlem's Hero."

"I don't think you should trust the detective for your safety." Rafael corrected her stance. Shoulders back, feet apart, stand straight and sturdy. She was reminded of the little lessons her aunt would put her and her sisters through. Perfect posture, perfect walk.

But her hands shook. Visibly. She tried to steel her nerves. He was right. After the raid at Maggie's, she knew the only person she could trust was herself.

"Come on, Lovie." His voice was soft. She closed her eyes, letting the feeling of desperation and fear wash over her. She had gone through so much. This was about protecting herself. Protecting her sisters. Rafael stood next to her now, his hands in his pockets. He was grinding his teeth together. "I know you're nervous. I am too. I just want you to be safe."

They had been friends for a decade. He was trying to help her. He was doing what he thought was right. If she stopped fighting him, maybe she would learn something.

She was grateful. She exhaled, letting everything fall away from her. She held herself as steady as she could, and she opened her eyes and shot.

It was still not perfect. She had missed the center of the target. But her bullet hole had ripped clean through the paper.

"Aim for the heart," Rafael said. For a moment, she had forgotten he was still there beside her, his hands guiding her body into the correct position. "If you shoot, you shoot to kill." Protestations bubbled up, but she bit her lip. She couldn't imagine having to use this weapon. She'd always gotten by on her wits, her smarts.

But the world was harder now. She couldn't afford to be soft.

Rafael showed her again. He was a good teacher, calm and patient. They had been at this place, this gun range outside the city, for hours, and she had just barely gotten the hang of it.

"Will I really ever need to use this?"

"Just in case, Lovie. It's yours." She held the tiny pistol in her hand. She was aware that it was the same type that Gilbert carried. She had seen it in his office a couple of times, lying on his desk, cold and harmless. "Try again."

She did as he asked, keeping her arm straight and staring directly into the target.

She shot once, twice, and a third time, emptying the barrel.

She had gotten close but not close enough.

26

⌖

THERE WAS NOTHING ladylike or graceful in climbing down the trellis in a gown. Louise owned one very nice dress. It was a dress she had bought on a whim a couple of years ago after seeing it in a store. It had cost a lot of money: emerald green with black beading, trailing to the ground. There was a matching little cape-let, but she hadn't put it on. She always thought that green made her look older. She had even succeeded in putting on her makeup herself, and against her forehead, a glitzy diamond hair band spar-kled.

Rosa Maria followed her out of the window. She was wearing an ornately beaded dress that landed just past her knee. In the low night-lights, the silver and green and purple beading danced and sparkled. She had pulled her dyed blond hair from her face. She was in a mood, and although she looked gorgeous, she had been glowering ever since Louise had told her about the raid.

Rafael watched as they approached. "You gals look sublime."

"Ritzy, aren't we?" Louise knew she looked good, but that did nothing to temper the waves of nerves in her stomach. She pushed a stray hair from her eyes. Rafael had done his part too. He was wearing a tuxedo with a wicked smile on his face. Louise knew that they would be the best-looking people in the joint.

"Let's go," Rosa Maria said. Louise took her hand and Rosa Maria didn't pull away.

They began to walk down the path. Lately she felt safe only when she was with someone. Even though Maggie's was silent, music blared from clubs that were supposed to be discreet. She kept hold of Rosa Maria as they marched down the street. Rafael led them to a rather large, unassuming building.

"Here we go," he said as he pulled open the door.

It was different from the Zodiac. Not much of a dance floor, although there was a small bandstand with a singer crooning away, tables scattered around. The average age of the patrons was about thirty. Louise was not surprised to see that girls, dressed in white with wine-colored beading on their dresses, flitted between the tables with smiles on their faces.

Rafael had been right to tell her to dress up. Everyone was dressed up in their finest.

Louise surveyed the building as Rafael escorted them to a table. It was a central table where they could see all the action.

"When do you come here?" Louise paused as Rafael pulled her seat out for her. So far, he was being quite the gentleman. She sat. Rosa Maria settled in next to her. Louise offered her a cigarette and she took it, finally relaxing into a smile.

"I try not to." Rafael sat down across from her.

Everything about Snake Eyes was gilded and ornate, the perfect location for a more mature night out. Rafael's dark eyes rolled around as if he was taking it all in, making mental notes. Rosa Maria stared at the singer on the bandstand.

"What are you thinking about?" Louise tapped her fingers on the table.

"Nothing much." Rosa Maria was still smiling as she smoked. "I'm trying not to be such a fire extinguisher."

"I know and I love you anyway." Louise felt out of place and she wasn't sure what she was supposed to do at a table like this.

She leaned toward Rafael. "You never really answered my question. Why do you come here?"

"I come here when I need to," he answered after a moment. His dark eyes watched one of the girls as she made her way through the tables.

"You're being very mysterious. Girls don't like that," Louise said.

He stuck his tongue out at her, and she rolled her eyes. She couldn't picture her friend in a place like this. Apparently, there were things she didn't know about him. "Oh, Lovie, when have I ever liked a girl?"

"How can I help you?" A sweet girl in white approached their table with a smile.

Rafael placed a few bills on the table. "Three glasses of the good stuff. And bring the bottle." The girl in white nodded and collected the bills. "I'll be right back with that, Mr. Moreno."

"She knows your name!" Louise said, pointing to the girl as she left.

"I think if Maggie's is closed, Frank Lister will be here," Rafael said, pulling Louise's attention back to the matter at hand. She had almost forgotten. For a moment, it felt like just a night out with her friends.

"And if he isn't?" She leaned back in her seat. She couldn't help asking even if she didn't really want to hear the answer.

"He's laying low. I'd give it a couple of days. Is this for the case?" Rosa Maria said. She was still smoking, still watching the singer.

"It is."

Rosa Maria narrowed her eyes. "That's too easy, isn't it? The owner of the club?"

"Leave no stone unturned."

Rafael looked up as their waitress returned with three glasses. She placed them and the bottle on the table, and Rafael slipped her another bill before the girl disappeared.

"You're not getting me drunk tonight, Mr. Moreno," Louise said. Rafael busied himself with pouring the glasses. This was real alcohol and Louise knew it. He only smiled in response. He handed her a glass and she drained it. "So, what's the appeal of a place like this?"

There was a small smile on Rafael's face, something unreadable. "I told you that you'd hate it."

She couldn't shake the feeling he was hiding something from her.

THREE DRINKS IN and Louise excused herself. The restroom was hard to find. She had to slide behind the bar and go up a set of stairs. To make matters even worse, she was tipsy.

Her shoes pinched. They were a little too small; she had ordered them from a catalogue years ago. There were holes in the sole, and she couldn't fit into them comfortably. She paused to pull them off and held them by their straps as she padded down the hall.

She wasn't even very sure there *was* a restroom up here, but she used the opportunity to look around. A couple of the doors were closed. She pushed her ear to one of them, listening. It was silent. The music was distant. The world tilted around her and she tried to keep herself upright.

"You can't be up here." The voice came from behind her, and she whirled around. The girl in front of her was tall and long, a cool look on her face. It was Ida Callahan. She must have begun working here after the raid.

"I just got a little turned around." It wasn't a very good excuse, but it was true.

"You're that nosy girl from Maggie's, aren't you?" Ida Callahan's nose wrinkled.

"I am, but I'm nosy for good reason." Her words slurred together. "I'm trying to find out what happened to your friend. Elizabeth."

At the mention of the name, Ida softened. "So, you're snooping around?" She crossed her arms over her chest. She was wearing the white club uniform, her hair out of her eyes and her lips dripping in red.

"I'm actually just looking for the restroom."

"Downstairs," Ida said. "There's a door near the bandstand—it's that one."

Louise nodded and moved to push past the girl.

"Wait. I thought of something." For the first time the younger girl sounded scared. Louise turned back toward her. "I keep going over it and over it, and Lizzie was mad, but I don't think she was mad at me." Ida paused, biting her lip. "She kept mentioning this man. She wouldn't tell me his name or anything."

"She was seeing someone?" Louise placed her hand on the wall next to her. It was so hard to stay upright, and she knew that Rafael would have ordered yet another bottle of alcohol.

"I'm not sure. She talked about him a lot. The gifts he sent her. Roses. I think she was just trying to lead him on." Ida trailed off and cleared her throat.

Louise took another step toward the girl. In the dim lighting, Louise could see she had tears in her eyes. She pretended not to notice. "I have a friend, like you were with Elizabeth." She was saying it because she was drunk, and she was sure that no one was listening to them. "If anything happened to her, I know I'd never forgive myself." The younger girl wiped away her tears, pulling herself together.

"I just miss her so much." Ida's voice was soft. "She wanted to leave. She wanted to leave Maggie's, but I told her that we should stay and save up, and she listened to me. She never listened to me. . . . I've got to get back down there. I'm just filling in for a friend here."

Ida pushed past her and moved toward the stairs. There was something about her stare that still managed to be so cold. "I have your handkerchief."

"Keep it."

Louise stayed there for a moment, waiting for the world to stop spinning around her before she made her move. She was sure that she had found something, even if the person she was looking for wasn't there. Her shoes were still in her hands, and she paused to put them on. She was going to throw them away when she got home. Life was too short to wear uncomfortable shoes.

She clutched the banister tightly as she descended the stairs. Rafael and Rosa Maria were still at the table, their waitress leaning in. She stayed there for a moment, watching as Rafael smiled up at her. Louise smoothed the wrinkles in her dress and approached, feeling her shoes pinch her feet every step of the way.

"Lovie!" Rafael, too, was drunk as Louise approached. She let him pour her another drink.

"I'll be right back with that, Mr. Moreno," the girl said, and moved away from their table. Louise had been right. A new bottle was waiting for them. Rosa Maria was in better spirits now too, or she was thoroughly drunk, waving a cigarette around as she so loudly explained something in Spanish.

This was what she wanted, time with her friends, nights out. She wouldn't let that be taken from her.

27

⧫

MEETING IN MORNINGSIDE Park was much more natural than sitting in the detective's office. It was the middle of the day and she found that she needed to be outside. No one who passed stopped to look at them. They were perfectly invisible.

"Have you found Bernie yet?" Louise had asked the moment she had sat down.

"I told you." Gilbert was always patient, always quiet. "We're working on every lead available."

She didn't believe him, but she thought that moving on would be smarter. "I have to ask you something." Louise adjusted her sunglasses. She was sipping a Coke and feeling the warm afternoon sun on her skin. She was sitting with her back straight, legs crossed at the ankle. She was consciously trying to keep as much space between them as she could.

She didn't want anyone passing to assume anything.

"Go ahead."

She had hoped that the relationship between her and Gilbert had changed a little. He no longer saw her as someone he had to manage. She hoped she could actually talk to him. But still, something about him made her nervous. She avoided looking straight at him. "Why do you care so much?" She had thought about storming into his office, placing her hands on the desk, and asking the question with so much force, he'd be stunned and have to answer.

But this was better. Less combative, at least.

He lit a cigarette and didn't reply for some time. Now, in the delicate sun, she could see how old and haggard he looked. She fidgeted in her seat. She didn't like when he took too long to answer her questions. The silence was always formidable between them, and she never knew how to read between the lines to parse what he really meant when he was quiet. "I knew this was coming."

"So?"

"I want to tell you the truth."

She could trust him. She could trust him. The words rang through her head so many times, and she wasn't sure she could believe them.

She knew he had his own motives. But people in the community spoke highly of him.

"So, tell me." She thought he had figured she was weak of stomach or heart.

He took another drag on his cigarette. "Laura." He said it so gently.

"Who is that?" Louise couldn't resist a good story.

"A woman I loved once," he said. She pursed her lips. It was hard to imagine that he had loved anyone at all. "I met her here, after the war." He had never talked about his own efforts in the war. Louise had been barely the twins' age when it had started. Those few years were long and cold.

"Did you fight?"

"Briefly. My brother did too. We left our sister behind."

She didn't expect him to open up about that. She knew it had been a hard and painful time for many people. She stared at the vibrant grass, not making eye contact. "Who was she? The woman?"

"A seamstress. I met her when I started with the police."

She looked up at him. He wasn't looking at her; she caught his side profile. He felt dreamy and faraway. "She was stubborn and smart and funny and . . . a lot like you, Miss Lloyd."

He didn't have to spell it out for her. She tried to imagine the Black woman this white man had, against all odds, fallen for.

"What happened to her?"

"Died. In a fire." This was the most forthcoming he had ever been with her. He was facing her now, and she was resisting the urge to look away. "A couple years ago now. She was better at my job than I was. She'd help me, sometimes. You remind me a lot of her. I . . . loved her." He trailed off. "We were supposed to get married. It was stupid, and reckless, but you love who you love."

Her heart squeezed. He said it so simply, but she knew he wouldn't feel the same about Ida and Elizabeth. He wouldn't feel the same about her and Rosa Maria.

It was interesting, those divides. It was interesting how rules were broken.

"Then she died. I tried to save her. I tried to convince her to stay with me. Nothing worked." His voice was so quiet, so devoid of emotion. He was staring at his hands now. "When I realized . . . I . . ." He paused. "It was my fault." He cleared his throat. She looked toward him. He was so careful, making sure never to touch her. She kept her space, but now he was staring her in the eye, something so raw and real that she pulled herself a little farther away from him. "You remind me of her, Miss Lloyd. You have all the good parts." Here he smiled. "And most of the bad."

She wrinkled her nose. She tried to imagine what this woman

was like, how she laughed, what she wore. As hard as she tried, she couldn't picture her.

IT WAS RARE that Josie contacted her. They met in the back pew of church, in the middle of the day, in between Josie's errands.

Josie sat straight and still, staring at the pulpit, not blinking.

"Hey, Sunshine," Louise said, sitting down next to her. Josie barely acknowledged her. "What's eating you?"

Josie leaned back in the pew. "I'm worried about Celia." They had been spending more and more time apart. Celia was drawn away with her marathon wedding planning and daydreams. Josie had always been more practical.

"What's going on?"

"She's mixed in with bad people." The answer came after a little pause. Louise reached out and took Josie's hand. Josie had always been more mature and sensible than her sister. She tried to see the world as it was, whereas her sister tried to see it how it could be. Celia often lost her head or heart. Josie wasn't like that.

"How do we help her?"

"I don't think she's getting married because she wants to." Josie spoke as if Louise had not said a word.

Was this jealousy? Josie was still upset her sister was choosing to leave her. Even though they'd be together for a few more weeks and spend their birthday together, her one main support was starting a new life without her. "How do we help her?" Louise asked again. Josie was clutching onto her rosary, dangling the beaded string from her fingers.

"She won't listen to reason."

Louise longed to be able to take their problems away, like she used to. "I'll talk to her, Sunshine. I'll try."

"You should meet him." Josie was glowering at the pulpit. The familiar quiet sounds of the church surrounded them. They weren't alone in the pews, but they were the farthest back. Other people held hushed conversations; some silently said their prayers. Louise knew her father and Sam were both in the bowels of the building. "He's taking advantage of her. She can't see it."

"Josie, it's okay. It'll all be okay." She didn't know if that was true, but she wasn't sure what else to say. Louise hadn't felt like this when Minna had gotten married; in fact, she had barely felt anything at all. But she doubted this was just nerves about Josie losing her twin.

"But it won't be." Josie hadn't yelled in all of her sixteen years, but she did now, raising her voice as loud as she could muster. People turned to stare at them. Louise pulled her sister up by the arm, gripping a little too tightly, and dragged her out of the church.

"What is going on, Josephine Lloyd?" she asked the minute they were outside, facing each other on the street. Her grip remained on her sister's arm, and Josie didn't pull away, just looked defiantly at her.

She recognized that look. She had seen it on herself, defying her father, waiting for the brutal reprimand.

But she wasn't her father.

She let go of her sister. "Josie, please, you have to talk to someone. You can talk to me." Josie stepped away from her. Again, she was getting nowhere. "Come with me. Come to dinner at my house. Then we can talk, okay?"

It was nearly time to eat anyway. Her matron liked the girls to be prompt. Josie considered this. "Okay," she said.

There were so many things in the world she could not solve, but hopefully, she could solve this.

28

THE EDITOR OF the *New York Tribune* insisted that there be people in the office at all times. He believed that news never stopped, never slept, and neither should his employees. Even with about half the regular team, all the typists had to be in. It had taken about four minutes for Louise to convince Rosa Maria to slip her into the archives of the *New York Tribune*. Rosa Maria had been reluctant to sneak her in, but Louise had made her case.

She was in the basement of the building, sitting behind a pile of papers from years ago. She was going to begin with the year the war started and work forward. She was prepared to spend all day in the archives if she had to, but she wouldn't leave until she found something.

She pulled her sweater closer to her body, keeping the chill off her arms. She placed her hat on the table and picked up a pen.

It was quiet, but then she didn't know what news sounded like. The *Tribune* offices were actually located on the second floor of the building, below a tailor's and above a law office. So the noises she was hearing didn't even belong to Rosa Maria's office.

It was strange seeing years she had lived summarized in a few words per article. She tried to think about what she'd been doing during the war years, and then remembered: being kidnapped, escaping, and experiencing a few moments of fame.

She skipped over that part. She didn't want to be reminded of her sixteen-year-old self, tired and hungry, being paraded for articles that would bring some prestige to her father's congregation.

She looked around, realizing that this small room was much like the one where she was once held. She took a deep breath, a sip of water.

It was a decade ago. She was fine.

A fire she could do. The *Tribune* was more meticulous about reporting the goings-on in the Black parts of the city, and the *Tribune* would be more thorough. Even years later, that memory would haunt her and everyone she knew.

It couldn't have been in Harlem. She had no details, except a first name, Laura, and that could have been fake as well.

She thought about Gilbert. She really didn't know anything about him. He was so private, so hard to read.

Maybe he was telling the truth. She did want to believe him, but she couldn't let herself. Not yet. There was something that didn't click with his story. She stared at the shelves of boxes, chronicling every paper from every month since the inception of the *Tribune*.

She'd have to whittle down her research. Gilbert hadn't given her much to go on, but she'd be sitting there for a year trying to find something helpful. Louise tapped her fingers on the cold metal table. She was sitting under one lone lightbulb.

Maybe she'd be able to find something else helpful to the case.

Maybe this wouldn't be a waste after all.

The boxes were daunting. She read the articles until the words swam in front of her eyes, blurring and not making much sense.

When she finally pushed her chair from the table, two hours had passed. She had skimmed through the years 1914–24 and no mention of a young woman killed in a fire.

She was sure the detective was lying to her. She didn't know what to do with this information.

———✦———

SHE CLIMBED THE stairs to the *Tribune* offices, past the front-desk girl, who was enthralled with a book and not paying attention. She pushed open the glass door to find a few men staring at their desks. Rosa Maria sat next to a man's desk, dutifully typing as he dictated to her.

She shouldn't be up here. She knew that. But the basement was cold, boring, and not helping.

Besides, the man Rosa Maria was sitting next to was rather familiar. Rosa Maria didn't notice her as she walked forward. No one did. No one expected her to be there, so no one looked.

She stepped into the bullpen. One man slammed his phone down with a yell. Louise jumped, bit the inside of her cheek so she wouldn't cry out.

Rosa Maria and the man looked up as she approached. Rosa Maria got to her feet. "Louise, you were supposed to call me."

"I got bored."

Rosa Maria cleared her throat and turned to the man behind her. Now that Louise was close, she could see he was the same man who had accosted her outside Maggie's.

"Miss Lloyd?"

"Yes, we've met already, haven't we? How do you know who I am?"

"Every reporter in Midtown knows who you are. You're . . . you've grown. You're beautiful. Thomas. Bernard Thomas." He extended a hand. She didn't shake it. "We were just writing about you. And about the new murders."

Rosa Maria's eyes were huge. Inadvertently, Louise had caught something she had been trying to hide.

"Another story about me, about those girls."

"You're really the main angle."

She stared at the reporter, then Rosa Maria, unsure of what to do or say. "I don't want to be the main angle. I don't want to be any angle." He started to say something, but Louise, seeing red, continued. "What is your obsession with this case? Why do you focus on it, on me?" He blushed, stammered for words. Louise barreled on. "Have you considered that we don't want your help? That you sticking your nose in our business doesn't help, but it hurts?"

"I'm not trying to hurt you." The answer was quiet and resolute. He really thought he was helping, doing something good. "Someone needs to inform the people about what's going on."

She was going to get herself into trouble. A thought came to her. His name sounded rather familiar, but she couldn't place why. She took a moment to compose herself. His coworkers, who were also Rosa Maria's coworkers, had stopped to watch the proceedings. She was attracting the wrong sort of attention wherever she went. She eyed him. "And that has to be you?"

"Louise." She had never heard that tone, cold and imperious, from Rosa Maria. It made her stop midthought. Rosa Maria was wearing a thin, deadly smile. "May I?"

Louise allowed herself to be escorted away.

29

⌁

DETECTIVE GILBERT NEVER left her alone in his office, but today he had left her sitting in her chair across from his desk. She was going to use this time to her advantage. Something had been bugging her since her run-in with one Bernard Thomas. She was still thinking of the name.

Louise had been glaring at the detective all morning, for the better part of their meeting, just allowing him to talk. He had been going over evidence, piles of paper stacked on the desk. If he thought she was being strangely quiet, he didn't say anything. Then he had left her alone in his office with a mumbled excuse. It was almost as if he had *wanted* her to go through his things.

It was his fault.

She pulled his desk drawer open. The bottom one, the biggest, was locked. Officially, she was just looking for the list she had stolen from Maggie's. Unofficially, she was looking for anything that would confirm his story about Laura. She found an envelope from an Emily Gilbert, with his home address on it. She folded it in half, sliding it in between her garter strap and her thigh. She rifled through the papers he kept in the drawer. None of them looked to be very important.

She knew she had very limited time. She was focused on finding something that was relevant to the story he'd told her. He had been so convincing. But as Louise really thought about it, something didn't add up. She lowered herself into his chair, flicking through the drawers as fast as she could.

She found the list of names she'd taken from Maggie's buried in a pile of papers in the middle drawer. She folded that and also slipped it in with the envelope.

The door banged open, triumphantly and obnoxiously, announcing the arrival of Officer Martin.

Louise looked up at him, caught. She slid the drawer closed, fighting to retain her composure.

"What are you doing?" He always spat the words he said to her. He never looked directly at her, or he tried not to. A smug grin was working its way across his face. Louise wrinkled her nose.

"Just looking for a bottle opener." Bad lie. Her bottle of Coke was sitting on the desk, open and untouched. "Handkerchief."

"Lying bitch."

"Smug fucker."

He took a step toward her. His eyes blazed. She was lucky the desk was between them.

"I know what you're up to."

"Then tell me." Louise pulled herself to her full height, not letting him shake her confidence. He couldn't *prove* anything. That was the important part. She knew it would be her word against his.

He could take her. He could, if he wanted to, drain the life from her body in this office. She narrowed her eyes. Her heart pounded, gearing up for a fight. She would fight him until the bitter end, if she had to.

"You're spying on Detective Gilbert." He took another step toward the desk. She took a step back. She recognized the calm, cold look in his eyes. He was determined to get his way. He wouldn't stop until he did.

"Can you prove it?" Louise asked. She was so tired of him thinking he knew better than her because he had been gifted with a penis. She was so tired of him thinking he knew better than her because he was white.

He looked her up and down. She had thought he had ignored her, mostly, preferring to pretend she didn't exist.

But that wasn't true.

He had been waiting for her to slip up, and now was his chance.

"I'm keeping my eye on you. I have no idea why the detective would trust a nigger bitch like you." The insult no longer stung. In fact, she had grown a little bored with his lack of creativity. He was so proud of being able to hit the same note over and over again.

It had begun to wear thin.

"I'm sure you are." She kept her voice calm and still. She was not going to let him know how much he scared her. She moved from behind the desk so she was facing him. "Tell Detective Gilbert anything you want."

"Tell me what?"

She kept her gaze trained on Martin, waiting for his reply. "Go ahead, Officer. Don't you have to tell Detective Gilbert something?"

He was smarter than she initially took him for. He sighed, lit a cigarette. "Nothing." It was a little petulant, but he sat in his regular seat. Louise lowered herself into her regular seat, feeling the pieces of paper settle against her thigh.

"Right." Gilbert must have sensed something strange between

them, but he ignored it, pushing ahead to the next parts of their plan.

LOUISE DIDN'T DARE pull the list out until she was safely back in the pink room. She placed the envelope on her vanity and sank down into the chair. She had discarded her coat, hat, and gloves, tossing them on the floor. She unfolded the paper, now worn in its creases. It still smelled like ink. The paper was starting to tear and the writing beginning to fade from being manhandled so.

She scanned the list until she found it. Bernard Thomas. His name in red ink. It appeared he owed Frank Lister a tidy sum of money, several hundred dollars. She stared at the name until her vision began to swim. Could this be the man who'd given Dora the ring? The Thomas that Timothy Draper had referred to as he threw her out of his store?

What was Bernard Thomas hiding?

ROSA MARIA WAS still angry. Louise understood. She had embarrassed her in her workplace, but Rosa Maria would barely look at her at dinner, and didn't join her in the pink room afterward.

Louise had to wait for her matron and housemates to be asleep before she crossed the hall in two easy steps and knocked twice on the door of the blue room.

Rosa Maria barely slept. She was more productive in the middle of the night, when there was no one else to bother her. She usually stayed up late, writing her novel by candlelight. There was too long of a pause before the door opened. Rosa Maria was wrapped in a dressing gown, glasses low on her nose.

"What do you want?"

"I am sorry," Louise said. She felt as if she had been apologizing a lot lately. But this was her fault. "I am sorry. I didn't mean to embarrass you."

"You acted with no decorum." Rosa Maria still refused to look at her, and maybe that was the worst part.

"I lost my temper. I couldn't help it."

"You always lose your temper and you can *never* help it."

"I'm at the center of everything that newspaperman does." Louise didn't know if this was exactly true. She had never stopped to read the *Tribune*, but it felt like that some days. "He accosted me outside of Maggie's." She was making the incident more dramatic than it was. Rosa Maria rolled her eyes.

"You just do whatever you want with no concern for anyone or anything else."

"Rosa Maria, please. I didn't mean anything. I'm sorry. But you . . . you should have told me what he was working on."

"I didn't know." Rosa Maria took a deep, steadying breath. "I just started working with him. And, anyway, this isn't about me."

"Then what is it about?"

They were standing so close together, their argument in whispers so they didn't risk waking one of the other girls up. Rosa Maria was pulling away from her. "I could have been fired."

"The editor wasn't even there."

"Do you think Mr. Thomas would wait for the editor's opinion if he wanted me out? And I was doing you a favor. You only think about yourself."

"But I may have found some—"

"I don't care."

"I apologized."

"You should sleep in your own room tonight, Louise." The way Rosa Maria said her name sent shivers down her spine. Louise pulled away. She was holding the list; she had been wanting to talk about the case, about the possibility that Bernard was involved somehow. "I have a lot of work to do."

It was a dismissal and not a polite or gentle one. She had thought that Rosa Maria would be on her side.

"I am sorry. I really am."

30

ANOTHER GIRL IS missing," Louise said. That morning she
had run into a terrified Annie Taylor hovering on her doorstep. Over a cup of tea, Annie had told her that Nell hadn't been
seen in a couple of days.

The girl had simply vanished. Louise knew that they didn't
have much time left. She was sure it was about to get worse. They
were in the middle of a chess match with someone who was clearly
deranged, and Louise wasn't sure if they were smart enough to win
it. The timeline the detective worked so hard to try to straighten
out no longer mattered. Louise knew that they were behind. She
looked to the board. Nell's name had been added. They were lurch-
ing, stumbling, trying to hold on to the ground as it shifted from
under them.

She eyed him. Gilbert's eyes met hers. She couldn't be sure, but
she thought she saw a ghost of a smile on his face.

"There's also something else. I seem to be missing that list of
names."

"You know."

"You're not exactly subtle."

A blush rose to her cheeks. "I needed to verify something."

"What?"

She cleared her throat. "I'm still in the middle of it. Following a hunch and all." His eyebrows wrinkled together. He was parsing her sentences, trying to find the weakness.

She knew he didn't believe her. She rose from her chair so fast she knocked it over. "I should keep going on that. I'll see you later."

She righted the chair and exited the office before he could say anything. She took a moment when she was outside the precinct to calm down. She looked up and down the street, always feeling like someone was watching her.

She pulled herself together. She still had a lot to do.

◁╎▷

DINNER THAT NIGHT was tense. Lately, dinner was the only time that all seven girls and the matron saw one another. Louise sat at her place while conversation wound around her. She wasn't much for talking these days. She had been thinking about the case. She was tired and Rosa Maria still wasn't speaking to her. Louise yearned to be in bed.

However, Maeve was glowing. From her hair to her perfect white skin, she was radiating from the inside out. Her green eyes rolled around the table. She was filled with news that she couldn't keep in.

"I'm in love!" Maeve's words cut through the commotion of their dinner table and settled over them.

Louise snorted. She had to say something. "Maeve, you say that every week."

"Right," Rosa Maria said. "First it was that businessman."

"Then that boy from the Zodiac," Catherine Gordon said. She was seated next to Maeve, her fork in her hand.

"And that man you led on for three weeks because he was rich," Helen Roberts said. She was seated on Rosa Maria's left side. Maeve blushed, but she wouldn't let this dissuade her.

"It's real this time. He saw me at work. Decided he couldn't leave until he had a date with me. Quite romantic, really." Maeve had the best job, objectively, out of all of them. Her job at Saks Fifth Avenue made her the most stylish girl in the house, and the girls clamored to borrow clothes from her.

"What does he do?" This was Helen again. She was, much like Celia, susceptible to silly romantic whims and daydreams. Most of the girls were, really. All of them were leaning in to hear Maeve's story, even though this was the seventh time this year that she had made this announcement.

"He's a police officer. Officer Andrew Martin," Maeve said. "But that doesn't matter. He still wants to take me to the Zodiac."

"He's using you," Louise said. Six pairs of eyes shifted to her. Louise could feel her heart stutter. She knew it was too much of a coincidence. Louise also knew that she wouldn't be able to explain *how* she knew that. She wished she hadn't spoken up at all.

"You're just sore."

"Am not."

"You are." She had never seen Maeve be so cold. "You're just jealous, Louise Lloyd. Because he loves me and he wants to marry me. He told me so. And once I get married, I can move out of this damn house and leave my damn job and make something of myself. And I want that. But you . . . you've never brought a boy to this table. What are you hiding, Louise? Are you some type of bulldagger or something?" The words rang in her ears, and Louise could feel heat rise to her face as anger pulsated through her. Everyone was staring at her, waiting for a reaction, waiting for her to do something.

Louise had risen from her seat and Maeve had too.

"Girls, sit down, now," Miss Brown said. Usually this order would have been obeyed, but Maeve and Louise were focused on each other.

"Louise." This was Rosa Maria, but not even her soft voice could pull Louise away from this. She was so angry that her vision blurred, that she couldn't see straight. All she could see was Maeve, and her smug, self-satisfied grin. She thought she knew everything. She had everything so easy, and she thought she was slumming it by living in Harlem.

"It's not my fault no one likes you." Maeve's eyes were narrowed into slits. "Nobody likes you and nobody will."

Louise reached up and hit Maeve as hard as she could across the face. She knew there were better ways of conflict resolution, but there was part of her that was overly satisfied with the way her palm made contact with Maeve's cheek.

"Nobody may like me, but at least I won't be some idiot of a housewife," Louise hissed.

"Ladies!" Louise had never heard the matron yell. The room sprang into motion. Maeve raised a hand to her cheek, now very pink, and began to sob. She tore herself away from the table, and Frances rose as well, following her to the bathroom. The rest of the girls watched Louise. They were waiting for her to explode.

"Miss Lloyd," Miss Brown said. Louise stared at her hand in pure elation.

"Lou," Rosa Maria said. She said something else, in Spanish. It was something Louise thought she understood, but her brain was still too stunned to translate. Miss Brown was staring at her, but the matron didn't say anything. This was a first in her house, and they were all unsure of what to do about it.

"I'm tired. I'm going to bed." Louise never left the table before dessert, but she knew she couldn't stay there another minute.

It wasn't until she made it up to her room that she exhaled. She didn't realize that, in those couple of minutes, she hadn't breathed at all. She didn't feel bad about slapping Maeve, even though she thought she should have. Maeve got what was coming to her. She paraded through the house all high-and-mighty because she could so effortlessly get boys to like her. It never occurred to Maeve that the other girls in her house might not want the same thing.

Louise changed, leaving her day clothes in a pile, and crawled into bed and pulled the covers over her head. She wanted all of this to be over.

31

SNAKE EYES WAS full when they arrived. They were given the same table, where they could see everything in the vicinity. Again, they were dressed in their best possible clothes and ready to stalk Frank Lister. Trying to find him was exasperating. She almost wished that he would come to her.

"You know, I'm worried about you, Louise." Rafael was watching her closely. He must have been serious; he rarely ever used her real name.

"You don't have to be." She placed a hand on his wrist. "I promise." She looked around.

"Positive?" This was Rosa Maria. After the incident with Maeve, they had decided to forget their fight. It was an unspoken agreement, but it just seemed that there was enough tension in the house as it was. They both had to move on and let it go.

Louise slid her a smile. "You bet."

She'd brought them with her to make sure that they knew she was okay. Working the case was changing her, which made them worry.

Louise looked around. "How do we know if Frank Lister is here?" It had been a week since the raid. He couldn't stay underground forever.

Rosa Maria smiled. "I bet he likes a girl who can dance." Louise and Rosa Maria rose from the table. The song the band was playing was slow, and they were the only two with this idea, but Louise allowed herself to be escorted onto the dance floor.

They had to waltz, or do an approximation of the waltz. For one moment, Louise tried to fight it. Her waltz was rusty. After a few seconds, she could feel everyone watching them. Louise let Rosa Maria lead, praying this would work.

It had been ages since they had danced together, but they slipped back into their easy partnership. Every time she danced with Rosa Maria, Louise got the same little thrill of excitement in the pit of her stomach. They so perfectly knew how to move with each other, it was as if they were linked by one brain, one heart. Dancing was easier now than talking to each other. They glided across the floor, making difficult steps look simple. Louise realized she was grinning. It was different from dancing at the Zodiac. At the Zodiac, everyone danced. Here, there was a spotlight on them and everyone watched. As the song ended, Rosa Maria twirled her once, twice, three times, and she sank down in a curtsy. Louise looked around. People were watching them, unsure of what to make of two girls dancing with each other. It was bold. It was a statement.

"Do you see him?" Louise asked.

"We should probably do another song," Rosa Maria said. This was fun for her.

"Fine." She looked behind her, to the singer. She counted in a slightly faster song—a foxtrot would do—but before she and Rosa Maria could connect and begin, someone tapped her on the shoulder.

"Might I cut in?" He was tall and flawlessly dressed in a black tux. His dark eyes twinkled with mischief.

"Be my guest." Rosa Maria pulled away from Louise, leaving her alone with Frank Lister.

⧖

"YOU LIED TO me, Sheba." Frank Lister's voice was calm as he took Louise in his arms. She always found it hard to have a casual conversation while dancing. She never liked it; it was tough to concentrate on the two things at the same time.

"I don't know what you're talking about." Louise kept her own voice to a murmur. This was what she had needed, but now she wasn't sure what to do.

"You said you weren't a dancer. You're too pretty to be lying like that."

"I won't make it a habit," Louise said before she could stop herself. It was worse when everyone was watching. She had him right in front of her, and she didn't know what to say.

"You know, I didn't realize—" He paused to effortlessly twirl her around. Louise preferred the foxtrot to the waltz. He was a much better dancer than she'd imagined he would be, and it was hard to keep up with him. He expertly guided them across the floor. Louise's heartbeat matched the pace of the music. She had always found the foxtrot rather calming, something she and Rosa Maria did together often. "The girl who worked in my mother's café was the girl sneaking around my club, talking to my employees."

"How do you know it was me?"

"Put two and two together, Miss Louise Lloyd."

She thought back to the articles hidden in the desk. He knew much more about her than he was letting on.

"Then you know why I'm here."

"Where's that detective that arrested Jimmy?"

"This is my domain."

"You know, Miss Lloyd, you're not one of them." It was eerily similar to what Jimmy Olson had told her in that interrogation room. Her blood ran cold and she was sick of trying to explain that she didn't want to be one of them. "What do they have on you?"

"I'd rather talk about you, Mr. Lister. You're aware that four girls from your club—"

"Former club."

"Your club have turned up dead. And another is missing."

"You don't suspect me, doll, do you?"

"Please don't make me explain how the evidence is stacked against you."

Another twirl, another pause. "Those girls are my employees, Miss Lloyd. It's bad business to kill your employees."

"Not when they're little girls who just won't listen." She knew he, at least, had to have an idea of who the Girl Killer was. He knew every name on that list. There was no way the club functioned without him knowing everything that was going on.

"I'm hurt, Miss Lloyd. To think you think I'm capable of hurting those girls."

"I think we all know what you're capable of, Mr. Lister."

"I'm innocent, Miss Lloyd." His lips hovered near her ear; he was pressing her to him. Louise's heart was in her throat.

"Can you prove it?" Louise looked up at him for the first time. His eyes still rested on her. A small smile was on his lips. She could feel the eyes of everyone watching them as he gracefully moved her across the floor. She didn't try to fight his lead. He made it nearly impossible to do that.

"Apartment 1C. Say 'Thank you,' Miss Lloyd."

She didn't respond. The song ended and Louise again sank into a deep curtsy. It was a moment later she realized Frank Lister had departed, disappeared, and Louise held a key in her hand.

32

⬥

THE FIRST THING she did was consult the list. She knew that she should give it back to the detective, especially since he knew she had it, but she wasn't ready to do so yet. Louise leaned over the paper by lamplight in her bedroom, her dress and combinations discarded for a nightdress and her robe. She sat on top of her bed, her legs curled under her, her hair tied tightly.

Frank Lister's writing was calm and familiar at this point. She had been spending most of her free time committing the list to her memory. When she was anxious, or scared, she'd slowly go through the names, making sure she remembered them all. It was a strange thing that helped soothe her.

It was past three in the morning and everything was a little hazy. Rosa Maria had declined to stay, kissing her good night after they climbed into her room. Louise needed to sleep, needed it so desperately that her bones creaked when she moved, but she stayed awake.

It was a normal key. Frank had slipped it to her so effortlessly, and now she was unsure of what to do with it. The silver glinted in the low light. There was no inscription, nothing on it that would make the meaning clear.

Her conversation with Frank Lister ran through her mind. She didn't get the feeling that he was trying to hide something. In fact, it was the opposite. He was being as helpful as he could. But why?

Maggie talked warmly about him. And Louise knew how he had grown up, before Prohibition. Maggie talked about the near-destitute conditions she, her son, and his family had endured. Louise knew what that was like too, although she was far removed from that life now.

And so was Frank. Now he ruled Harlem with an iron fist. He didn't trust anyone, used everyone in his life for his own gain. And it had worked for him. She knew that. Maggie's was his flagship establishment, the café the cover for the nightclub. He had several other places too.

There was something about him that could seem so sincere. He always made sure to give back to his community when it suited him. And now he had given back in the most mysterious way possible. She was back to staring at the key on her bed, lying on the sheets that matched the walls. The pink sheets were pulled taut and straight. She picked up the key again.

She was going to figure it out.

⋖⋔⋗

ANNIE STARED AT the key. They were sitting in Morningside Park. Louise knew that the only people who would tell her where this key would lead were the girls who worked for Frank Lister. Annie was toying with the key in her fingers, her eyes closed.

Louise had given her the entire story of the previous night at Snake Eyes. Annie hadn't said anything when she finished.

"He owns a building or two." This was the first helpful thing

Annie had said that afternoon. Truthfully, Louise was in a foul mood. She felt like she was on the edge of something, and wanted desperately to know what it was. "I can give you the addresses."

"That would help."

She had spent the morning wandering around Harlem with no real aim. She figured whatever the key opened was close to Maggie's or Snake Eyes. She had to tell the detective about it. She knew that. But she wanted to know where it would lead first.

Annie avoided her gaze. She had also avoided saying much that afternoon. "It hasn't been easy with Nell missing. I've looked everywhere I can for her. She's simply vanished."

Louise was two steps behind, letting the Girl Killer take her bishop with his rook. She knew the key would lead her to where Nell was.

And she had to act fast.

Time was ticking. And she was going to do whatever she could to get Nell back alive.

33

⬥

IT WAS RAINING when Louise woke up, and it continued into the midmorning. Louise pulled a hat over her hair as she waited for the detective. She had forgotten her umbrella and was letting the rain fall on her. It was the cozy kind of day that she would have loved to have spent in the café, serving tea and coffee and biscuits and watching the rain fall.

She missed working in the café. She missed the stability of the job she once had. She could barely call this a job at all.

"You're going to catch a cold, Miss Lloyd." Detective Gilbert strode toward her, Officer Martin a few paces behind. The detective clutched an umbrella. He sounded exactly like her aunt.

Louise looked up at the angry stormy sky. "Then I suppose I'll catch a cold." The threat of a cold was so minor when she could have the glorious feeling of the rain falling on her. She wasn't even wearing a jacket. "Officer Martin." Louise looked toward him. His eyes were rimmed with red. Louise thought she wore her hangovers better than he wore his.

"Miss Lloyd." The officer tipped his head toward her.

They were standing in front of a building near Maggie's. Louise had passed this building over so many times in her life. It was a shabby little apartment building where Harlem favored houses. Of the two addresses Annie had given her, this was the one that had an apartment 1C.

The detective entered the building, closing his umbrella. Louise and Martin fell in line behind him. They passed an empty lobby desk, took a right, and found apartment 1C. Louise pulled the key from her purse. Trepidation flooded her senses.

She put the key into the lock and turned, fumbling for a moment as she got the key to fit inside. Every part of her was telling her to leave, to turn around now. Using the tips of her fingers, Louise pushed the door in.

<hr />

THERE WAS AN odd scent that lingered, and the little apartment had been in a whirlwind. An unmade bed sat in the corner, the grimy curtains pulled over the window. There was a small writing table with papers covering it, a typewriter on top. The room was empty. There was no trace of Nell or anyone at all.

Louise stepped inside, although she didn't want to. She surveyed the small space and then took a right into the tiny bathroom. The toilet was crusted in urine; dirt caked the bathtub. Louise felt her stomach, full for once after breakfast, revolt. She pressed a hand over her mouth as she pulled open the cabinet door above the sink. There was a giant roach in the sink, and Louise bit her tongue to keep from screaming when she saw it.

Louise listened to the detective and the officer in the other room. The space was small. It was meant to be used only for hours at a time. It was about the size of her bedroom. She heard Martin say that he had found a handful of pearls sitting on top of a pool of blood under the bed.

She stepped back out of the bathroom and looked around. She knew she was standing in the room where four girls had died. She felt something crawl up her spine, and she thought that she should say something, but she wasn't sure what. Anything she thought to say felt wrong. It wasn't often that she was rendered speechless. She turned to the detective, whose mouth was a firm line. He had a grim look in his eye. Louise wandered toward the desk. On it were clippings from newspapers, but they went further back than Dora's body being found. The clippings traced their way to a decade ago and were about Louise herself. She had seen the newspaper articles before. Louise stared at a photograph of herself a few years younger. It was hard to believe that she had ever been that girl. It was hard to believe who she had grown up to be. She wondered what that girl would think of her now. She hoped the girl in that photograph would be proud of her now. She was glad to continue the legacy, glad to be able to help girls in need. The work was infuriating and depressing all in one, but the further she got into the case, the more she thought she was meant to help people.

Louise had discovered that she liked this sort of work more than she'd thought she would. She liked searching for people, tracking them down, finding answers.

But this was the bad part of the job.

They were standing in the middle of a crime scene.

"I know, Miss Lloyd. I know." Gilbert was scanning the little room. "Officer Martin?"

"I know the drill," Martin said. He left them alone. Louise turned to the detective. She still was unsure of what to say. She was staring at a photograph of her at fifteen, the day after she had been kidnapped.

"Frank Lister gave you this key?" Gilbert was looking around the tornado of an apartment.

"He did." Louise pulled herself away from the desk. She knew where this was going. They would have to arrest Frank Lister.

"He's been watching me. He has stories about me. He . . ." She trailed off. She suddenly felt the need to get out of the little apartment, so she did exactly that, leaving the room and heading back down the hallway the way they'd come.

◁※▷

"MISS LLOYD." OFFICER Martin followed her as she made her way outside. The rain had slowed to a drizzle, and she took a couple of breaths before she turned toward him.

"Please just leave me alone." Louise didn't want to hear his snide comments, but instead he smiled.

"It can be intense, I know." Martin still left some space between them. He probably thought her skin color was an illness he could catch. He was looking at her and Louise realized that he was one of the very few people who understood how she was feeling. "But you've already seen the worst of it."

"I thought I was going to pull a Daniel Boone."

"It's natural. You'll get used to it," Martin said. "Do you want to know what I do?"

Why was he was being nice to her?

"What do you do?" Louise asked. She wondered if this was some mean trick, if he would report her to the detective or anyone else. But he simply smiled again.

"I hold my breath and count to ten. I know it doesn't seem like something you'll ever get used to, but it helps." For one moment, they were exactly on the same page. They clearly understood each other, and that, in itself, was a relief. He was smiling at her, quiet and beguiling. Louise wondered what he was really up to. Maybe the detective had given him the same talk, that he was to be nicer to her. It felt as if the detective was largely running interference between them. He stepped toward her, closing the gap. For one full moment, Louise thought they could be friends.

"I don't want your help." Louise pulled herself away. She couldn't forget that this man hated her. She couldn't forget that his goals were different from hers. His main goal was to make her life a living hell. "All we have to do is solve this and I'll be done here."

A smirk tugged at his lips. "You're a very interesting girl, Miss Lloyd."

She couldn't forget how he had intimidated her the last time he had seen her. She couldn't forget that if he had the choice, he would destroy her. For a moment, she had almost lost sight of the fact that he was her enemy, and that was what he wanted. "I would love to chat, but I think the detective needs me."

He had helped her, a little. She took a deep breath as she walked away, counting to ten before she released. She did feel a little calmer, the angry sea of her stomach stilled.

She could handle it. She had seen worse.

34

⌁

THE NIGHT FRANK Lister was arrested was a clear, calm night. Louise sat in her regular seat in the detective's office, waiting.

Detective Gilbert had entrusted this very important task to Officer Martin. It was one in the morning. Louise should have been at the Zodiac, or, God forbid, in bed, but she was sitting there wearing her most professional attire.

"What does the *S* stand for?" She had been staring at the silver cigarette case in its place on the desk. She was not sure that she had seen the desk without the case in its spot. It was little things like that that comforted her.

"Hmmm?" The detective had been poring over files in front of him.

"The *S*."

He looked up at her. "Stanley. It was my father's, actually. I'm named after him. Theodore is my middle name." Louise narrowed her eyes. He didn't seem like a Stanley or a Junior. She didn't say anything else. They were both on edge. Louise had been sitting in her spot for an hour and fifteen minutes, and nothing had happened yet. All things considered, it was still early in the night.

Louise wondered who was at the Zodiac that night. She tried to imagine the crowd of people on the dance floor, the heat between the bodies amplified as they changed partners. Rafael would be working. Louise pictured him behind the bar, jealously watching the dancing group. She pictured the woman singing on the stage, glowing like an angel under the lights above her. She smiled at the thought.

"Are you ready?" The detective didn't look up from his papers as he said this. Louise wondered what he was reading. She should have brought something to do. She hadn't known it would take so long.

Louise let her eyes flicker shut. "Stay on topic—don't let him control the conversation. Stay calm. Do not give in to my temper." Again, Louise was the only one Frank Lister would talk to. That was the condition of his self-surrender, that and he had to make sure Snake Eyes got up and running for the night first. He paid good money for protection and the right to keep his club running.

Gilbert looked up at her. "You were listening."

"I do listen when you speak."

"I'm surprised to hear that."

Louise wrinkled her nose but didn't say anything to that. She had been staring at the board since she arrived, even though she had every detail of the case memorized already. She stared at the photographs of the girls as if they would finally tell her something she didn't know.

There was a knock on the door and the detective looked up. Louise turned toward it. Martin stuck his head in. "Ready whenever you are, sir." The door closed with a soft click. Louise decided that the officer was best in small doses or not at all.

"Are you sure you're ready, Miss Lloyd?" Detective Gilbert was now staring intently at her. She felt something crawl over her skin.

Her eyes were locked on the door. She was as ready as she would ever be.

⌁⌁⌁

LOUISE DIDN'T LIKE the interrogation room. It was too small and too cold and she felt as if the walls would close in on her.

Frank Lister watched her. He leaned back in his chair as if this were a casual meeting. "It's just you and me, princess."

Louise sank into the seat across from him, crossing her legs at the ankle. "My name's not 'princess.' Your key led me right to a crime scene."

"You're still talking like you're one of them." The reply was quiet and patient. Louise didn't grace this with a response.

"How did you know?" She was not going to let him get to her. She kept her back straight, looking him right in the eye.

"How did I know what, princess?" The nickname was so degrading especially because she was sure he knew her name.

"Apartment 1C is a crime scene." The sight had been haunting her since she had been there. Louise knew that the detective's team was doing their best to remove any evidence.

"Well, that's a surprise." He was watching her closely. Neither one of them was breaking eye contact.

"As far as I'm concerned, Mr. Lister, you are the Girl Killer." She could barely hear her thoughts over the sound of the beating of her heart. A part of her was telling her to get out of the little room as fast as she could. The detective was close, but she was not going to call him in.

"I'm innocent."

"Continue." Louise leaned forward. She was wearing a blouse that was a little too small, and it was hard to move in.

"Bernard Thomas." The statement came after a few moments of silence.

"The *Tribune* writer? Do the girls call him Bernie?"

"One in the same."

Louise paused. "Why?" She found that that was the question bubbling up to her lips the most often. He watched her, beady dark eyes on her hazel ones. "Why do you think he's the Girl Killer? All the girls said that he's kind, buys them things."

"Annie said that, didn't she? Miss Taylor is a liar. He nearly broke her arm once."

"Why would she lie about that?"

"Why do little girls lie?" He bounced the question back at her, and she realized that she didn't know how to answer it. "He could be nice, but he's violent, angry sometimes."

"Why did you let him near your club?"

"I just collect the money," Frank Lister said. He paused, and Louise could see that even though he tried not to show it, there was a thick veneer over his true emotions. The murders had shaken him. Made him more human. "I'm no angel, but I'm no murderer either." Louise bit her lip. She had no reply to that. There was something about his gaze that was hypnotic.

"Why did you give me the key?"

"If anyone is the Girl Killer, it's Thomas, princess."

"My name isn't 'princess.'" He was only doing it to get a reaction from her. She did think she believed him, however, and that was the worst part. Maybe Bernard Thomas was the Girl Killer. Although she had never thought about it, of course Frank Lister would have his own theories. "Why do you keep renting to him?"

"Bernard Thomas pays me each month for use of apartment 1C. That's how it works. Man's gotta make money somehow."

Louise was suddenly sick and tired of staring at his face. She pulled herself up from her chair and exited the little room without another word. Officer Martin was waiting for her as she left. She expected him to say something mean, and she didn't have the mental capacity to spar with him tonight. "You think he did it?" Louise tried to ignore it. He was there only to watch her fail. Those minutes with him outside the apartment building did nothing to change the fact she knew he hated her. He was smirking as he watched her. "Miss Lloyd, I'm talking to you." He put a hand on her wrist, stopping her in her tracks. They were in the middle of the station. A few of the other officers who seemed to be there all the time—Jones, Tucker, a couple others—watched carefully.

Louise knew they would protect him. She cleared her throat. The fact that he clearly thought he could make her obey him infuriated her.

"I don't think Lister did it," Louise said. She pulled herself away, her heart racing. "I have to talk to Detective Gilbert."

"We'll see about that." Martin raised an eyebrow. He was able to rattle her even when he did nothing to her at all.

35

NELL—ELEANOR HAWKINS—was lying on her back, wearing her black club uniform. Her lifeless eyes stared at the sky. Louise and the detective shared a look. At the exact same time, they made the sign of the cross against their chests.

She wasn't surprised. She wasn't sure if she was supposed to be. The only thing she felt was a rock form in her stomach and her heart fill with dread. It was a beautiful, cloudless day and the heat was making the smell around the area worse.

Nell's body was almost the same as Ruth's before her. Her skin was waxy, and of course, in her right hand, she was holding a small card with the Virgin Mary on it.

"She had to have been placed here early morning," Gilbert said. Officer Martin and Officer Tucker were talking to the people who had found the body in front of Maggie's. Louise was doing her best not to look at Nell. But she had already seen what was done to her. Like Ruth, Nell had been sliced open, deep, precise cuts on her arms and legs and from her sternum to her belly button. She could imagine that the torture was slow and cruel, that the killer had drawn out Nell's death until she was screaming, crying in agony. Louise could picture him bringing her right to the edge of death and holding out until she was begging for him to take her life. She inhaled, felt her stomach shake. Nell was practically in tatters, blood seeping through her and onto the ground around her.

"Before the sun rose." She knew the drill by now. By dinnertime the news of Nell's death would spread through Harlem. She could feel a change in the place she had grown up. The world felt a lot bleaker than it used to be.

"Miss Lloyd."

Louise glanced at Gilbert. She knew she looked shaken. She couldn't erase it from her face. She ignored him. She thought she would vomit if she opened her mouth. She could see it now. Gilbert was right. They were losing and it was clear.

"Excuse me." The voice pulled Louise's attention. There was a small crowd around the body now, and the speaker was a doughy white man she recognized. "What can you tell me about this girl?"

She stared into his watery green eyes. He looked into hers. "Hello, Mr. Thomas."

That caught Gilbert's attention. "Officer Martin?" The younger officer approached. Louise took a step back, knowing what would come next. "Bernard Thomas, we're bringing you in for questioning about the murders of Dora Hughes, Elizabeth Merrell, Clara Fisher, Ruth Coleman, and Eleanor Hawkins. Take him in," Gilbert said.

Louise watched Bernard sputter about how he was innocent. "He might be the one."

"We're about to find out." Gilbert was staring at the body, refusing to look at her. She had known it would come to this. Louise just wasn't ready.

BERNARD THOMAS HAD no idea what they were talking about. The detective sat at the table across from him while Officer Martin and Louise hung near the back. She was there to watch, not say anything.

They had been sitting in silence for ten minutes when Louise spoke. The silence was unbearable and she knew she was speaking out of turn. She'd be scolded for it later, but anything was better than standing there and waiting for Bernard to say something. It was so quiet, she was sure she could hear the tick of all the men's watches, secreted in their respective pockets.

"What is your obsession with this case?" All three men looked to her when she spoke.

"It's the one I was assigned, sweetheart. I assume you know how my job works." His answer was flippant.

"You're behind the eight ball." Louise stepped forward, placing her hands on the table. "I'd be very careful about what you say next."

"Mr. Thomas," Gilbert said. His tone was sharp and she jumped. "Talk to me, not to her." The writer pulled his eyes away from Louise, and she exhaled softly. She hadn't realized she was holding her breath.

"I don't know what I'm doing here," Bernard said. Louise stared at him. Those watery eyes had dropped to the table in front of him.

"Elizabeth Merrell. Clara Fisher. Dora Hughes. Ruth Coleman. Now Nell Hawkins. You were seeing all these girls before they died." This was the detective taking command of the interrogation.

"I might have, but that doesn't mean anything."

"You sent them all things. Little presents, tokens of your appreciation, even a small diamond ring. And you hired them all the nights they went missing. Then you lured them away and murdered them." Detective Gilbert continued as if no one had spoken. Louise wondered how the detective managed to not lose his temper.

"I didn't give them anything."

"Annie told me. She said you admitted it." She pulled his attention back to her. She kept talking out of turn and she couldn't help it.

"Annie Taylor's a little liar." The writer's jaw tightened. He sounded bitter about it.

"Why should I believe you?"

Bernard stared at her, one hard, long look. She wished she had that necklace and the ring to show him the proof.

"And I never sent anything to those girls—I just let them think I did."

"Why?" This was Martin. For a moment, Louise had forgotten he was in the room. Even Gilbert turned to look at him. The officer stepped forward, taking his time as they watched him do so. He shoved Louise out of his way, and she went stumbling to the side. "Why would you do that?"

There was a moment of silence. Several moments of silence, stretching into a few minutes. Louise moved toward the wall, crossed her arms over her chest, uncrossed them. She wanted to be doing very basic dance steps, something to get her energy out. It was hard to stand still and wait.

"My wife will leave me." Bernard's voice was soft. He didn't look at any of them. "If she knew I went to those types of places, she would leave me." He would deserve it. Louise wondered what sort of woman had married this man. She couldn't picture her, but she probably had low self-esteem. "He's blackmailing me. I don't know who he is, but I'll get a message telling me to hire one of the girls. I rented apartment 1C. I pay for it monthly. I didn't even know until . . ."

"Those girls ended up dead?" Martin was leaning on the table.

"Exactly." The writer was sweating through his shirt, and Louise fought the urge to pull herself away. He still refused to make eye contact, so she looked at the detective. She didn't know if he was believing this story. His face was hard to read at the best of times, and this wasn't the best of times.

"So you're an accessory to murder." This was Detective Gilbert. He spoke after a couple of minutes of silence. His silence was always calculated, and he always made the most of it. When he did speak, his voice rang with authority. Louise pulled herself up to her full height. She wondered if it was possible for her to command that type of attention. "That's not better." But he was thinking. Louise could always tell when the detective was thinking. His eyebrow was raised, and he was casually sitting in his seat. She just didn't know what he was thinking. Gilbert paused again. "But I suppose we can work something out."

"Like what?" Bernard asked. He was dripping sweat now. Louise took a step away from the table. For the first time, Gilbert smiled, a slow smile that did nothing but chill her to the bone.

"Let's talk."

36

LOUISE SIPPED ON a bottle of Coke as she sat across from the detective in his office and waited. He and Officer Martin were in an intense discussion of half sentences and runaway thoughts, and she was fighting to keep up.

"We have to let Lister go," Martin was saying. "There's no way it's him."

Bernard Thomas, writer, philanderer, and possible murderer, was still under observation. He was sitting in the little room, and time was running out.

"Haven't we found anything on him?"

"Nothing related to the murders." It was the first time in an hour that she had spoken. Both men had forgotten that she was in the room. That was typical. She found that she was rather superfluous during this part.

"Right." Gilbert stared at her for a moment. Louise placed her glass bottle on the desk. Her hands were slick with condensation and she wiped them on her skirt. The detective watched as she did so. "I want you to go in there."

"I . . ."

"She can't," Martin said. "She's not an officer. She's nobody." The officer rose from his seat, yelling, blustering, and angry.

"Sit down. She'll do as I say." Gilbert was not amused with the show of dramatics. Martin, his cheeks turning pink, did as he was told. Louise bit back a smirk. It was nice to see Martin be treated like a child. At least she wasn't the only one.

"I can't do it," Louise said. It was more like she didn't want to do it. She didn't want to be near the reporter. They had a suspect in custody. Wasn't this the part where the detective granted her freedom? Wasn't this the part where she was allowed to go home, leave and never return?

She had been focusing on that. They had a habit of talking about and around her, deciding things for her before she had a chance to say yes or no. They argued about her and didn't give her a chance to speak. As much as she wanted to help those girls, she was tired of how they tried to control her.

"I'm not taking no for an answer, Miss Lloyd." He had been kind to her, so far, and she knew that could change in an instant. He wasn't looking at her. He was frowning. She wanted to ask if he thought this was it, the resolution at last. "Take him some tea." He looked at her now, blue eyes boring into hers. "He deserves something to eat."

The tray, with a cup of tea, a kettle, and a sandwich on a plate, was ready.

She said a quick silent prayer. Her heart drummed through her body.

"Fine," she said, "I'll do it." She didn't have a choice, but giving her consent made her *feel* like she did. She rose from her seat, smoothing out her skirt. Her palms began to sweat.

"You look green, Miss Lloyd."

She didn't respond. Simply picked the tray up.

She wasn't scared.

***

THE INTERROGATION ROOM was always ten or so degrees colder than the rest of the station. She placed the tray on the table and sat down. Bernard looked tired, drawn, his skin a ghastly gray.

"When will they let me out of here?"

"We just want to talk." Louise placed her forearms on the cold metal of the table.

"I don't know anything."

"But it seems like you do. Go on, eat something." She tried to be kind to him. She thought he needed that.

"I don't know anything," he repeated. He eyed the tray warily. "You didn't do anything to this, did you?"

Louise poured him a cup of tea. "I just want to know the truth. I just want to get to the bottom of this."

He didn't pick it up. "I don't know anything. I— My wife . . ." He trailed off. He picked up the bread, tore into it. He chewed noisily. Louise refused to watch him eat.

"If you know anything that'll help, I'm sure they'll let you go."

"Why did they send you in, huh?"

Louise looked at him. She didn't have to answer that question, but she did. "Because I'm exactly like the girls you like. I'm like the girls they think you killed."

She let the words hang in the air between them. He was staring at her, something gleaming in his eyes.

"I'm not a murderer, doll."

"Lloyd. My name is Louise Lloyd."

He didn't say anything. He still saw her as that nervous, shy sixteen-year-old. Most people who knew her name thought of her like that. It was a humiliating way to be seen. "I've made mistakes." He didn't add on to his sentence, still staring at the cup of tea on the table between them.

"Like what?" Louise was sure that this was going nowhere fast.

"My wife would leave me if she knew."

"Knew what?"

He took a sip of tea. Coughed. Put the cup back down. "I'm not a bad man. I wanted something different."

It was the only thing she could empathize with. She also wanted something different. She wanted the chance to leave the community she'd lived in her entire life. She wanted to be someone who wasn't Louise Lloyd.

He reached up, undid his tie. Beads of sweat appeared on his forehead.

"Are you okay?" Louise asked.

He nodded, but couldn't speak. His face was starting to drain of color. Instead of running to get the detective, like she knew she should, she was stuck to her chair.

He took another sip, the cup falling from his hands and hitting the floor, shattering.

"I don't know what is happening to me." His voice was light, wheezy. She stared at him, unable to move.

"Tell me."

"I did nothing wrong."

"Tell me what you did."

He was becoming worse by the moment. He was sweating, his hands shaking, erratic. He was pulling off his tie. "I'm being black-mailed." The words came after a moment. "He wants something from me, but I don't . . . know . . . what." His breathing was labored. "If I don't do what he says, he said he'd kill me. I write about them. I write about . . . you. I keep the story in the papers because he wants the attention. And if I don't . . ." He took another deep breath, trying to regain his senses.

"What? What will happen?" she asked. She rose from the table, opened the door. She called out for the detective, her voice ringing through the empty, ghostly precinct.

He came running, quickly followed by Officer Martin, but it was no use.

By the time they made it to the little room, Bernard Thomas had died.

37

THE ZODIAC WAS closed, but that had never bothered Louise. She and Rosa Maria went together, knowing that Rafael would be there early. They entered through the side door, like employees did. Rafael was at the bar, wearing a bold suit of dark green. He was wiping the bar down, and Louise and Rosa Maria sat down in front of him.

She liked the Zodiac when it was closed and quiet just as much as she did when it was open and loud. She liked the hush of reverie that fell over the empty bandstand and the dance floor, like it was a church. Louise looked around, feeling something sweep over her. The Zodiac had been a home to her more than any other place she had lived.

The first thing Rafael did was give them that one-dimpled smile. She didn't smile back. She was still occupied with the afternoon's events, but she was careful not to mention it. She didn't want to explain and have her and Rosa Maria end up in another fight. She knew Rosa Maria could sense something was wrong. Louise was quiet through dinner and washing the dishes. She had been quiet while getting dressed for the night. Louise was scared that if she opened her mouth, she'd never stop screaming. Now it was quarter to eleven; the club was due to open for the night. "What's wrong, Lovie?" His eyes fell on her. Louise inhaled. She had to tell someone. She closed her eyes and told them the whole story, the afternoon at the station, the writer dying in front of her.

"Holy fuck." Rafael was breathless when she finished.

"Mr. Thomas is dead?" Rosa Maria asked.

"I think it was a heart thing," Louise said. She had been escorted out before an examiner had arrived, told to leave. Bernard Thomas' death was above her nonexistent pay grade.

The three of them sat in silence for a moment, unsure of what to do. Then Rafael began to pour them glasses.

"I shouldn't drink tonight," Rosa Maria said. Rafael raised one eyebrow. They all knew that wasn't true.

"One drink and then we drink water all night," Louise said. It was a modest proposal.

"Two drinks," Rosa Maria amended. This happened every time they went to the Zodiac together, and they always ended up drinking too much. Rafael watched them both, knowing how this would go.

The front door opened and Louise looked up. She hadn't even been aware that it had been unlocked. She watched as Detective Gilbert strode in, hat in hand.

"Detective," Louise said, "what are you doing here?" Rafael stiffened up. Louise gave him a look. "He's here for me, not you. The Zodiac isn't in trouble." It was strange seeing the detective, so formal, in a place like the Zodiac.

"I don't drink," Gilbert said.

"You're in the Zodiac. Everyone drinks in the Zodiac," Rafael said. He leaned on the bar, popping a bottle of the Zodiac's best bootleg alcohol. He poured another glass, and Gilbert and Louise shared a look. Louise was correct in assuming that Detective Theodore Gilbert was exactly Rafael's type.

"You arrested our Lou, didn't you?" Rosa Maria added. It was hard to keep up with both Rafael and Rosa Maria. She wondered if Gilbert could handle it.

"He did," Louise supplied the answer.

"It's lovely to see you again, Miss Moreno." The detective gave Rosa Maria a small smile.

Rosa Maria returned it with one of her own. "You've been working our Lou awfully hard these past few weeks."

"I don't mind it," Louise said quickly.

"How did you know I would be here?" she asked.

"I called your home. Miss Walsh said that you weren't currently there, and I figured there was one place you could be."

"You talked to Ma—Miss Walsh?" she asked.

Gilbert eyed his glass again. "She's very charming."

"A real bearcat." Louise winked. Gilbert didn't ask for a translation.

"Detective Gilbert, it is 1926. Live a little, won't you?" Rosa Maria asked. As if moving before he could change his mind, Detective Gilbert lifted his glass. The women did the same. The detective coughed and Louise bit back a smile. Whatever he wanted to talk about, it could wait. Rafael filled their glasses again.

"I know you were shaken this afternoon," Gilbert said, looking between the three of them. "Shaken" was an understatement. "I wanted to make sure you were all right."

"Where are you from, Detective?" This was Rosa Maria interrupting. She was already drunk.

"I'm from London." Rosa Maria nodded as she took this information in. Louise watched her carefully.

"That's far," Rosa Maria said. Louise hid a laugh behind her hand. The detective nodded his agreement. Louise felt as if she knew next to nothing about the detective, and he knew so much about her.

"You didn't have to come all this way, Detective. I'm fine," Louise said. Always obliging, Rafael leaned on the counter, ready to fill their glasses again. The detective raised an eyebrow. Theodore Gilbert was not one to back away from the challenge. Rafael was smirking, watching the proceedings before him. The detective drained his glass again, and Louise and Rosa Maria did the same. Louise wondered how long he would be able to keep up with them. He wasn't a regular drinker and he was older than her.

He wouldn't be able to hold it. "Truthfully, I was curious too. This place is a badly kept secret. I wanted to see what all the buzz was about."

She liked this side of him; she liked seeing a part of him that she didn't see when she was sitting across from him in the tiny office. He had even placed his jacket on the bar.

"Then you have to see it open." Rafael nudged his way into the conversation. His light brown eyes were focused on the detective in front of him, and Louise could see a little bit of a blush rising to his cheeks. "It's fine now, but there's nothing like it open."

"This is what you do? You sit and drink?" the detective asked. It wasn't a rude question. She thought he really wanted to know.

"I dance. I dance more than I drink." She felt weird admitting that, like she was a child with a childish pastime.

"Louise is the best dancer I have ever seen, and I taught her myself," Rosa Maria said. Rafael was watching the detective carefully, almost totally lovestruck. It was funny seeing her friend like this. The usually unruffled Rafael was most definitely ruffled.

"I used to be a chorus girl," Louise said. She sometimes missed being onstage, being under the lights.

"You must be good, Miss Lloyd. You too, Miss Moreno," Detective Gilbert said. This was after a long moment of silence. Louise still wasn't sure what to say to him.

She cleared her throat. "Thank you." Rafael poured them another drink.

"So, Detective," Rosa Maria said. She was slathering on the charm in a way that was obvious and adorable. "Tell me about yourself."

38

❖

THE RIDE HOME from the Zodiac was quiet. Rosa Maria was
staring out the window. The city passed by rapidly, a view she
had seen so many times.

"What do you think?"

Rosa Maria was staring with one eye open, out of the opposite
window. "About what?"

"Detective Gilbert."

Rosa Maria pulled herself up so she was sitting straight in her
seat. The road before them was long and strangely quiet for New
York City. "He's something." She searched for the word she wanted
to use.

Louise turned to face her. The driver in the front stayed silent.
"What? He's what?"

"I'm not sure I like him," Rosa Maria said. It was rare she didn't
like anyone. It was a trait that Louise admired, one she didn't have,
herself. "I don't know."

"Yes, you do." That was something else Louise admired in Rosa

Maria. She was always so sure of herself. She made every choice and didn't think about whether it was the right or wrong one.

Louise really did value her opinion, but she saw that it wasn't going to be a good one.

"It doesn't matter." Rosa Maria rolled the car window down and lit a cigarette.

"It does matter. What do you think?"

"I think he's being very charming to hide something."

The words took a moment to settle. "Why do you say that?" Louise estimated that she'd spent the better part of the past eight years on New York roads going to the Zodiac and back. It was a calming place to be now, the stretch of road acting as a lullaby.

"No, I might be wrong." Rosa Maria was now trying to cover for herself.

Louise locked eyes with her. "Say what you were going to say."

"I just don't trust him."

"He's already told me what he's hiding." Louise still wasn't sure she believed his story.

"What is it?"

Louise reached out, entwining her pinkie with Rosa Maria's. It was as much physical contact as they allowed each other in public. "He told me about this woman he was in love with. She was Black and she died in this fire and he couldn't do anything to save her. I went to your archives to find out if he was telling the truth." Even as she recounted the story, she felt it ring false.

"Did you find anything?"

"No," Louise said. It was the one part of the puzzle that still didn't make sense to her. It was the one part of the puzzle that maybe wasn't connected to the rest of it. But she couldn't let it go. She wouldn't let it go.

"So how do you know he's not lying to you?"

She had had her doubts and they were crashing into her now that she was faced with no one but her and Rosa Maria in the back of this cab. "Why would he do all this? Why would he find me and have me work with him on this case?"

"He didn't find you. You assaulted a police officer. And you were lucky that you weren't thrown in a jail somewhere."

The memory made Louise smile. She thought about it often. "If he's lying, then what is his endgame? Where do I fit in with all of this?" It was something she was trying not to focus on. She had learned at a young age that it was better to keep her head down and do what she was told. She had never been able to make that work.

With the death of Bernard Thomas, she wasn't sure what would happen next. She figured that would be it, that the case would be closed. The detective had made no mention of it—he had left before the club had opened—but she would have to talk to him.

"My brother is no help," Rosa Maria said. They shared a look. Rafael had been shamelessly flirting with Gilbert, and nearly burst into tears when he had left. She had never seen Rafael so uncouth. It was rather amusing. "But if you think there's something wrong, I think you should follow it." Louise allowed herself to lean into the other woman. She shut her eyes and let the lulling motion of the car calm her.

There was a time when she was scared of cars, when she did anything she could to avoid being in them. It probably went back to when she was kidnapped. She liked being able to move freely and at her own whim. But that had changed so quickly with going to the Zodiac.

"I think you're right," Louise said. She didn't mention that Josie had also had her doubts about the detective. It was something she decided to disregard altogether.

Louise suddenly had a sinking feeling of regret in her gut.

39

WHEN LOUISE SAT down in front of the detective the next day, he declared the case closed. "It makes sense," he said. Louise didn't know if he was saying it because he believed it or because he was so tired of this summer. "It does make sense."

Louise could feel something in her that had been tense for weeks relax. She exhaled and pushed her doubts from her mind. The summer seemed to relax too. It was cooler than it had been in days, and that felt like a sign. She was willing to accept Bernard Thomas as the Girl Killer. The man was dead and Harlem could be just like it was before.

Gilbert rubbed his temples, his eyes shut. The Girl Killer case had taken a lot from both of them. "I suppose this is it," he said. He looked at her, and again; he was so tired that his eyes couldn't produce the right shade of blue. "Congratulations, Miss Lloyd. You're free." She had spent ages dreaming of this moment. He extended a hand and Louise shook it.

He picked up his silver cigarette case. It was all rather anticlimactic. She had thought this would be a bigger moment. But a man was dead.

The *Tribune* had run a front-page story claiming their late employee was not guilty of the murders, featuring a photograph of him and his wife, a rather average blond lady named Virginia, with a line or two from her also proclaiming his innocence.

Louise had talked to Annie. With a small, resigned sigh, Annie had told the truth, and agreed: Bernard Thomas could have been the Girl Killer. Annie admitted that he had gotten rough with her, and other girls. Annie told her it made sense.

Louise had thought that Annie wanted this over as much as she did.

"What will you do now?"

Gilbert thought about it for a moment. "I suppose there's always a murder to solve. What about you, Miss Lloyd?"

"I'm going to see if I can work at another café," Louise said. She didn't divulge her real plans, that she and Rosa Maria could finally move in together. "And tonight I'm going to celebrate, although I shouldn't tell you that."

"You did a good job, Miss Lloyd. Congratulations." In the end, it had been worth it. She would never know if he had been serious about sending her to prison. Now she wouldn't have to find out. She would have to lie low for a few weeks, let this story blow over. She was still planning on helping young women like herself when she could but was happy to let the legend of Harlem's Hero die for good.

She could go back to being Louise. She could go back to being a young woman and not a story. "If you ever come back to the Zodiac, we can have a rematch." Louise hadn't thought she would come to like the detective in the way she had. She still didn't trust him completely, but she had warmed to him in a way that surprised her. Here it was, at the end of whatever this was, and she thought they could be friends.

"I'm never returning to the Zodiac. I told you I don't drink." Gilbert was still bitter about losing to Louise. She looked around the little office. She had spent more time in these past weeks in this office than her bedroom, and it had sort of become a home away from home for her. She pulled herself away from the desk.

"I'll still win, sir. I should be leaving. Uh, dinner and everything." He rose as she did, accompanied her to the door. It felt as if there was nothing else to say.

She was going to go home and celebrate for the first time in a while. He shook her hand again and with that, Louise departed from the office.

SOMETHING JUST DIDN'T sit right. As Louise dressed for the Zodiac, she knew something was off. She was sitting on her windowsill clad in a dressing gown as the moon spilled onto her, smoking and exhaling into the sweet summer night.

She should have been rejoicing. She should have been ready to go to the Zodiac, revel in the freedom that she had just gained. She was going to return the gun Rafael had given her.

And this would all blow over. She would really be free to move on.

How glorious that would be! How wonderful it would be to be someone other than Harlem's Hero.

Something that had defined her for a decade. Something that had nearly suffocated her.

She had been a showgirl, a waitress, a lover, a dancer.

And now she was a detective too.

The case was wrapped up in a bow. But as she sipped from her glass of wine, legs straddling the windowsill as she smoked, Louise knew that *something* wasn't right.

She could chalk it up to nerves. It felt like she could, for the first time in weeks, relax, exhale. She hadn't even known she was holding her breath until Detective Gilbert said she could go.

Even dinner was more tolerable. The other Wayward Girls didn't bother her as much as usual. She found their talk of men and clothes rather charming.

But now, as Louise was trying to get dressed, she found that she couldn't let it all go just yet. The precious time she used to decide between dresses was taken up by chain-smoking and thinking.

She hated it. She hated being so contemplative. She hated not being able to put a name to her feelings as they coursed through her with no regard for the rest of her.

She used the butt of her cigarette to light a new one. She always felt soothed by the view from her window. Knowing she was a trellis and a subway away from her favorite place in the world always calmed her.

Louise leaned back on the sill, the ridge hitting her back. She had spent so many hours in this exact spot. Her dressing gown was falling off her shoulder, revealing the strap of her combinations. Hardly decent, but it wasn't like anyone could see her clearly enough to be offended or anything.

The knock on the door was a familiar three pattern. Rosa Maria opened it and stepped in.

"You scared me. I could have fallen." Louise didn't need to look to know that it was Rosa Maria. But she did look. Rosa Maria was wearing a red dress, a silver band against her forehead. Her lips were dripping with red, and the urge to tear the dress off her ripped through Louise.

But they'd have to talk eventually. They couldn't rely on making whoopee forever.

"I wanted to see how you were." Rosa Maria sat down at her vanity, crossing her long legs. "It's finally over, Louise."

She wished that were true. She pulled herself in from the window, letting her dressing gown fall to the floor. Then she stepped over it and pressed her lips to Rosa Maria's, pausing every movement in her body. She felt Rosa Maria react, her tongue pressing between Louise's lips. She always tasted the same, sweet and soft, and she always wore the same perfume. It was comforting, her taste, her smell. Louise remembered falling in love with her years ago. There was a part of her that would always belong to Rosa Maria. She kissed her again, still unable to be apart from her for too long.

This was something she didn't want to give up. Rosa Maria wasn't someone she wanted to give up. She knew that. She pulled away, pressed her forehead to the other woman's. "I don't think it is. I think we're still in the middle of it." Rosa Maria sighed and moved away from Louise.

The detective had told her that one of the rules of the job was to always trust her gut.

But Lou could leave it alone. She could ignore the swelling in her stomach telling her something was wrong.

She just hoped she wasn't making a terrible mistake.

40

L OUISE HADN'T BEEN expecting a scared call from Annie
Taylor. Especially not one from the closest hospital. She had,
up until the phone rang, been in the games room. She had never
known why Miss Brown, mother to three grown daughters,
had a games room, but Louise had gotten very adept at billiards
while living there. It was late enough that all her roommates had
returned from work. She was still wondering about Bernard
Thomas.

Maybe she was overthinking it. He was the perfect suspect.

And he was dead. He had died right in front of her.

And the case was closed.

It had happened too fast. They worked on this for weeks and
then they careened into a conclusion. The world would move on.

She didn't trust easy. And this felt too easy.

It might work itself out. But she couldn't let it go. She had always been like that. Her aunt always said that she was unable to
move on. Harlem was letting out a slow exhalation. She could al-

most feel it. They had been wrapped up in fear for so long. But mothers were letting their children play in the streets. From the window, she could see them, their shorts and dresses getting covered in dust. Mothers sat on the steps to the houses, braiding their daughters' hair, talking, or disciplining their children.

It was home.

It just wasn't right.

She thought about it all again. She had been focused on nothing but the facts of the case since the night before. She had been running over them in her head. She had been trying to decipher what the reporter had been trying to tell her, trying to figure out how he had died so suddenly. The detective had written it off as a heart attack, all the stress and the shock. It had happened so quickly, no one would have been able to save him.

She leaned against the table, staring at the felted top. Louise had spent so long staring at her notes the night before that she thought she went cross-eyed.

It was so easy to get consumed with these thoughts, trying to figure out the how and the why of it all. Officially, they had the how and the why. Bernard Thomas had kidnapped and killed five girls, strangling the first few, then stabbing the rest, letting them be seen by all of Harlem. They had the why. He was cheating on his wife. He was committing a crime. He had hated himself, hated Black girls, but was a sick man and had to go further.

Louise thought about the man that she had met, the one who had hounded her outside Maggie's, the one who wrote stories about her.

That brought her to a new train of thought: what did she have to do with any of this? She had been Harlem's Hero and she could finally be done with all of that.

The phone, ringing in its booth, brought her back to the present. She had no obligation to get it, and she almost didn't, but something told her to pick it up.

The voice was weak, quiet. "Louise." She would recognize it anywhere.

"Annie."

The girl spoke in a whisper. "I need you to help me."

"Of course." Louise could feel her heart leap in her chest, pattering and stuttering. She had to remain calm. She wouldn't help anyone if she wasn't calm.

"I . . ."

The voice on the line changed. "Miss Lloyd, I presume." This tone was all business and no-nonsense.

"Speaking," Louise said.

"My name is Cristina Morgan. I'm a nurse at Harlem Hospital Center. You're the only one Miss Taylor would allow me to call."

"What happened to her?"

"I believe it's best if you come in. Right away."

"Of course," Louise said. "Thank you."

⧌⧍⧍

SHE WAS LUCKY enough to have never needed a stay in the hospital. Cristina Morgan, in a starched white uniform, a stern frown on her face, was waiting for her.

Cristina was about her height and age, but she managed to command a room in a way Louise had never seen. She walked and talked and talked and walked, every part of her moving as fast as possible. "She was found early this morning. Some bloody cuts, she was in and out of it. Miss Taylor is stable now, but still weak. She can talk, but not for too long."

"What happened, exactly?" Louise struggled to keep up with the nurse.

Cristina stopped outside a small room, turning to her. Her eyes were wide and brown, her lips pulled downward. Louise wondered if she had any other facial expression. "You should let her explain. Will you leave out the back when you're done?"

That was something Louise recognized. The subtle art of doing favors. The subtle art of breaking the rules. "Of course."

"Thirty minutes, then I have to call security." Cristina pushed the door open.

The girl lying in the bed was Annie; she knew that. But it didn't look like her. She was smaller, more frail than Louise had ever seen her. She was just under five feet, weighing nothing, and Louise had never realized that before. Annie was lying with her eyes closed. Her skin was colorless, the blankets up to her neck. Her hands were pressed, palm down, into the white sheets.

It was eerie. That was the only way to describe it. There was a free chair and Louise sank into it, placing her hand atop Annie's own. "Annie, it's Louise."

Annie opened one eye. She swallowed, hoarse. "He almost got me."

She knew it. She *knew* it. "Tell me everything."

Annie struggled to pull herself up so she was sitting. Her lips were cracked. There was a paper cup next to her. Bags had multiplied under her eyes. She had aged a decade over the course of the last day. "It was late, but I was heading home. I knew I shouldn't be walking alone, but I was so close to home. I was grabbed from behind, and something was placed over my mouth." She stared at the sheets as she talked. She paused, taking a sip from the cup next to her. Louise leaned forward. She was speaking so softly it was hard to hear her. "I tried to fight back. He stabbed something into me."

"You think it was . . ."

"I heard him say that he was going to save me. He said that he was going to absolve me from all of my mistakes. I don't know what happened next. I woke up in the street."

Her heart dropped.

The Girl Killer had struck again.

How was she going to go about this? She had to be careful. "I hope you're not lying to me."

At that, Annie sat straight up. She groaned in pain. Louise could see now there was a deep wound on her abdomen. Annie glared at her, full of seventeen-year-old ire. "You're the only one who's ever believed me."

The words cut deep. Louise deserved it. But Annie Taylor had lied to her before.

Was she lying now, or was she doing what she had to do to survive?

"What are you gonna do about it?" Annie asked. She refused to look at Louise. The little hospital room had a window, and Annie was afforded a view of the street down below. The girl was looking out of it, her nose scrunched up.

Louise didn't say anything for a long time. For the first time in her life, she didn't know what she would do. What she did know was that she would have to proceed with caution.

Her hand was still on Annie's. Louise squeezed gently. It was still so easy to see her as one of her sisters. She was just as gentle, just as kind, just as sensitive and sweet. Annie didn't pull her hand away.

"Bernard Thomas died two nights ago. Everything points to him being the Girl Killer."

"He couldn't be." If she'd had any doubts or any second

thoughts, they all disappeared. Annie looked into her eyes now, and all Louise saw was a scared little girl. "Will you call Andrew for me?"

"We should call Ida." Louise's thoughts were racing. She didn't want to call Officer Andrew Martin. She had to make sure Ida knew.

"Ida left." Annie's voice was devoid of emotion. "Out of the state. A couple days ago." This was *news*. Louise had wondered why she hadn't heard from the long-legged, strong-willed young woman in days. She hadn't been able to find her to tell her the case was closed. Apparently, Ida had other things to do.

Louise looked over her shoulder, then lit a cigarette. Why didn't they all follow Ida's lead? Leave the city. She didn't know where she would go.

"Please, call Andrew for me," Annie repeated her plea, and watched as Louise smoked.

Louise nodded. What else could she do?

There was a soft knock. "Miss Lloyd, I hope you got what you've come for." Nurse Morgan was standing at the door. She didn't want to leave so soon. But it was time for her to go.

"I'm going to figure it out." Louise pulled herself up from the chair. Annie nodded. Louise allowed the nurse to escort her out.

⎯⎯⎯◁▽▷⎯⎯⎯

"SHE'S STABLE FOR now. I'm afraid she may be imagining things." The nurse led her down a hallway, away from the rest of the people. She avoided the looks of other hospital employees.

"I don't think she is." Louise kept her head down. She spoke softly.

"Why would she want to call you? Does she have any family that you know of?"

"She has a family. Will you let me know if she says anything else?"

"She'll be getting out soon. We can't keep her for much longer. She's stable. She'll be fine." Cristina pulled her into a hallway.

Louise considered this. "How bad was the attack?" They were reaching a secret entrance. She didn't know if the nurse was going to get in trouble for getting her in and out.

"Not bad enough to kill her, but she needed stitches. She was really shaken up. She's just a kid."

"She shouldn't be going through any of this." The day the Girl Killer case was announced closed was the same day Annie was attacked. The past twenty-four hours sprawled out in her mind. She knew now that there had been a mistake, that Gilbert and the rest of his team had closed the case too early.

And maybe that was what he had wanted. He wanted the case over and done with so that they could all move on, even if it meant that it wasn't actually finished.

"She'll be fine. She'll recover." Cristina pushed the door open for her. The sun was beginning to set. At this rate, Louise would be late for dinner.

"She will. She's a tough thing," Louise said. Unlike her friends, Annie survived. She would be the only victim to survive, and she didn't have much of a story for it.

Louise had known it. It was all too neat. She had passed something over, missed something vital.

Louise owed it to Annie to see this thing through.

41

I T WAS LOUISE'S idea to return to the gun range. As she returned from the hospital the night before, she had felt as if she needed a refresher. Just to be ready for anything. That morning, Louise was unaccompanied at the range, surrounded by men who were working on the same thing. Rafael was late, or not coming. She could only assume that he had gotten caught up with a handsome boy and was now unable to leave his apartment.

She would have been insulted had she been surprised.

She was trying to remember what Rafael had told her. Keeping herself steady, Louise shut one eye, staring down her target.

Every time she pulled the trigger, it was a bit of a shock. She had to hold herself through the recoil. She never could have imagined needing this.

She tried to fight the thoughts running through her mind, but she was no match. Had the dead girls gotten justice? Would they be able to rest now? This wasn't about her. This was about Dora Hughes, Elizabeth Merrell, Clara Fisher, Ruth Coleman, and Eleanor Hawkins.

This was about Annie. She had been released from the hospital and was doing fine. But she refused to leave her house, just in case someone was waiting for her.

Louise could pretend. But she knew that they wouldn't rest easy if this case wasn't properly solved.

She owed it to them, she figured. And not just the dead girls. The families. The ones who would have to suffer. And if this killer struck again, she would be to blame.

She figured that some of what Jimmy Olson had told her that night in the interrogation room was true. She was there only to act as a police scapegoat. As much as she hated thinking that man was right about anything, he was right about this.

It was happening again. Annie was lucky to still be alive. The job wasn't done yet, and she had to see it through, and she couldn't ignore it.

She was playing with fire and she knew it. But she couldn't let it end like this.

"Lovie." Rafael had arrived, late but in style in a striped short-sleeved shirt and navy trousers.

"You should never surprise the person holding a gun." Louise didn't turn around. "You're late."

"I'm sorry." Rafael stood next to her. He hadn't missed much, anyway. She had gotten off only a few shots while standing in front of the target. "Keep your arms straight."

"You know the case is closed, right?"

"You solved the case? Put the gun down!" Rafael demanded.

"Why?" Louise stared at him, wondering what he wanted.

"Do as you're told," Rafael said. When she did, he picked her up in a tight hug. "You are the most gifted and talented girl in the world!" She could always count on Rafael. He put her down, kissing her forehead. "Why are we here? We should be celebrating, dancing!" He twirled her into a complicated box step, ignoring the fact that it was eleven thirty in the morning on a Thursday. People were staring at them, talking behind their hands.

"Because. Stop." Louise stopped him from twirling her around. "I just want this to pass peacefully, okay?"

Rafael frowned. "Why? Lovie, you're gonna be famous."

"No, I'm not—with any luck, they'll keep my name out of it."

Rafael placed a hand on her cheek. Louise blinked up at him. "This isn't the Lovie I know. What are you hiding?"

"Just because I don't want to be famous doesn't mean I'm hiding something. That chorus girl Lovie was twenty-three. And she didn't want to be famous."

"But I still know you're hiding something."

"Annie Taylor was attacked the night before last." People were still staring at them. She didn't want this getting out. Louise stepped closer to him and lowered her voice.

"By him?"

"I don't know. Officially, it can't be. That man is dead. But it just doesn't fit."

"Is she okay?"

"She'll be fine." Louise had been thinking about Annie and only Annie since she had returned from the hospital. She needed to find out what she was missing. Rafael bit the inside of his cheek. It was a nervous habit, but Louise couldn't remember the last time she had seen him nervous. He was thinking it through.

"It could be a mistake, an accident, something completely un-related, right?"

"What did you think of Detective Gilbert?" The question came out before she could stop it.

Rafael let out a low whistle, turned away from her. That

was his way of saying that he didn't want to answer that question. He bounced back with one of his own. "What are you going to do?"

"Figure this out." She said it like it was so simple.

But she knew it would never be as easy as she hoped.

42

ART IN WAS WAITING for her when Louise and Rosa Maria
stumbled home. It was just after the Zodiac closed, and both
women had spent nearly every song on the dance floor. At the best
of times, the trellis wasn't easy to conquer. The two women stared
up at it when Martin announced his presence with the strike of a
match. "You're getting in late."

For one moment, Louise thought she'd be facing the Girl Killer.
The officer was dressed casually and for the day, a boater hat and linen
suit. She turned toward him. "What do you want from me?" She was
too tired to face Martin or anything right now. The only thing she
wanted to do was climb up the trellis and go directly to bed.

"Lou." Rosa Maria squeezed her hand.

Louise turned to her, pushing a stray hair from Rosa Maria's
lips. "Go in. Twenty minutes, leave the window open." She watched
as Rosa Maria climbed up, and when she was satisfied, she turned
to Martin. "What?"

He looked around. He seemed a little jumpy, nervous. He offered an arm. "Why don't we take a walk?"

They strolled a few paces away from the house. Louise had tried to match Rosa Maria drink for drink, as they were wont to do, and Louise had won, but God, at what cost? The cool, very early-morning breeze blew past and the world swirled in and out of focus. "What couldn't have waited until I had some coffee?" She always felt as if someone was watching her, waiting for a chance. Louise looked behind her and saw nothing.

"I can't talk about this in front of Detective Gilbert." His voice was quiet, shaky. He took a half second between each word to steady himself.

"Why not?" There was a distinct ache in her bones. Louise had the specific training of being a former chorus girl, and this pain in her bones wasn't from dancing in shoddy shoes on wood floors. No, this was worry.

"It's about Annie."

Louise was sure that she was the only person who knew about this ongoing affair. It was another secret she had to keep. She was getting tired of being the designated secret keeper.

"So?"

"He's been watching her."

Louise stopped walking, effectively halting them both. She turned to the officer. "What do you mean?"

He reached into his breast pocket, pulled out an assortment of photos and papers. The writing was the detective's—she knew it well—but what she was looking at in the low, oily light of the streetlamp was a full schedule of Annie's day. Since the club was closed, it was probably harder to keep track of the girls. But this was so thorough it was chilling. Annie's name was written in neat print at the top.

"Are you sure you're not overreacting? What if . . ." She couldn't think of a good reason the detective would have this.

"Miss Lloyd . . . Louise, you have to help me."

She could see the anguish on his face. It was killing him to have to come to her. But she wanted to be done. She wanted to go back to her normal life. She didn't want to have to be this person.

But he was scared and she knew Annie was in danger.

She swallowed hard. This information was enough to sober her somewhat. The cool wind that blew through her helped, and now she was just tired. She inhaled, sorting through her thoughts. "I think we'll need something concrete."

Something had been at the back of her mind for a while now. She doubted the detective. She thought Bernard Thomas' sudden death was odd, to say the least.

"I trust you have a plan."

She gave the papers back to Martin. "We're behind the eight ball here. Have you thought about what would happen if you're wrong?" He blinked twice, formulating an answer. His face was devoid of blood. All she saw in his eyes was panic. He was squeezing her hand, maybe an unconscious gesture.

"I have to take that chance. Haven't you ever been in love?"

There were so many things she could have said. She could have said that Annie was seventeen, still a girl. She could have said that he was deceiving Maeve, and the poor girl didn't deserve that, no matter how annoying she was. She should have said that Annie was Black, just like her, and he had been vicious to her from the day they had met. She should have told him that he was a hypocrite just for that. She wanted to tell him that he was an awful person and ruining two people's lives for his entertainment. But she bit her tongue. She maneuvered her hand away from Martin. He lit another cigarette. "Are you sure about Gilbert?"

He dropped the match to the ground. "I think so."

"Then we have to try, don't we?" She had the same thoughts.

The same doubts. The moment the reporter dropped dead in front of her, she had thought it was over. Then Annie had been attacked and the clock reset. But Louise would never tell him that. What choice did she really have but simple duty? Not to the city or the department, but to herself and the other girls in Harlem. If she could keep them safe, then she would. There was no doubt about that.

For the first time since they had begun talking, Martin began to relax. He exhaled, removed his hat, and ran a hand over his hair. "Do you want me to walk you back?"

"It's fine." Louise pulled a cigarette from her tiny purse and lit it. "Besides, I have a plan to come up with."

⊲╳⊳

SHE COULDN'T SLEEP. The ceiling swirled around her. Rosa Maria was asleep when Louise had pulled herself through the window. She had undressed to the sound of her drunken snores. Louise had climbed into bed without waking Rosa Maria, and now she lay awake.

Shadows danced on the wall, and in them, she thought she saw figures. As a little girl, she had been scared of the dark. It was the only girlish impulse she had been allowed, and now so much of her life was conducted in the dark.

There was a figure on the street too. She knew it. He was staring up at her window, eyeing the trellis. She pulled herself from her bed; she was still in her combinations, dress deposited on the floor. She knelt down and looked out the window. There was no one of significance there, some people making their way home from clubs or out to start their morning. She squinted, staring at the street.

Louise pinched herself on her thigh. The pain jolted through her. She lit a cigarette and inhaled, then exhaled. Maybe she was just overtired. She hadn't slept in a week, not really. She was trying to be the woman she used to be.

Behind her, Rosa Maria sighed. Louise looked over her shoulder. The moon accented Rosa Maria's hair, her soft skin, the pink of her nightgown.

She wasn't drunk anymore. The feeling had dissipated and now she was left with worry. Worry was an old friend. Louise pictured them walking side by side, hand in hand. Worry comforted her.

Louise would never be able to get rid of the worry.

Around her, the house creaked. The house was so small and the walls so thin that Louise could hear Maeve in the next room shift and sigh in her own sleep. The sun would rise soon. A new day would start and she was in the same place she had been weeks ago.

It was never-ending. Louise tapped her fingers on the windowsill. She looked down again, sure that someone was watching her. Rosa Maria exhaled a deep sleep breath.

When Louise climbed back into bed, she stared at the ceiling again, waiting for sleep that would not come.

43

THE LANDLADY DIDN'T want to let her in. Luckily, Martin had used his slick good looks for something useful. He pretended to be someone who was interested in renting a room while Louise climbed the fire escape and then into the open window.

Detective Gilbert's apartment was much like his office. Clean, almost ridiculously so. The bed was made, the window open, the soft wind blowing the curtains. The walls were white. There was a desk shoved into the corner, books on a bookshelf behind it. She had never been in a place this clean. Experimentally, she ran her finger over the dark brown wood of the desk. She came away with no dust or dirt. She supposed that he spent so much time in the office, so much time working cases, that he paid monthly for this room but never used it. She pushed open his wardrobe door, just for the thrill. His suits were neatly hung and color coded. She ran a hand over the fabrics, feeling the hair on her arms rise as she did.

It was almost eerie how quiet the building was. It felt almost empty, like it was missing something. She had gotten too used to the bustling noise of the girls she was always surrounded with.

There was nothing to go over on the bed, and she had checked under it, her own preferred hiding place, just to be sure. She moved to the desk. She pulled the chair out, and sat down, back straight. She was staring at blank walls. He had very few personal effects in this apartment.

A typewriter took up most of the desk, leaving room for a small lamp. She opened the drawers. The first had a spare gun in it, larger than the standard police issue. She picked it up, unsure if it was loaded. It was heavier than the one Rafael had given her, more serious looking. She could feel the weight of it and she didn't like it. She put it back in the drawer.

This wasn't who she wanted to be. Someone who snuck around, broke into places, snooped through other people's things. But now that she had become this person, she found it rather exhilarating. There was a chance that someone could catch her.

She opened the next drawer. It was empty. She tried to picture Gilbert in this place. He was too tall for it, like he would routinely hit his head on the ceiling when he got ready in the morning. She stood. Maybe he did.

It was also so impersonal, this room. Her room, and every other one she had been in, had some sort of mark of the person who lived there. For her, it was the fact that her clothes were simply every-where. She couldn't function in a room this neat. Something had to be out of place. She was tempted to move something, just mis-place it, even though she would never know if he noticed. She picked up the lamp, and then put it down. Too obvious.

But the lamp was heavy.

She picked it up again, wondering if it should *be* that heavy. She pulled the metal string, and in her hands, the base of the lamp released itself.

She sat back down at the desk, lamp still in hand. She pulled out a faded photograph, the initials *LC* and the year *1913* written on the back. Two other folded pieces of paper came out, as well as a ring with a diamond surrounded by petals. It was another copy of the Lily. Louise slid it onto her finger, feeling the cool, heavy weight on her finger. She watched it glitter in the low light.

She stared at the woman in the photo, the mysterious Laura. He hadn't been lying to her.

She looked like a woman Louise could have known growing up. Her face was round, eyes shut as she grinned. She had a nice smile; Louise could hear her laugh, charming and unrestrained.

She put the photo down. She next examined the two pages that made up a letter, a long one, sent in the summer of 1913.

Stanley, my dear,

The past two years with you have been better than anything I could have imagined. I sometimes think about how we first met, how you saved me, how you helped me.

And it pains me to write this. I have just returned from an evening with you and it was lovely, but I know now more than ever what I have to do.

I love you so much, but we both know we cannot be. My family expects certain things of me, as I am so sure yours does as well.

Louise stopped reading and stood. She pushed the chair back in again before she went to the bookcase.

She always thought that where and how a person lived reflected his true personality. And what she was getting from the room Detective Gilbert rented was cold and precise. It was much like the man himself.

She turned around, eyeing every corner, every place where nothing was hidden. Then she looked toward the lamp. How inconspicuous. But there was more to this room than she'd thought.

She moved back to the wardrobe, pulling the doors open and the hanging clothes to the side to see the back. She knocked twice, her fingers running over the fine wood. Her breath was caught in her throat; she was hoping, wishing, *praying*.

When she found the hidden compartment, on the left side of the wardrobe, the door springing open on invisible hinges, Louise nearly let out a yell of excitement.

If he was hiding something, she would find it.

And she knew he was hiding something.

44

LOUISE WOULD HAVE admitted that she had no idea what she was doing. In hindsight, she probably would have wanted a plan, but that had never stopped her before. She had never been to a morgue, and the thought of it scared her a little. She was dressed in her most professional clothes, trying to seem older than she was, more severe.

It was cold in the morgue. Her cardigan did nothing to protect her from it as she entered. There were bodies on slabs covered with white sheets.

The morgue attendant was a frazzled man about her age who looked as if he had forgotten something. She had never seen him before. He wasn't the coroner, the man who attended all the crime scenes. "Can I help you?"

"I need to see reports on Dora Hughes, Ruth Coleman, Clara Fisher, Nell Hawkins, and Elizabeth Merrell."

"What? All of them?" He looked toward the bodies, then back to the paper he was holding, and back to her. "Who are you?"

"It doesn't matter who I am. Detective Theodore Gilbert needs all of this information yesterday." He eyed her. His eyes were nearly the same shade of hazel as hers. He was pale and it looked as if he hadn't left the morgue all summer. She met his gaze with her most serious one. "I'm just the messenger. If you want to take it up with him, you can, but he is a very busy man and I can't promise you won't lose your job." She maintained eye contact, trying to intimidate him into doing what she wanted him to do. There was always the chance that he didn't believe her and would end up calling his superiors.

"I thought this case was closed."

"We need to archive everything."

He swore under his breath and rose from his seat. "Stay here and don't *touch* anything."

The minute he was gone, disappearing into an office, she looked around. She stared at the white sheets, daring herself to pull one back and see who was lying there. Louise didn't think that she could work in a place like this. It required so much of a person, and she didn't know if she had what it took to be around death all day. There was a clipboard lying on one of the tables. She looked around. There was no one nearby and the assistant was still puttering around the office. Louise could hear him humming to himself as he worked.

She picked up the clipboard, looking for anything pertinent to the case. Going through things was almost second nature to her now. People did need to stop leaving her alone in places. Louise went through the folders on the desk, trying to find anything that could be helpful.

"What are you doing?" The attendant was behind her.

Louise dropped the clipboard. "Nothing."

"You were looking for something." His tone was accusatory and he was right. "Who are you?" His dark eyes narrowed.

She eyed him. "I'm Maeve Walsh." She spat her housemate's name out before she could stop herself. She extended a hand. "Nice to meet you."

"You work with Detective Gilbert?"

"I'm his new assistant and he wants me to be caught up."

"Do detectives *have* assistants?"

"Secretary. On official matters only. And this is about the most official of matters, and it's my first case with him, and I really need to make a good impression. Papers, please." He looked her up and down, trying to decipher her lie. "Do you want to test me? I will get you fired." His job was more important to him. He gave her the file of papers and she took them. "Thank you, sir." She tucked the files under her arm and pulled away.

"Wait!" She turned when he called after her. He eyed her. "Detective Gilbert will want this as well, wouldn't he?"

Louise stared at him, trying to figure out if he was bluffing. He held out a small box and Louise stepped toward him. "You're right. He will want this. Thank you."

"Wait—you need to sign out," the attendant yelled after her. Louise walked faster and left the morgue, clutching the files and the box. She'd gotten what she needed.

And she hoped that she would find what she needed.

◁◈▷

SHE WENT TO Rafael's apartment. He had a little place shoved in the corner of Bed-Stuy, an apartment that was only sort of clean. He had a roommate, officially, but Louise hadn't seen him in months. There were large portraits of people Louise couldn't name on the wall, one woman in particular staring beautifully and imperiously over the proceedings in the living room. Rafael sat at the piano, which was almost the size of the living room. Louise sat on the couch, clutching a mug of coffee that had gone lukewarm in her hands. She knew that she shouldn't be in a man's apartment alone, but it was preferable to being in her home while Rosa Maria was at work and she still felt like she was being watched.

Rafael was playing scales, transitioning to a song she recognized from the chorus all those years ago. "You're being rather quiet, Lovie."

"I'm not in the mood," Louise said. Rafael had tried to ask her what she was looking over, but she refused to tell him.

He turned toward her and stopped playing. "You have to tell me. What are you working on?"

"Officer Martin and I have an inkling. I am going to see it through." She had the reports all in front of her in a row, as if reading them over and over would bring her some type of clarity.

Rafael moved so he was sitting next to her. He took the mug from her hand and she let him. "These are all the death reports. How did you get these?"

"I lied. I'm going over something."

"What?"

She didn't want to tell him and then be wrong. There was nothing she hated more than being wrong. Louise pulled her feet under her on the couch and considered the box. "So I went to the city morgue today and as I was leaving, the attendant handed me this box and . . ."

"And what?"

Her throat tightened. "You're going to think I'm crazy."

"I already do."

"I have a feeling." She didn't like classifying it as a feeling, as a thought. It made it sound impulsive, which it was. "I mean, it's nothing. It's stupid, you know? It's probably just nothing."

"I wonder if everyone in your family babbles when they want to avoid talking about something." Rafael picked up one of the reports. It was Ruth's; he stared at the list of things that had happened to her.

"No, it's just Celia, but she talks a lot as a general rule."

"Tell me what's going on, Lovie."

"Officer Martin thinks Detective Gilbert is the Girl Killer. I'm just helping to see if he's right."

Rafael inhaled. "Serious?"

"I'm serious." Louise turned toward him.

"Are you sure?"

"Well, no. But I'm going to figure it out. Because if he's not, then he's hiding something big."

Rafael flicked through the pages. It was somehow a relief to voice her thoughts. It was her first time saying it out loud. "So, what's in the box?"

"I don't know. I'm too scared to open it." She eyed it. It was a small box, a couple of inches long and a few inches wide. Rafael took it from her and opened the lid.

In it were a few pearls, possibly fake, although she couldn't tell for sure. There were ten of them rolling around in the box. They were all covered in blood. She stared at them.

"These are from Maggie's necklaces, right?"

Rafael looked into the box. "They look like them."

Louise closed the lid. It was a little anticlimactic.

"I also found these in his apartment." Louise reached into her purse and pulled out the few small vials that she had stolen from the secret compartment in Gilbert's wardrobe. They were all laudanum. Maybe the detective had an old war injury, or maybe this was how the Girl Killer was keeping the girls obedient?

"You broke into his apartment?"

"Martin helped."

"Where did you find them?"

"Secret compartment in his wardrobe. Left side."

Rafael whistled. "Impressive. Do you know if they were drugged?"

"That's what I'm trying to find out."

"Where does he even get these?" Rafael eyed the vials.

"I think a city detective has some strings to pull." She was trying to ignore him as he did his research. "Can you please go back to playing the piano? And be careful! Those are dangerous."

Rafael did as he was told, moving back to the piano bench. He began to play a merry tune. Louise flicked her eyes up at him and then elected to ignore him. She used her finger to trace her progress as she scanned through the pages, glancing now and then at the serious-looking vials on the low table in front of her, trying to decipher what was what. All the reports were written in shorthand, some type of vague references to what had been found in the girls' bodies. The handwriting was small and thin. Rafael turned back around to her after roughly two and a half minutes of playing. All the girls had been given nearly lethal amounts of laudanum, but Clara, Elizabeth, and Dora were strangled, and Ruth and Nell were stabbed. Why would he change?

"Why?" Louise lit a cigarette. Her vision was starting to blur from staring at the thin writing.

"I don't know." Rafael played a couple of notes.

Louise exhaled. "Maybe he didn't like it. Maybe he wanted something more personal."

"Lovie, why do you think Gilbert . . ." He couldn't even bring himself to say it. Louise raised an eyebrow. She wondered how many vivid and intense fantasies Rafael had had guest-starring the detective.

"I don't know! I just do. There's something not adding up with him. He's lying to me. And Martin's worried about Annie, and if there's anything else I can do to help, I'm gonna do it. Bernard said someone was blackmailing him and then he died right in front of me. Isn't that odd?"

Rafael moved to sit next to her again. He eyed her. "When was the last time you ate something? Slept? Did anything that wasn't this case?"

She never expected Rafael to be the rational one between them. "I am fine."

He wrapped an arm around her. She shut her eyes, inhaling deeply. "You don't have to save everyone. You're working yourself to the bone. You need to eat and rest."

"I'm on the verge of something." She pulled herself away from him.

"Lovie, I think you're a bit goofy. I think you're seeing things that aren't there. You're chasing ghosts." It was so gentle that it almost didn't feel like a blow. He touched her cheek with the back of his hand. She swatted him away.

"You're just saying that because you don't think I'm right. In fact, you want me to be wrong." She began to collect her things. She would much rather do this alone in her bedroom now.

"I'm saying this because I care about you."

She reordered the files, shoving them all into the folder. She straightened herself.

"Something weird is going on, and I'm going to find out what."

45

SHE HAD TO start at the beginning. That meant another visit to Dorothea Hughes.

Louise went in the middle of the day, when she thought Mr. Hughes would be at work.

Dorothea was glad to see her, waving her in. Louise paused to pick the baby up, hoisting her on her hip.

"Louise," Dorothea greeted her warmly. "What brings you back?" They sat at the kitchen table. Dorothea poured some water for them both.

"I have some more questions about Dora," Louise said. Dorothea didn't say anything, so she continued. "I know the case has been closed, but I still have some questions." Louise wasn't sure if Dorothea would be able to help her. If she knew anything, it was that sixteen-year-old girls were skilled at lying. "Did she mention anyone before she went missing? Any men, in particular?"

Dorothea paused before replying. "I have been thinking of those days before she went missing."

It felt like a lifetime ago, but Dora had been the one who started all of this for Louise. Dorothea considered the question. "She didn't mention anything."

"Are you sure?" Louise asked.

Dorothea nodded. "She didn't talk about anyone." Louise knew that she needed to get back up into Dora's room. "She was good at hiding things."

"Did she talk about him at all? Bernard Thomas?"

Dorothea took a sip from her water glass. Louise allowed the baby to squeeze her finger. She moved to press her nose to the baby's head. She still had that very sweet baby smell.

"She talked about a writer she met once or twice, but she never mentioned him by name. It must be him."

Louise cleared her throat.

"So the case really is closed." Louise could practically see her tears of relief. "It's over." Dorothea made the sign of the cross against her chest.

"Not exactly," Louise said. "I mean, yes, technically. I just . . . I'm just dotting the i's and crossing my t's. You know."

"Of course." Dorothea did not understand, but Louise didn't try to explain.

"I'm just going over everything again." She should be doing anything but. "I think he may have been working with someone else. Can I go upstairs to her room?"

Dorothea took the baby and led the way upstairs. Louise crossed over to the bed, got on the floor on her stomach, and reached as far as she could underneath it. The room was dark, drafty, and cold. Louise sorted through the assorted costume jewelry, matches, and cigarettes, finding nothing of use. Dorothea watched as Louise did so.

"Is this where she was hiding things?" She sounded surprised and Louise didn't know how she could be.

"You were her age once."

"I never disrespected my parents. And I hid things in the floor." Dorothea put the baby on the floor and knelt down, prying open a loose floorboard and bringing up a handful of hidden makeup: lipstick, rouge, and mascara.

And a dusty little notebook. Dora's initials on the front.

Louise stared at it. She took it. Of course the dreamy sixteen-year-old would keep a diary. She flipped open to a random page. In the girly script Louise had seen before was a phone number. The page was marked with one of the Virgin Mary cards.

"This is it." Louise pulled herself to her feet.

"What else was Dora hiding from me?" Dorothea remained on her knees, facing the spot in the floor.

"I don't know." It wasn't something Louise was qualified to answer. "I know she loved you, even if it didn't seem like it." She wondered what she would say to her own mother, given a chance. "Can I take this? Just for now?"

"Of course," Dorothea said.

"I'm so, so sorry for your loss." Louise remembered what it had been like seeing Dora's body on the concrete. She gave the baby one more quick kiss and departed the little house.

When she was outside, she pulled the book out again. She stared at the number. It wasn't the detective's phone number, not at his office. Maybe it was his home number. Maybe she was wrong and Martin was wrong and their doubt was misplaced. She no longer knew whom to trust.

She would have to make some phone calls.

⋯⋯

SHE SAT WITH her back against the small wall of the phone room. She had kicked out Frances to commandeer the little booth. Frances, a girl who was scared of virtually everything in the world, shook with nerves and nearly burst into tears.

"I just need it for a couple of moments," Louise had promised. That was nearly an hour ago. She would feel bad, but Frances annoyed her. She had called the number in the book. She had been told by a very polite operator that that number had been disconnected. The operator had also declined to tell her whom the number belonged to when she pretended not to remember whom she had called.

Not her best lie. She knew the operator would think she knew whom she was calling.

Louise was always paranoid that the operators were listening in on her conversations. But the phone was hung up now. Frances was tapping on the phone booth door.

She held the little book in her hand. She looked at the number. She was getting nowhere.

Louise got out of the phone booth. Frances nearly pushed her out of the way. "Who are you trying to call?"

"John."

Louise knew better than to ask. With the Wayward Girls, it usually came down to a man. "I'll leave you to it," Louise said. She went up to the pink room and shut the door behind her. She put the card on her vanity and collapsed into the chair. She had the key to the case in her hands, but she wasn't getting anywhere. There was something so private about going through this diary. But she opened the window and lit a cigarette, placing the book precariously on her knee. She flicked through the pages. Dora had started this diary nearly five years ago, and Louise read on as the years progressed. There would be months with her not writing much at all, and then lengthy whimsical pages filled with musings suitable for a young girl. It was akin to reading Celia's journal, she thought, if Celia was only a little bit less harebrained.

Dora talked in code, her handwriting running into itself as if her brain was moving too fast for her hand to keep up.

The case was closed. Louise didn't have to keep doing this to herself.

But she slowly went through the diary, line by line, staring at the initials Dora used for people she was talking about. It was exactly what Louise would have done if she'd kept a journal at sixteen. But she had never done that.

There was a knock on her door. Louise stubbed out her cigarette, just in case. She was always paranoid of Miss Brown coming in and seeing her smoking. It was Catherine Gordon, still dressed in stiff black from her work. "Didn't know you were home. Dinner."

"Thanks for telling me."

Catherine raised an eyebrow. "Can I borrow a dress for tonight? Maybe that red one? If you can find it, that is."

Louise smiled. That was one thing that would never change. Girls would always want to borrow dresses. "It's hung up. Give me a moment." Catherine was the newest girl in the house. She wandered in and sat at the vanity. Louise went to the wardrobe. "Will you tell Miss Brown I'm going to skip dinner?"

"Sparing yourself from listening to Maeve talk about her officer?" Catherine said as she turned to her.

"Yes," Louise said. The truth was she had too much work to do.

46

⬦

"ARE YOU SURE you're okay?" Louise asked for the seventh time.

Annie had been released days ago, given a clean bill of health, and her hands shook as she lit a cigarette, but she nodded. "I'll be fine. I always am."

Louise didn't believe that for a moment, but the girl was strong and proud. "Do you remember anything?"

"I've tried." Annie sounded sad about it. "I think someone saw him. That's why he stopped, but I think he was going to kill me in the street."

The officer was late. She was sure that Martin was doing it to her on purpose. She didn't say anything. Annie rose as she saw him. Louise did too, feeling much like the chaperone on a date.

"Andrew," Annie said. She sounded breathless about it, a nervous girl unsure of what to say. He wasn't in his uniform, dressed neatly in a slate gray suit. He smiled when he saw her, kissing her twice.

"Couldn't have picked an earlier time, could you, Lloyd?" He glared at her, but smiled at Annie.

Louise had the sneaking feeling that they were hiding something. She didn't want to know. They all sat on the bench in the park. Louise lit a cigarette. "Annie, we have to ask you something."

Annie looked between them. "I've told you everything I know already."

"We have a couple more questions." He spoke gently to her, instantly calming her down.

"Do you know my boss, Detective Gilbert?" Martin asked.

"We've spoken a couple of times."

"But have you seen him at Maggie's?" Louise asked. She was not about to let Martin show her up.

Annie closed her eyes, as if she had to think back. "We see so many people there."

"Think about the nights when Dora or Elizabeth went missing."

"Did any of the girls ever mention him outside of the case?" Louise asked. Annie gave Martin another look.

"Come on, Annie. Just tell us what you know." Martin lit her a cigarette. Annie took it gratefully. There was real, genuine love between them. Louise had never seen such tenderness between two people. And Martin was lying to Maeve every day. She didn't think Maeve knew; she wouldn't be happy with sharing a man. Louise figured Martin wanted to have his indulgences and marry the "right girl."

Annie inhaled. She had tears in her eyes. She shut them before she answered. "I think I've seen him a couple of times. I never knew what to say to him."

Louise wanted to wrap her arms around the girl and squeeze

her until all her pain went away. "I don't think I ever saw him with a girl. I maybe saw him at a table. Maybe with a drink. But other than that?"

"That's good, Annie. That's enough," Martin said. She smiled shyly at him. "I should make it to the station anyway. He'll be wondering where I am." Martin pulled himself up from his seat. Louise hoped he wouldn't betray her. She had no idea what he would say. They were playing a dangerous game, and while he had to trust her, she had to trust him too. And she knew she was playing with fire. He departed, tipping his hat to them.

When they were alone, Louise continued. "Will you be okay?"

"Of course. I'll do my best." Annie leaned back on the bench and stared up at the sky.

"Call me if you need me. I have some work to do."

Annie nodded, and with that, Louise rose, crushed out her cigarette on the concrete, and walked away.

◁◈▷

THE LIBRARIAN IGNORED her. She expected that. She wasn't even really sure if she was in the New York Public Library. It was silent, comforting, as she walked through the halls of the big building that could so easily swallow her up. She had never felt so small, the high ceilings, the slick floor. It was decadent in a way that only the Zodiac had struck her before this. It was a place for secrets. She could hide among the books and never be found.

But that wasn't why she was here.

She needed to discover something about herself, and the library held a greater wealth of history than Rosa Maria's paper.

She started with the time she'd been kidnapped. That brutally cold night in 1916. It was hard to believe that a decade had passed.

She had felt the weight of so many people's expectations of whom she should become after that. She had turned out to be a waitress who regularly broke the law.

Until this case.

She sat down at one of the tables, placing her purse next to her. She was reading from the *Tribune*, the *Times*, every major paper. It was strange to see how her story wasn't a story until it was. There was no mention of missing girls, no mention of her being snatched from the sidewalk blocks from her home, no mention of this utterly life-changing event, until there was a photograph of a fifteen-year-old Louise looking shell-shocked and dirty, accompanied by three other girls.

She remembered shepherding them to freedom, flagging down the first person she saw, the first person, a woman in a skirt suit, who would help them, listen to her.

What a strange time that had been.

They had been made to pose for photos. She placed her fingers on the photo of herself in the paper. She read through the stories; they were all the same. Young girl lauded as hero. Some headlines managed to blame it on her, calling her a frivolous and careless girl. She hadn't seen any of this when she was younger, but of course, she had had other things to deal with then.

Even her sisters had looked at her differently. The twins had been little more than toddlers, but Minna had been old enough to be wary of her presence when she returned.

And her father had used her. For fame, for visibility at least. He had expected her to fall in line with his demands. She had tried, but everything felt so strange after she came home. She had been scared. Scared for weeks to go outside, but she had to hide it. In her father's eyes, Louise's return meant that God was real and that she was the chosen one. For weeks he went on about Louise's miracle.

She let the memory wash over her for a moment. Everything in that period of returning and leaving again wafted in and out of her senses, as if she had watched herself go through the motions of those two years. Then she left. She had to. She couldn't be the girl everyone wanted her to be. The night she broke up with Sam, they sat side by side in the pews of the church, and she told him everything. Louise gave the little ring back. She had thought she was doing him a favor.

The favor was for her.

And now she was here.

She flicked through the papers. Some awkward quotes from her, from Lottie Haynes and Etta Hall, girls she could barely remember but whom she'd saved.

And then something in the corner of one of the photos caught her eye. She stared at it. It was blurry, but she was sure of what she was seeing. There was a photo of her on the steps of a precinct. Now that she saw it, she realized it was the same precinct that she went to every day.

And the man hovering in the corner was an officer. He was dressed in uniform and his features were younger. The photo was black-and-white, but she knew his eyes were blue. His nose was long and his chin was square and firm.

She was staring at a young detective, or, as he was then, Officer Theodore Gilbert.

Of course. He said he had heard of her, that night in his office, that he was impressed. She thought back to that night, shivering in her dress, thinking the worst.

He had *known* her. He had been there. He was glaring at her in the photo. Fifteen-year-old Louise didn't notice him. But now she knew she was right to be scared.

47

VIRGINIA THOMAS WAS more unimpressive in real life than she was in photos. She was a drawn lady, the skin over her face tight and taut. She didn't register any emotion. She was wearing black.

Louise was lucky that Virginia had even opened the door for her. The Thomases lived in a tiny one-bedroom apartment in the type of building where every noise was amplified. Louise sat uncomfortably on a couch. She had a cup of tea on her lap, but she hadn't taken a sip of it. Virginia was sitting across from her.

It had taken some work to find the Thomases' apartment. She had had to ask Rosa Maria for help, again. Louise had to promise that this was the last favor she'd ever call in. It was a promise she didn't know if she could keep.

Here she was, in a serious black dress to talk to the wife of a man who everyone thought was a murderer. They got down to business quickly. Virginia recognized her and she said as much. Her voice was tight and tense, matching her outward appearance. With her left hand, she slowly stirred her teaspoon in her cup.

"I'm sorry for your loss," Louise said.

Virginia ignored this statement. "You don't think he did it?" There were so many photographs of them, happy, smiling, around the little living room she sat in.

"I think he might not have."

"He so rarely talked to me about his work. But I loved him and he loved me." Virginia refused to look at her. When she did, her dark brown eyes bored into Louise's. She seemed dead behind those eyes, totally devoid of emotion. "I know what you must think."

"I'm sure he loved you more than anything in the world, but I'm not here to press into your relationship."

"But you do want something from me." It was a statement, not a question.

She was about to protest, but the widow was right. She wondered how many visitors darkened the doorstep of the apartment to demand something from the grieving woman. "Did he say anything about being blackmailed? Being watched? What about a club called Maggie's?"

"He never spoke about Maggie's. Just that he was there for his work. He was writing something."

"I assume he would be."

Virginia looked up at her sharply. "I'm very serious, miss." Louise bit her tongue. "He was there for research purposes." She believed it, and that was the worst part.

"I'm sorry. I shouldn't have insinuated anything."

"You're right." Virginia's voice was thin. She stopped stirring her tea. Louise had tried to block out the chime of metal on china and was relieved when it stopped.

"What was he working on?" Louise asked.

"He was going to expose that den of iniquity for what it was."

"And did someone want to stop him? Did he mention that? Anyone?" She placed her teacup on the little coffee table in front of her. She hadn't taken a sip. She was sure Virginia had offered the tea to be polite. She had accepted it to be polite.

"I don't think so."

"Did he get any strange correspondence? Letters or phone calls or anything."

"No."

"Did he have an office?" Louise asked. "I'm sorry. I wouldn't ask unless it was necessary."

"He had a desk. You could look through it."

"I would like that."

THEIR BEDROOM WAS small and cramped. But it was perfectly clean save for the desk. Virginia left her alone in the bedroom. Louise sat down at the chair. She was sure this corner of the room hadn't been touched since his death.

It was sort of eerie, really, going through the dead man's things. She started with the pile of papers on top. She was looking for anything that could be of use. She needed to prove that Gilbert had been blackmailing him. Louise didn't know what she would find. She needed to be right. But if she was right, she had no idea what would happen.

Most of his notes were neatly handwritten. She found a list of story ideas. He really was committed to telling stories about her community.

Maybe she had been too hard on him.

She had been too defensive. She never gave him a chance to truly tell her what he wanted when he approached her that day outside Maggie's.

She regretted that now. She thought she had to keep her guard up all the time. Maybe that wasn't true. But he had gotten rough with the girls—she had to remember that. He wasn't a good man.

He *had* been writing about Maggie's. The draft of the Maggie's story was buried in the second drawer. Louise folded the papers up. They wouldn't fit under her garter strap, so she placed them in her brassiere.

There was a photograph shuffled between the papers. Louise had to look briefly to know it was Annie.

What she really was looking for was well hidden. She wondered if Virginia had ever gone through her husband's things. Louise knew that if she was ever to marry, she'd never be stupid enough to let her husband have his secrets.

They were all kept in a file. Several letters, all unsigned, but typed, and threatening.

She didn't know if Bernard had believed all of this. He had done as he was told, anyway. Which girl, always apartment 1C. All the Girl Killer had to do was lie in wait.

He had been sending the girls to their deaths, and he didn't do anything to stop it. He tried to save himself, for his story.

Whatever small bit of compassion she had felt toward him dried up instantaneously.

He could have helped them.

But the weight of it all. Outlined in the letters was what the Girl Killer would have sent to his wife, incriminating photographs and other proof. The letters threatened to kill Bernard, kill Virginia, if anyone found out. Maybe he was too scared.

She had learned, quite early on, that people really cared only for themselves.

As far as she was concerned, he had let himself burn.

48

⎯◈⎯

THERE WERE ONLY a few cars when she walked up to the lot. The garage doors were closed. She knocked loudly.

The same man as before answered her. He raised an eyebrow accompanied by a smirk. "You came back."

"I wanted to know why you lied to me, Isaac White." Louise entered the little shop without him asking. She had known he had been lying to her since their first meeting. It just didn't seem important until now. She wanted to know what he knew.

"A man can't be too careful these days." Isaac placed himself behind the counter. She could understand that. He extended a hand. "It's nice to meet you, miss."

"Louise."

"Miss Louise." He opened a small refrigerator and placed two bottles of Coke on the counter. "Why'd you come back? I thought that case you're on was solved. The killer is dead." She liked the way he talked. His voice was gentle and smooth. He opened the two bottles of Coke.

"You read the papers."

"That's how I know who you are."

"Impressive. The case is technically officially closed, yes. I'm just checking over some things." She leaned on the counter, watching him as he leaned against the wall.

"Sounds like a good use of your time."

"I just want to be sure." She didn't say anything about Annie's attack. She was keeping those cards close to her chest, just in case.

"Strange."

"I know." She couldn't get a read on him. His eyes danced and he was watching her intently. "I just like being sure about things. We need to talk."

His eyes narrowed. They were a striking light brown that glowed, even in the low light of the shop. "Ladies first."

"I'm here to talk to you about Detective Theodore Gilbert." There was no use in playing around. She had a job to do and so did he. "Have you ever been arrested by him?"

Isaac raised an eyebrow. This couldn't be where he'd been expecting to go. "A couple years ago. I think he was newly promoted then. He started small."

"What did he arrest you for?"

"Officially, I was drinking, and a lot. Enough for any man to arrest me." It was nice getting to hear someone else's story for a change. She reached over as he talked, and took one of the glass bottles. She took a long sip from it. "I had to pay a fine, and a hefty one, but I was just more careful after that."

"He arrested me too." Louise leaned forward on the counter. "I mean, not him technically, but he—"

"Made you work the case, didn't he?"

"Yeah." She took another sip from the bottle.

He tapped his against hers. "He always rubbed me the wrong way."

"Yeah. You spend any time at Maggie's?"

"The café? Every week. Pity it closed." He was teasing her, earning some joy from annoying her.

"You know what I mean."

"I do. But it's not what you think."

"Why do you owe Frank Lister so much money, then?"

Isaac took another sip. He placed the bottle on the glass counter, avoiding her gaze. "I don't have sex with any of those girls." It was so forceful. He was angry at her for even insinuating the idea. "I gamble. We play poker, me and some of Frank's boys. I'm not very good at it."

"Clearly."

"Was I?" Isaac hesitated for a moment. He drew his eyes away from her.

"Were you what?"

"A suspect."

"For a moment, but that's what I wanted to talk to you about." Louise lit a cigarette. It was the only thing she could think to do with her hands. "What do you know about Bernard Thomas?"

"Not much. He joined us at the tables, sometimes."

"You ever see Detective Gilbert there?"

Isaac laughed. It was a genuine laugh, as if her question was just hilarious. "A city detective. In the largest and loudest den of sin in Harlem? I've never seen him there."

"Is it possible you just didn't recognize him?" Louise watched his face. His nose wrinkled as he tried to recall. "Maybe you did see him?"

"I'm not in there that often, Miss Louise. And I will never forget what that man looks like."

Nor would she. This summer would never let her forget. "You're right. I'm sorry. I should go." She wasn't sure why she was apologizing, but it felt right. She wasn't getting anywhere.

"Wait, Miss Louise," Isaac called after her as she turned to leave. She turned back to him.

He started his sentence a couple of times, false starts. It was as if he was trying to figure out what he wanted to say. "I'm sorry I lied to you. Sorry I couldn't be a bigger help. But I've never seen him there. I'm barely there as it is."

"It's fine."

"Good luck, Miss Louise."

◅▽▻

THE CURE FOR anything, everything, was a cup of coffee. Louise took the morning to stay in bed, drinking slowly to ease her hangover. She sat on top of her bed, cross-legged in her combinations. Her papers, her research, were all out in front of her.

She wished she had a chalkboard, like in the detective's office. She had to make do with a piece of paper, writing things out in a haphazard fashion.

She had read what Bernard Thomas had written about Maggie's. She was equal parts pleased and annoyed to find that he had simply described her as an "ornery waitress."

He had been doing his job rather diligently, and she was surprised to find that out. He had spoken to the girls who worked at Maggie's. He had laid out a timeline of Louise's life leading up to the case. It was all very thorough.

And the story wasn't even finished yet.

Louise put the handwritten pages aside and closed her eyes. It was early enough in the morning to make her feel as if she were the only one in the house. She clutched her mug in both hands. Her coffee had long gone cold and she was still sipping at it. She clipped her hair from her face, stared at the papers, the notes she had taken.

She didn't know if Gilbert knew she had broken into his apartment. She didn't know if he knew she had stolen things from him. She had copied Dora Hughes and had hidden the glass vials of laudanum and the ring under the floorboards in her bedroom. She had spent some time with Martin going over all these findings. It wasn't enough to prove their theory yet.

She went through the letters that had been sent to Bernard Thomas. She couldn't believe the detective would have been stupid enough to incriminate himself, so it didn't surprise her that even the letters sent to the *Tribune* were typed.

Had he kidnapped her? She hadn't even thought about saying it out loud. It was something she had been juggling over and over in her head. It had been too ridiculous to really consider. But now, in the creaky light of day, as she thought about it over cold coffee as the sun fought its way through the curtains and onto the rug on the floor, it was more sobering than anything.

She was scared about what it meant for her. How had she, unwillingly or otherwise, been complicit in the deaths of these girls?

Her head was spinning. She took another sip of coffee. If she was right, she had to figure out his next step.

She was never too good at being a chess player. Minna was annoyingly good at it and would goad Louise into games when they were younger. She would always lose, and she hated losing to Minna.

The detective was ahead; she could see the board. He had her in check, but since the city thought Bernard Thomas was a murderer, the heat was off him. If she were him, she would leave.

She needed him to confirm it. She just needed to scare him.

Louise rose from her spot, grabbing her dressing gown and

pulling it close to her. She propped open the window and lit a cigarette. She lowered herself to her knees, exhaling smoke into the morning. Her hands shook. She fought to hold them still as she smoked. The morning sun was quiet and bright, rising over Harlem and bringing a new day.

"Louise." It was Maeve standing in her doorway. She had red rings around her green eyes. "There's a girl at the door for you. Let her know it's too fucking early."

Louise stubbed her cigarette out and tied her dressing gown tighter. She hadn't heard a knock or the doorbell ring. As she descended the staircase, she saw Celia hovering at the door. "Come upstairs, Dove," Louise said, and waved her sister up the stairs and into her bedroom.

They crawled into bed. Celia took a look around Louise's pink room and sneered, wrinkling her nose. "You should clean up."

"Hush, you."

"What is all this?"

Louise didn't know how to tell her sister what, exactly, her days now entailed. So she piled everything up and discarded it messily on the floor below. "Just some things I'm working on. What's going on, Dove?"

"Nothing." The answer was too quick to be the truth.

"Celia, what is going on? Is it your boy?"

Celia didn't respond for a very long time. They lay in bed, in silence, as the house around them began to wake up. "I just wanted to see you." The twins prided themselves on being independent and needing only each other. "I miss you."

Louise didn't pry into it. Instead, she cleared her throat. "Remember the detective?" she asked.

"Yeah." Celia had shut her eyes. Her breathing was low and slow; she was half-asleep. Louise didn't blame her.

"What did you really think of him?" While she knew Josie wouldn't mince her words, Celia was always harder to read.

Celia opened one very bright hazel eye. She wrinkled her nose. "I think you can't trust him. I think he was too nice."

"He hasn't talked to you or Josie since, has he?"

"No. Not Josie. She doesn't like him. We've seen each other in the park. We've talked. I've talked to him."

"About what?"

Celia closed her eye again. "About you." The way she said it was innocent and chilling.

"You know Father uses you as a cautionary tale," Celia said.

"Of course he does."

"Aren't you scared?" Celia curled into her, an arm on Louise's stomach.

"Of course I am." It was nice to admit her real feelings. Louise hadn't done that in a long time. She hadn't even stopped to think about what she might be feeling. She leaned over, grabbing the paper. "Do you wanna help me? I could use a second pair of eyes."

Celia nodded. "Okay."

It was a way to get Celia's mind off whatever was bugging her. It was something they both needed.

49

BEFORE SHE KNOCKED, Louise cleared her throat and adjusted her skirt. She'd almost brought Rosa Maria with her, if only to hold her hand through the process.

But she was a grown woman of twenty-six. She could handle things on her own.

Beyond the door, she could hear the sounds of Josie and Celia practicing scales in perfect harmony. She closed her eyes and knocked.

Her aunt Louise opened the door. The older Louise peered down her long, straight nose at her. Louise had always been envious of that nose: it highlighted the sharp angles that were in the Lloyd genes. Louise had inherited soft lines and features from her mother's family. She stared at her aunt and then forced a smile on her face. Her father and aunt looked rather alike. They both had firm faces, sharp eyes. Joseph's eyes were darker than the older Louise's. Looking at her aunt, in a modest dress that was covered by an apron, Louise realized she had nothing in common with the woman.

"Louise." Her aunt always sounded disappointed to see her. "What a pleasure it is to see you."

"I need to speak to my father," Louise said. "Can I do that?"

"He's a very busy man, as you know."

"This is a matter of life and death." Louise pushed past her aunt and stepped into the tiny house.

It was more suffocating than she remembered. The twins were in the sitting room, wearing identical dresses that had gone out of style a decade ago. Louise was sure that she and Minna had worn the same ones.

"Louise!" Celia saw her first and rushed to her, wrapped her arms around Louise as tight as she could.

"Hello, Dove. Where's Father?"

"Study. I think we should go for ice cream."

"Maybe after I go talk to Father," Louise said, and kissed her sister on the head before pulling her off.

The reason Louise and her three sisters had had to be stuffed into one bedroom was so that her father could have an office. The house wasn't very big as it was, and the third, precious bedroom was one that she wasn't even allowed to step foot in as a child.

She knocked twice on the door, which she always remembered being closed, but didn't wait for him to answer.

She had been thinking about this for the past few days. She knew now that the key to this case was her past.

Which meant she had to talk to her father.

Louise wasn't looking forward to it. She had tried to think of a way to avoid this, but she had failed herself. The last time she had been in this room, she was ten and her father was informing her that her mother had died.

"Louise."

"Father."

Joseph looked up at her. "What do you want?"

Louise cleared her throat. She had had a lot of time to come up with what she was going to say to him. She wanted to tell him that he had been a terrible parent, that he had forced her to grow up way too fast.

But she bit her tongue and looked him in the eye. "I need to talk to you about when I was fifteen. When I was . . ." She was talking slowly in an effort to have the words she wanted to say come out in the correct order.

"I know, Louise. What of it?"

She didn't know how to say it. "Do you remember the officer on the case?"

"I don't, Louise. Why did you feel the need to bother me with this?"

"It's just, I didn't think I was bothering you. I think—"

"Spit it out, Louise." He had never had any patience for her dancing around a subject. This was going south and fast.

"I just need to know what you remember." She closed her eyes for a moment, unsure of how he would react.

"I remember you being an idiot girl. I remember you—"

"This isn't why I came here." She didn't know why she expected her father to be even a little helpful.

Joseph sighed. Sometimes, Louise could see certain shades of him in her. "You only come when you need something."

"You kicked me out."

"You never wanted to do what was best for you or for this family." He never yelled. His voice dropped, sending a shiver down her spine. He always accused her of doing everything wrong, even when she tried to do what he wanted.

"I was kidnapped and you used me to expand your congregation." She had blocked out those weeks following her return.

Joseph had used her story as a miracle, and preyed on unsuspecting people. "You used me," Louise said. She rose from the chair. She didn't know why she had bothered to try to talk to him.

But there had to be something else in the house that could help her.

She exited without saying goodbye.

<hr>

HER OLD BEDROOM had changed a lot. The walls were still white, beds still pushed up against the walls, but it was now the twins' domain. She could tell which twin occupied which side. Josie's side was clean and orderly, her bed made. Celia had somehow managed to strip off the bedsheets. A small tornado had whipped its way through her half. Louise bit back a laugh. Celia loved to throw stones at glass houses.

Underneath the twins' lives, the letters, jewelry, and perfume, she could still see shades of her and Minna living there. The bookcase was only half-full; the rest was lined with trinkets. Coming back to this room, this house, always made her feel like a kid again.

"Lou. What are you looking for?" It was Celia who entered the room after her.

"I'm not sure." She needed a moment or two to get her bearings. "Did you two throw out everything Minna and I held dear?" Celia considered the question. She dived under Josie's bed, and pulled out a serious brown box. It had Louise's name written on it in a messy girlish script, a heart hovering over the *i*.

"Not all of it." Celia sat down on her bed. Louise joined her.

"Dove, this may be my last time coming here." She curled her legs under her and placed the box in front of her.

Celia didn't say anything. Beyond the bedroom, Josie was at the piano, playing a lovelorn tune. Aunt Louise was in the kitchen.

Louise shut her eyes for a moment, remembering what it was like to be a child in this house.

She opened the box.

A lot of it was garbage the twins interpreted as romantic history. But there were a couple of things of use. A black, flat, velvet box that she knew used to be her mother's. She took it, pulling the lid open to reveal a choker necklace with red stones.

"What are you looking for?" Celia asked.

It was on the tip of her tongue, but she still couldn't figure out what she was hoping to find. Maybe she was looking in the wrong place. But she couldn't break into Gilbert's rooms again. And if they were really connected, she might be able to find something to show for it here.

"I . . ." She was about to answer her sister when she found another photo of herself. It had been taken when she was fifteen, right after she had fought her way out, and it was similar to the photo she found in the library. Celia stared at it too.

She squinted, trying to find the young Officer Gilbert in the background. He wasn't there, like he had been playing games with her from the start.

50

THE PLAN WAS formed the way most of her plans were formed: half-thought-through and made after a night of dancing. However, when she laid it out to Officer Martin, he thought it was a good one.

They had the laudanum; she had the ring. They had the meticulous documenting of Annie's movements. She knew Detective Theodore Gilbert was the Girl Killer.

Now she just had to prove it all, without a shadow of a doubt.

They had to invent a new victim, invent new evidence, and goad the detective into thinking something new was happening.

Louise knocked on the door of Detective Gilbert's office. Then she stepped in, sitting down in front of his desk. She had made sure to look a little disheveled, a little in a panic.

"Detective," she said. "I don't think this is over." She placed an envelope on the desk. It had her name, typed, and spots of blood on it. "I think he's watching me. I keep getting these strange phone calls at home. My matron said that she saw someone outside. I'm not safe." She was laying it on thick. She could feel it as she spoke but couldn't stop herself.

Gilbert scanned the envelope. If he registered it as a fake, he didn't show it on his face. Louise had used her own blood on the envelope, using her letter opener to slash a cut on her left wrist. The cut still throbbed; she'd slipped and it was a little deeper than she'd intended to make it. She had sat at her vanity, her right hand shaking as she made the incision a couple of inches long. It was currently hidden under the sleeve of her jacket. She watched as Gilbert pulled the paper from the envelope. It also had traces of her blood on it.

"But it's blank. It's empty."

"It's not blank," Gilbert said.

Louise leaned forward, watching as he held a match toward the paper. "You'll burn it!"

"Not if I'm careful, Miss Lloyd."

This idea had been Martin's. It was a rather good one. They had thought long and hard about this message. They needed something subtle. They had argued about it too. Louise had reminded him that she had the power to ruin his life, and he caved almost instantly.

As the words appeared, the detective exhaled. "I thought this was over." She couldn't bring herself to look at him. Did he know? He must have known.

"Me too." She swallowed hard. She never liked lying, especially to people in positions of power. But this was a necessary lie, and maybe necessary lies weren't grave sins.

"When did you get this?"

"Came to my house last night." Did he suspect she was lying? She had gone over this part so many times. He was hard to read.

Louise watched as the heat from the match revealed the carefully scrawled words.

"An old army trick."

"Where did you serve?"

His blue eyes flicked up to meet hers for a moment. She paused, not willing to let herself look away first. He didn't answer her. "Everywhere."

Martin had written this, with his left hand. The words she had chosen were few and simple: *One more girl.*

"I have an idea. It might be a little strange. But I think I know how to get to the bottom of this," Louise said.

"How?"

"Meet me in Maggie's club tomorrow night. We'll figure it all out," Louise said.

"What are you thinking?" Gilbert leaned back in his seat, looked at her. His eyes bored into hers.

"You'll see." She was only half-sure that this would work. The doubts settled into her until she couldn't ignore them. If she failed at this, she would be back at square one. The detective looked over the note.

"Right." He didn't sound convinced. His eyebrows knit together, the perfect picture of worry. He cleared his throat. "Thank you for bringing this to me. You are dismissed."

⌘

LOUISE FOLLOWED MARTIN outside, paces away from the precinct. Martin leaned against the building, smoking.

"He fell for it," she said. "Let's hope he falls for the next part." Louise lit a cigarette. She hadn't realized that she had ceased breathing the entire time she was sitting in his office. "The invisible ink was a nice touch."

"I thought he'd get it. What happens next?" Martin asked.

"I take it from here." Louise shifted in her spot, full of nervous energy. The next part was more intimidating than this. "He believed it."

"Will you keep me updated?" Martin asked. He was still worried and she couldn't blame him. They had to be careful. They were trying to outwit a murderer.

"Of course." She didn't know what the future held for them. She hoped that she would never have to work with Martin again, that this would be it. For all she knew, he could run back to the detective and tell him her entire plan.

It was why she hadn't let him know her entire plan. She knew she couldn't trust him.

"I've got to go." Louise dropped her cigarette, stamping it out with the heel of her shoe.

"Good luck, Miss Lloyd. With it all."

She knew she would need it.

51

IT WAS SAD seeing Maggie's like this. It was midnight, and Louise was flanked by Rosa Maria and Rafael. They were all still dressed in their day clothes.

"Is he coming?" Rafael tried not to sound too excited. Rosa Maria and Louise focused on dragging a table and enough chairs to the center of the dance floor. Rafael, ever helpful, clutched a bottle of bootleg alcohol. He had claimed that they were going to need the liquid courage. Louise had immediately bet him all the money in her tiny purse, about seven dollars, that Gilbert wouldn't touch the stuff.

"I assume he is," Louise said. "He didn't say no."

Rafael couldn't stop grinning. Rosa Maria, on the other hand, was a little nervous. She had seated herself at the table. "This is so strange. To think this was where those girls worked."

Louise hadn't been back to Maggie's since the night of the raid. The only thing she could focus on was Jimmy Olson trying to rape her.

Even now, weeks later, she could still feel him pressed against her, demanding things of her. She sat next to Rosa Maria. Rafael sat down across from her and placed the Ouija board between the three of them.

"I heard Myrtle Collins had one of these at her last party," Rosa Maria said. She pressed a finger to the surface.

"This was a waste of money," Louise said. Rafael poured into three glasses, dusty and obviously taken from behind the bar, where they hadn't been touched since the raid. Louise tapped hers against Rosa Maria's and drained it. "Ghosts aren't real. The afterlife can't talk."

"I'm sure you're wrong about that, Lovie." Rafael had, more than once, staunchly expressed his views. Louise hadn't told him, but she thought he was being stupid.

Rosa Maria remained neutral. "If something happens, then it happens." She had brought a notebook to record details. Louise had done the same.

"He's not showing," Louise said. On some level, she felt like a kid again, trespassing on private property to do stupid things with her friends.

"Do you know how this is supposed to work?" Rosa Maria was staring at the board.

The hair on Louise's arms rose. It was cold, but she attributed that to the fact they were underground in a glorified basement.

"Lou, you should be the questioner." Rosa Maria was still staring at the board.

"No. It should be Rafael."

"It was your idea," Rosa Maria said.

Louise sighed. She looked around the little circle. She didn't believe in these things. She had just put this plan in place. Rosa Maria was well aware. She had let Rafael believe they were going to actually communicate with the dead. It was more entertaining that way. "All right," she said. They placed one finger on the planchette. Louise closed her eyes. "Dora Hughes, Clara Fisher, Elizabeth Merrell, Ruth Coleman, Nell Hawkins, if you're here and present, please talk to us."

A breeze brushed past them, making the hair stand on her neck. Her heart was pounding in her chest; she could feel the walls of the former club closing in on her.

And then the planchette moved. To the yes.

"Who's there?" Louise asked.

It took a moment for the planchette to move again, going to the C, the L, the A, the R, and back to the A.

"What are you doing here?" The voice, the smooth, real voice, boomed in the silence around them. All of them turned to find Detective Gilbert striding in. He removed his hat and coat, laying them on the dusty bar. He sounded angry. Well, not *angry*, but definitely displeased.

"I thought we'd see if we could connect with the dead girls." Louise looked up at him as he took a seat at the table.

"This is ridiculous."

"It's just a lark," Rosa Maria said. Louise tried to hold as still as possible.

The detective glared at her. "How is this supposed to help, Miss Lloyd?" He frowned and she felt a knot of guilt in her stomach.

"Maybe the spirits of the victims can guide us." It sounded ridiculous as she was saying it. But she needed him to believe that this would work.

Gilbert did not look convinced, but he raised an eyebrow and sat down at the board. "How does this work?"

"You ask a question and the spirits answer." Louise swallowed hard. "Clara Fisher, are you still here?" Louise could feel her throat tightening. With everyone at the table touching the planchette, it began to move to the *yes*.

"You're moving it," Rosa Maria said.

"I'm not, and if you want to go ahead, go for it."

"No," Rafael said. "One person should be the questioner. We can suggest things, but, Lovie, you have to be it now."

She swallowed hard. "Miss Fisher." Apparently talking to the dead was a formal affair. "How old were you?"

The planchette moved over the numbers one, then six.

Rafael exhaled sharply. Rosa Maria shot a look at her brother.

"Rafael, stop pushing it," Louise said. She raised her eyes to him.

He frowned. "I'm not."

"Detective?"

"Not me."

They shared a round of looks. Before they continued, Rafael poured them all another drink.

"Can you tell me where you were murdered?"

The planchette breezed over the numbers 126.

"Miss Lloyd," Gilbert said. There was a sense of urgency in his tone. A cool wind blew past them again.

There was a creak coming from the back room, soft taps that sounded like high-heeled shoes coming toward them.

"What was that?" Louise asked.

Rafael looked up. "Nothing."

"Ask if she knew her attacker," Rosa Maria said.

"Miss Lloyd." Gilbert sounded unnerved.

Her heart was pumping, pattering in her chest. She didn't believe this; she knew that. None of this was real. None of this was happening. Louise and Rosa Maria were making this up. But it still felt real.

She ignored him and focused on the board. "Miss Fisher, do you know who killed you?"

After a long moment, the planchette moved to *yes*.

Louise and Rosa Maria shared a long look. "Who?"

Minutes of silence.

Then the planchette moved again, *S-T-A-N* . . .

"Everyone, take your hands off," Louise said. They all did as she said, raising their hands in the air. The air was thick with heat. Louise's breath fell from between her lips, ragged and loud. The planchette went skittering off the table, hitting the ground. The noise broke the spell around them. Louise drained her glass. She looked up at the detective. He was glaring at her with exceptional anger in his light blue eyes. This was a mistake; she knew it. She had made the wrong move.

"This was a ridiculous experiment." Gilbert was angry now. "You've wasted my time and yours, Miss Lloyd."

With that, he collected his things and exited the abandoned club.

"Who the hell is Stan?" Rafael was still staring at the board, unable to comprehend what had happened.

Louise used one of the candles to light a cigarette. She leaned back in her chair, feeling her heart slow to normal.

"Detective Stanley Theodore Gilbert."

⊲▽⊳

THEY ENDED UP at Rafael's apartment. It was two in the morning. They were all dead tired, but they curled up in the small living room.

They hadn't spoken in the cab, hadn't spoken as they took the elevator. Rosa Maria made some coffee. Louise poured a generous helping of alcohol into her cup.

"What . . . was that?" Rafael asked. For the first time in his life, he was shocked into silence. He was sitting on the piano bench.

Louise lit a cigarette before she said anything. "Detective Gilbert is the Girl Killer. And now I'm sure."

Rosa Maria looked at her. "How?"

She was quite proud of herself, actually. She pulled herself up so she was sitting on his couch, and curled her legs under her. "Quite simple, really. Once Martin discovered that he was watching Annie, and I became fairly certain that he kidnapped me, I dug a little deeper. Then we set this up." Rosa Maria sat next to her. Louise continued. "I knew there was something strange about the way he devoted himself to his case, and I found all that laudanum in his apartment."

"You broke into his apartment?" Rosa Maria asked.

"Yes, I did."

"But what about the board?" Rafael asked.

"It was me and Rosa Maria, really. And magnets." Louise drained her mug, coughing as she did.

"So, we can't talk to the dead?"

"No."

"But what about the noises we heard? The wind?"

That was something Louise couldn't explain. She cleared her throat. "Atmosphere."

"What are you going to do now?" Rosa Maria asked.

"I don't know." She closed her eyes. It had been a long day, leading into a long night.

"The detective . . . ," Rafael said.

"Is a murderer," Rosa Maria finished his sentence.

They sat in silence for a little while more. Louise was jittering from the coffee and the nerves. She tried to calm herself down. There was nothing to be scared of. She had engineered the situation. She had made it happen. But her heart was still skittering in her chest. She felt as if she couldn't quite catch her breath.

"You need to relax," Rosa Maria said quietly next to her ear. "You're fine. We're all fine."

It was as if none of them knew what to do with this information.

"But are you sure he killed all those girls? Then pretended he didn't?" Rosa Maria asked.

"That's how it works, I think."

"What about Bernard?"

"I think Gilbert slipped something into the tea I gave him to make it look like a heart attack or something." She couldn't get the image of the man dying in front of her out of her mind. She still saw him when she closed her eyes.

"What about you?" This was Rafael, a rare moment of selflessness from him.

"What?" Louise opened one eye, against everything in her body wanting to just go to sleep.

"What about you? Why you?"

That was something she didn't know the answer to. That was a question she didn't want to focus on. She was connected to this case in more ways than she understood.

And she didn't know what lengths he would go to.

Part of her wanted this all to be a mistake, to be a coincidence. But it wasn't. After seeing the look the detective had on his face tonight, she knew that now.

"We all need to get some rest," Rosa Maria said. They did need rest. But none of them moved. They all stared at different spots in the apartment, unable to function.

"What a strange night," she said, and lit a cigarette, concentrating on inhaling and exhaling.

"What a brilliant plan," Rafael said. If he was disappointed it was all a ruse, he didn't show it. Louise felt bad about not letting him in, but she knew he couldn't keep a secret.

"I was just trying to scare him. Let him know I'm onto him," she said. And she had done that. It was a risk, but hopefully he'd slip up and Martin could catch him.

But the next move was his. And she wasn't sure what Gilbert would do in retaliation.

52

THIS TIME, IT was Josie knocking on the door. Louise and Rosa Maria were sitting in the kitchen, waiting for coffee to bring them to life.

Louise answered the door. It was early in the morning, but Josie was disheveled on her doorstep. She had been crying. Tears were still running down her face.

"Sunshine. What's going on?" Josie had so often run to Minna for help that this felt like a little victory in the constant war with her sister.

"It's Celia." Josie could barely get the words out.

Rosa Maria had joined her at the door. "What's wrong with Celia?" Louise asked.

"She didn't come home last night."

Josie's words sank into her, freezing her. "Come in, come in." Rosa Maria waved them all inside.

They reconvened in the kitchen. Rosa Maria began to brew tea. Louise sat across from her sister. "Josie, you have to tell me everything."

Josie looked right past Louise. Her hazel eyes were bright with tears. She hiccuped, tried to catch her breath. "She didn't come home last night."

"Where was she? Where did she go?"

"I don't know."

"Josephine Sylvia Lloyd, if you're lying to me."

"I really don't know!"

Louise and Rosa Maria shared a look. Another set of knocks rang from the door. Rosa Maria went to get the door and led in Rafael, looking similarly disheveled. He was smoking and neither girl told him to stub it out. "There was a raid at the Zodiac."

"What?"

"When?"

Rafael flopped into a kitchen chair. He was bleeding, a cut on his arm. "Last night. I just barely got out."

Louise looked toward her sister. "Rafael, is there any chance you saw my sister at the Zodiac last night?"

Rafael had closed his eyes. Rosa Maria nudged him and whispered something in Spanish. Their conversation was rapid, with one twin starting sentences and the other finishing them.

"I didn't see her at the Zodiac. I would have told you," Rafael said.

Louise knelt down in front of her sister. Josie was still crying, wiping her eyes with the back of her hand. "Josie, do you think Celia went to the Zodiac last night?"

"I don't know. She didn't say a word to me yesterday."

"Josephine, I need you to concentrate." A horrible feeling settled into her. "Did she say anything? Do anything strange?"

"She didn't even talk to me. She just was gone all day and never came home." Rosa Maria nudged Louise, who could feel her heart pounding in her chest. She didn't like where this was headed.

"Louise, what do you think?"

"I think I should go try to find my sister." Louise pulled herself up. She went to the entryway and wrapped herself up in a coat, making sure nothing indecent was visible.

"I'll go with you," Rosa Maria said. Louise hadn't realized that Rosa Maria had followed her.

"No, stay here with Josie. Make sure she calms down. Okay?" Louise couldn't resist kissing Rosa Maria quickly. "This is probably just a misunderstanding."

She didn't believe the words as they came out of her mouth. She knew it was anything but.

⋖⋇⋗

AT ABOUT SIX that evening, Louise climbed the stairs to her childhood home. She knocked twice. She wasn't expecting anyone to answer. She was expecting her father or her aunt to know it was her and leave her standing on the stoop for the rest of the evening.

"What are you doing here?" Her aunt Louise opened the door.

"I just wanted to come by," Louise said. "See Celia. Is she home?" The older Louise exhaled and opened the door, letting Louise the younger in.

She was in the door. That was a good first step. Her aunt led her to the parlor, where her father was reading a paper. She stared at the headline about the Zodiac.

He was reading the *Tribune*.

"Father," Louise said. She was met with silence. She didn't know what she was expecting. She was standing in her childhood home, and she couldn't imagine what she was doing there. She should have gone home. Celia would probably have called by now, or she'd be sitting in the parlor, talking her housemates' ears off.

It was too late to go home. She was already standing there.

"Joseph," Aunt Louise said. She stared at her brother. "I'm going to make something to eat. Your daughter is here." That was the most help that she would get from her aunt. She was lucky that she got that much.

Louise had drawn her lines a long time ago.

She knew that her father was going to murder her when he found out. That was probably the scariest part.

"Father." She hadn't been in this parlor since she left the house. It was frighteningly the same. A clock ticked away on the mantel. An old piano stood in the corner, and she remembered sitting with Celia as she learned to play. Louise had learned too, but she had never been very good at it. Her father was sitting on a worn couch, and on the table stood a photo, one of the only photos of Janie Lloyd, heavily pregnant, just before she died. Louise stared at the face. They had the same nose, the same eye shape and color, and the same wide smile.

She really did look like her mother. She had heard it so often. She had begun not to believe it, but the photograph was there.

"What brings you home, Louise?" She stood in front of her father, hoping he wouldn't see her shaking.

"I wanted to speak to Celia." Louise was lying and she knew her father knew that. Joseph raised his eyes from his paper to look at her. She always felt as if she was under inspection when he did so.

"She's not home," Joseph said. "She hasn't been home all day." Louise felt something within her cave. She had been hoping that Celia would be there, upstairs.

Now she could feel herself spiraling to the worst place possible.

"Of course." She felt stupid coming here.

"What did you do?" her father asked. He knew; of course he knew. And he was sitting, reading the paper, and not trying to find her. Louise felt a flash of anger. He didn't care enough. He never cared about his children. He cared about how the community perceived the family but not about his actual children, his own flesh and blood.

Except for Minna. But then again, Minna had always been the exception and not the rule.

"I didn't do anything," Louise said. She cleared her throat. At least that part had been the truth. She honestly hadn't done anything. "I just thought Celia would be here, but if not, I should go." It would have been a good excuse. She stepped back.

"Stop."

She froze in place. She was an adult and she hated that her father still scared her. She stared at him, trying to pull herself up to her full height.

"What?" she asked. There was a pause as Joseph, still seated, looked over his oldest daughter. Louise tried not to break eye contact as he did so. She wondered what he was thinking. His face gave nothing away. Louise had inherited that trait.

"Where is Celia?" Joseph asked. Louise paused and shifted in her seat.

"I don't know," she said. That was the truth and it hurt to say it. She had no idea how he would react to that.

He paused. There was a moment when she thought that he wouldn't be angry. That was foolish of her. Before she knew what he was doing, his hands were at her shoulders, slamming her against the wall. Her head hit the wall and she groaned in pain.

"Joseph." This was the other Louise. "Let her go." The older Louise crossed her arms over her chest. "This won't help."

"If she turns up dead, Louise . . . ," Joseph said slowly.

"I know," Louise said. He didn't have to say it. She knew it all too well.

It would be on her.

⌁⌁⌁

THE LAST STOP Louise made was to apartment 1C. She held her breath as she approached, feeling something grip her heart. She wouldn't be able to rest if she didn't check this room. She had to know. Louise had had to go back to Miss Brown's to get her gun, shoving it into her handbag. Josie was still at the house, curled up asleep in Louise's bed, wearing a spangled dress, while Rosa Maria read in the chair in front of the vanity. She felt the weight of the gun in her little purse as she walked through the halls.

For one moment, she thought about her mother. Janie would have hated that she was so stubborn.

Louise inhaled. She was taking her time, because she had to. If anyone was in there, she wanted the element of surprise. She wanted to be able to barge in and save Celia. Her heart was in her throat. It stuttered and stammered as she made her way down the hallway. Her shoes echoed. She could see that this building, like most of Harlem, was falling apart. She had seen a mouse scuttle down the hallway and into an unknown crevice. A smell had settled over the building, but she wasn't sure what it was. The smell was musty and murky.

Louise pulled herself together. She couldn't allow herself to be scared. She thought of her mother again, the most brilliant of her memories of Janie. *Always be brave.*

Blood pounded in her ears, and although it was another very hot day in a summer of very hot days, Louise's whole body was cold.

She took a deep breath. She had to bypass the red rope that blocked the door, marking the space a crime scene, and pick the lock. It took her a little longer than normal. Before she pushed the door open, she took her gun from her purse. Her heart was in her throat. She was so sure that Celia would be behind this door, that she could save her sister and this nightmare would be over. She held on to the gun as tightly as she could to keep from shaking. She raised it and entered the little apartment.

She didn't know what she was expecting, but the little apartment was immaculately clean and empty. Louise lowered her gun. It was startlingly empty, as if no one had ever been there. Celia was nowhere to be found.

What if she was wrong? Louise moved to the square window, moving the shutters so that the last afternoon sun breezed in. She looked around. There was no trace of her sister or the person who had kidnapped her.

Louise was totally out of options.

She let the shutters go, casting the room in near darkness again. She was alone. As odd as it sounded, she had to think like the detective. Louise exited the apartment. Something about it was enough to make her skin crawl. She shut the door behind her, shoved her gun carelessly into her purse, and walked down the hallway as fast as her legs could carry her. No one questioned her; the halls were empty and a Black woman wouldn't look out of place in the Black part of town. She pushed her hair from her eyes. She hadn't really bothered putting herself together that morning—there were other pressing issues—and she suddenly realized how messy she must look. She was slightly embarrassed for her state: hair and makeup not done, a mismatched blouse and skirt. She exited the building and went back out into the setting sun. Suddenly she wanted to fall apart. Returning home without Celia was a loss.

But she didn't know where else to search, so Louise headed down the street toward her home. It felt as if she was giving up, and she went right up to bed without going to dinner.

53

LOUISE DIDN'T LIKE walking past Maggie's ever since the building had been closed. It was too sad. She didn't realize how much she loved her café until it was gone.

That morning, the day after Celia had gone missing, Louise and Rosa Maria had to walk past it. Louise was running an early-morning errand for Miss Brown. She had been doing more of that since the café closed, Miss Brown believing that she was wholly unemployed.

She had begun looking for a new job, something similar to what she'd had before the case threw a wrench in her life.

It was going to be another dry day, and Louise was dressed in white, a hat pulled over her hair. She could get through her errand and go back to bed. That was all she wanted: to sleep through the day. She and Rosa Maria walked with linked arms.

"I think tonight we can try the stations again," Rosa Maria was saying. "Maybe you missed something by the Zodiac." Louise nodded. She knew she wouldn't be able to focus until she got Celia back.

There was something lying in front of the café. There was *some-one* lying in front of the café. Louise's heart froze.

She paused. Her brain was trying to make herself move closer, but everything in her resisted.

"Louise," Rosa Maria said. Her voice sounded like it was miles away as the world swam around her.

There weren't many people on the street now, and everyone was giving Maggie's a wide berth.

Louise pulled herself together and approached the body.

She was small, wearing a dress of bright emerald green, one that was a little too long for her, black shoes on her feet. Gemstones sparkled in her hair, and her eyes stared up at the cool, calm sky.

Underneath her, blood seeped. There were stab wounds on her chest and her abdomen, deep slashes on her bare arms. Beside her was a little card with the Virgin Mary on it.

Louise stared. She knew she was staring at the body of her youngest sister, but there was a part of her that didn't want to believe it.

She opened her mouth to say something but couldn't formulate the words. Instead, her knees buckled and gave way. Rosa Maria moved to catch her before she hit the ground. Celia's lifeless hazel eyes were the last thing she saw before she passed out.

<hr>

"MISS LLOYD. MISS Lloyd . . . Louise." Louise opened her eyes to see Officer Martin hovering over her. She moved to sit up, but he placed a hand on her shoulder. Rosa Maria was right next to her, holding her left hand. "Slowly."

"Celia," Louise said. She blinked rapidly, trying to make the world fall back into place. They were a few feet from where her sister's body lay on the ground. She had no memory of who'd moved her or of what had happened. "She . . ."

"Miss Lloyd, I need you to breathe." Martin kept his calm demeanor as Louise pulled herself to a sitting position, doing as she was told. She was covered in dust and she tried to brush it away. Louise's head rang as she looked around, tried to pull herself from the ground.

"Celia . . . ," Louise repeated. It was the only thing she could focus on, the only thing in her head. She shut her eyes, taking a deep breath. She felt her stomach revolt.

"It's okay, Louise," Rosa Maria said.

"Miss Lloyd." Officer Martin did not finish his sentence. Louise didn't know if he knew what to say. Louise didn't know what she wanted him to say. "I'll get someone to take you home, but I need you to breathe for me." Louise took exaggerated breaths. It helped in trying to steady herself. She felt empty and tired. Martin kept his hands on her shoulders. He surveyed her closely, his eyes taking in every detail of her tearstained face.

"I can take her, Officer," Rosa Maria said.

"I'm having you escorted home." There would be no arguing with the officer. He watched her for a moment. His lips were in a firm frown. "I am so sorry for your loss, Miss Lloyd."

Louise started crying again.

54

LOUISE SPENT THREE days in bed. Every few hours, Rosa Maria would come into her room and set out a cup of tea and something to eat, and every time, it would be left untouched and then replaced.

Louise lay on her back, staring at her ceiling. She was unsure if she was sleeping, or if she was awake. Every part of her body ached. Her face was red and puffy from crying.

She didn't move, didn't leave bed, didn't say anything for three days. She just cried and slept. She could feel the pain so acutely within her that she couldn't move. She thought about Josie. Her partner, her other half, had been taken from her. If Louise felt this bad, she couldn't imagine what Josie was feeling.

The world stayed still around her. Her blinds were closed and yet the sun fought its way through, casting a pale light over the pink room.

On the fourth day, Louise pulled herself from bed. The first thing she did was pray. She was doing a lot more praying recently.

She didn't know if she believed what she was saying, but she had to try; she had to attempt it.

She knew that her family would be doing the same thing. Louise was reminded of saying the same prayers when Janie Lloyd died.

Louise thought that her mother dying was the worst thing she would ever have to withstand.

And here she was.

"Louise." The door opened. Rosa Maria stepped in. "You're awake. You're up." She had a teacup in her hands, one she placed on the bedside table, right next to a teacup that was identical to it. "Louise, I'm so sorry. She knows you loved her, and she knows you tried to save her," Rosa Maria said.

"I shouldn't have pushed it. I should have left it alone." She was sure that the guilt would follow her around for the rest of her life. Her father's words rang in her head, and she squeezed her hand into a fist. She couldn't let him get to her like this. She wouldn't let him get to her like this.

Rosa Maria kissed her gently. Louise hesitated for a moment, and then kissed her back. For one single moment, everything was right in the world.

"I'm hungry," Louise said as she pulled away. It turned out that not eating for three days made someone very hungry. Her stomach growled.

"Miss Brown just made lunch. Rafael has been here every day wanting to see you. And . . . your sister came."

"Josie?" Louise asked. For a moment she was filled with relief.

"Minna," Rosa Maria said. Louise had forgotten just for a second that she had another sister. She deflated again, then wrapped her red robe around her body.

"I'm hungry," Louise said again. Now it was the only thing she could focus on.

"Come, we'll get you something to eat." Rosa Maria took her by the hand and led her down the stairs. It was a day where almost everyone was home. Louise took her chair at the table, feeling more out of place than ever.

The girls watched as Louise sat down. Her stomach growled as she placed her napkin on her lap.

"We wanted to be here," Catherine said. "For you."

"I canceled my plans," Maeve said, as if that were something that Louise should have felt bad about.

"I would like to eat something," Louise said. She was light-headed. She wasn't sure she would be able to keep anything down.

"Of course," Rosa Maria said quietly. "We'll all eat something." As if that were a solution to her problems.

They sat and ate in silence.

━━━◆━━━

AFTER LUNCH, LOUISE returned to her room. She didn't want to get into bed, so she sat at her desk and stared at herself in the mirror. She wanted to bathe, to change from the clothes she was wearing into something mostly clean.

But she couldn't persuade herself to move from her chair.

There was a knock on the door. She was vaguely aware that time was passing, that the world was still moving around her, but she was stuck.

"I'm fine," Louise said. "Please leave me alone. I'm fine."

The door opened. She was expecting to see Rosa Maria or another girl. She didn't think that they would leave her alone, even though she'd asked.

But Minna, dressed in black, stood at her door.

"Louise," Minna said.

"Leave me alone." Her younger sister was the last person she wanted to see at that moment.

"We have to be with family right now. And like it or not, I'm family." Minna seated herself on the bed. "Don't you ever clean up around here? Louise, it's a mess and you live here."

"My sister just died."

Minna rolled her eyes. "Louise, you can't be mad at me anymore. We're all you have."

"No, Minna," Louise said. "You have your husband, your son, Father, and Aunt Louise. Those two are everything I had. You'll be fine. Josie's just lost the one person she's been with since birth."

"You know, I expected better from you, Louise Lovie Lloyd." Minna rose from her seat and Louise did too. The two sisters squared off. Louise wondered if she would have to fight her sister. "I expect this behavior from anyone else, but we're Lloyd girls. We don't mope or whine or pity ourselves." Minna stepped closer to her. Louise crossed her arms over her chest. "If something is wrong, we go out and fix it. And then we clean our rooms."

She hated that her sister—rational, calm Minna—was right. She managed to be right about many things. She inhaled, and then exhaled again. "I'm sorry, Minna. We need each other now more than ever." She hated saying it. She and Minna had been constantly at odds—they had been fighting for seventeen years—but maybe it was time to put their feud aside.

"She was going to get married." Minna collapsed back on the bed, and Louise sat next to her.

"How are you feeling? How is Josie?"

Minna sighed. "It comes and goes. I miss her. Josie does too. I think she's still in shock."

"It's not going to get better anytime soon. Remember when Mother died?"

"I remember you clutching onto my hand and never letting go."

"I didn't want you to do something that would make Father angry."

"I wasn't going to," Minna retorted. She cleared her throat. "You should come to the funeral."

Louise paused. She wanted to be at the funeral with everything she had. She wanted to be there with her family for her sister. "We'll see."

Minna turned to her, took Louise's hands in hers. "That breaks my heart, Louise. I know we've had our differences, but we're sisters, and now Josie and I are the only ones you have. We're your family." That was something she would have to get used to now: having two sisters. Louise wanted to counter that. Rafael was her family; Rosa Maria was her family. "Do you think we'll be able to get along now? She would want us to get along."

"Maybe." Louise gave a measured response. "I think we can try to get along."

55

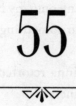

SICK OF HER bedroom, Louise moved herself down to the parlor. She curled up on the old fainting couch. It was the middle of the day and she still felt as if she could not really leave her house.

She had a book in her lap, but she wasn't reading. The house was still and silent around her for once. It was nice to know that the house could occasionally be silent.

There was a knock on the door and Louise pulled herself up. She didn't want to get it.

It was Rafael. The first thing he did was wrap her into a tight hug.

"I am so sorry, Lovie," Rafael whispered in her ear. She had been doing a very good job of not crying, but she burst into tears again. "I'm sorry. I'm so, so sorry."

"It's not your fault," Louise said. He held her tightly. "Come inside," Louise said. She led him into the parlor and took her seat on the fainting couch. Rafael sat beside her, pulling her close.

"How are you doing?" he asked her. She was quickly coming to hate that question. She was still numb, pain radiating from a point in her stomach. Celia had been dead for less than a week and she thought the pain might never go away. "Was that a dumb question?" He held her so her head was on his shoulder. "I'm so sorry."

She had to direct her sadness into anger. She closed her eyes and let herself relax. She pretended it was a long night after the Zodiac and she had just spent hours on the dance floor. Except the Zodiac was closed. She had nearly forgotten, and she felt her heart squeeze again.

"Hey, go get dressed. I want to show you something."

"Raf."

"Go, Louise. It's important." It must be serious. Louise pulled herself from the couch and went up the stairs to bathe and dress as fast as she could.

She didn't want to leave the house, but she wanted to know what Rafael had in store for her.

⋈

RAFAEL CALLED A cab.

"Where're we going?" Louise asked. She had managed to dress herself in a solemn black day dress, makeup free, her hair swept from her face. It was more effort than she wanted to put into herself that day.

"You'll see."

"I hate when you try to be mysterious."

When they got out of the car, he led her to a storefront, then pulled out a key, unlocking and opening the door.

It was dusty and quiet and dark. Rafael let go of Louise's hand and moved to turn on a lamp. She was standing at the edge of what could be a dance floor. A bandstand was toward the back, and there was a bar nestled in the corner. She could picture it if she tried: a band on the bandstand, someone behind the bar, and people on the floor.

"What is this?" Louise asked.

"My new club," Rafael said. Louise raised her eyebrows. It was impressive. Small, but not too small—with some proper work, the floors and bar could shine. Rafael crossed back to her, sticking his hands in his pockets. "Cost a fortune, but the old owner headed to Chicago. Wanted it sold fast. He wasn't even using it."

"So it's yours now? How copacetic."

"Mine, all mine." He extended a hand toward her and she took it. He led her to the middle of the dusty floor. Rafael took her by the waist and began to lead her in an elegant waltz. Louise fought the urge to groan loudly as he did so. "It's fine," Rafael said. "Just waltz with me."

She didn't know that this was what she needed, but as they moved across the floor in silent, perfect harmony, she could feel something loosen inside of her. He twirled her once, twice, and she was grinning when he brought her back to him.

"This could be a nice place."

"Needs a name," Rafael said. "I wasn't sure what to call it. Before we can open, we need a name." He paused and looked around. "What was it that you called Celia?"

"Dove?"

"Yeah," Rafael said. "I could name it after her. I know that wouldn't bring her back but . . ."

Louise had to smile. "She would love that." Celia would have loved to have a club named after her. Louise knew she'd have adored it.

It felt right that the first dance in the Dove was them effortlessly moving across the floor.

"I didn't know you wanted one of these."

"I wasn't going to be the Zodiac bartender forever, and when it was raided, it just felt like it was time. Should be safe." He twirled her around again. Their steps were carving out places in the dust, tracking their progress across the floor. She could see it so clearly, this club full of people, a place that kept secrets for them like the Zodiac had.

"Is this why you go to Snake Eyes?" Louise asked.

"I was hoping to poach the band. No dice," Rafael explained.

The Zodiac wouldn't open again, but that didn't matter. The Dove was a few short blocks away and Rafael was smarter, more clever, than the Zodiac owner had been.

When they had tired of waltzing, he led her to the bar and set a bottle of real champagne on top.

Louise didn't ask where he'd gotten it. It was better if she didn't know.

He popped the bottle and poured two glasses. He passed one to her.

"To change?"

"Growing up?" She hadn't realized it; she wasn't the person she had been when she had walked into the Zodiac for the first time. She had been young and idealistic, and now she was a grown adult.

"To not getting arrested," Rafael said with his sly smile and a wink. Louise rolled her eyes, but she drank to that. Rafael filled her glass again.

56

Louise dressed to go out. Rosa Maria was on Louise's bed in the pink room and watched as Louise tried to choose between dresses, holding them up in the light to decide what to wear. They were aware of the plan. Louise would meet Martin at the Zodiac with the intention of luring Gilbert there; Rosa Maria would head to Rafael's apartment, where Annie and Josie were waiting.

"The blue one." Louise held it up to her body.

"No." Rosa Maria pulled herself from her chair. "Neither. Louise, you've worn both those dresses a lot. You do know that, right?"

"I know." She wanted to look her best.

Rosa Maria sighed and departed her room. She returned with her arms full of clothes and placed them on the bed. She picked up a black pair of trousers. "Wear these."

"I don't want to cause a scandal." Louise took the trousers and held them up. Truthfully, she never thought she really was that type of girl.

"You should," Rosa Maria said. "I grew out of these. You should wear them. I know I'd like to see you in them." Louise pulled them on. They were soft and light and she immediately realized she liked wearing them. Louise pulled on a red shirtwaist she had bought with the intention of wearing and then never did.

"See?" Rosa Maria had placed herself on the bed again, watching Louise get dressed. "You really are a choice bit of calico."

"I guess so." Louise still wasn't convinced. Her hands wouldn't stop shaking. She hadn't told Rosa Maria what she thought would happen at the Zodiac.

"Louise, are you okay?" Rosa Maria watched her.

Louise inhaled. That was a heavy question. "I'm fine. Some days are better than others." Did it sound convincing? She was trying to convince everyone that she was okay. She still felt like one stiff breeze would blow and she would fall to pieces. She was barely stitched together.

"You're sure?"

"On the level." Louise placed her hands on her waist and looked around the little pink room. Now that she had cleaned the room, it looked a lot bigger than it used to.

"Okay, sit," Rosa Maria instructed. She pulled herself up from the bed. Louise did as she was told, sitting at the vanity table. She shifted in her seat.

Louise stared at herself in the mirror. She did look good. It was possibly the best she had looked in her life.

From downstairs, a girl called for Maeve, reminding her that they were not alone. Louise picked up the black velvet box that held her mother's necklace. When she put it on, the inset rubies gave the appearance of blood shimmering from her throat.

Louise rose. "I should go." She picked up her purse. She had already placed the little gun inside it, and every time she lifted her purse, she was reminded of the weight. She wasn't going to need the gun. In fact, she was going to give it back to Rafael. But she liked the feeling of having it with her. Just in case.

"Be careful." Rosa Maria still had to dress for her own night out at Rafael's. Louise put her purse down again, and crossed the one and a half steps to where Rosa Maria was standing, taking her by the waist and kissing her deeply. She hadn't told Rosa Maria or Rafael the whole plan. She needed them to be able to deny it if they were questioned about anything. She needed to keep them safe.

Louise could feel her heart stop, then speed up as the other girl reacted. They moved back in synchronized steps, so that they were pressed against the wall near the door. Louise couldn't let her lips leave, couldn't pull away. There was a part of her that was convinced that she would die if she let go right now. For the moment, they were totally and completely connected.

"Someone is going to come in." Rosa Maria's lips were still against hers. Louise paused, pulling away ever so slightly. Their foreheads touched and Louise could feel the heat radiating from Rosa Maria's body.

"I don't care." Louise kissed her again. She didn't know how desperately she needed to be close to the other woman, but she didn't want to be pulled away again.

"Be safe." Rosa Maria's voice cracked.

"I'm always safe."

"You're all bravado."

"And you love it."

"You know it may be dangerous."

"You love when I'm dangerous."

"Louise."

"I love you. I don't care what happens. I love you."

"I love you too," Rosa Maria said. They weren't much for the public declarations of love or affection, but they were the only two people in her room. No one else was going to see.

Louise kissed her again, long and lingering, then pulled away from her. No matter what she wanted to do, she had to go.

She picked up her purse, then her shoes. Anticipation flooded through her veins. "I'll see you very soon." Louise kissed Rosa Maria one more time before she climbed out the window.

57

⊽⊼⊽

THE ZODIAC WAS cold and dusty, quiet from a week of no use. Louise picked the lock to the front door. Nostalgia washed over her. She hated seeing her favorite place like this, and she had missed it more than she had known. She paced for a few minutes as her eyes adjusted to the low light. Everything must have been exactly as it had been the night it had been raided. Broken glass covered the floor, alcohol making her shoes stick as she walked. The band equipment was toppled on the stage. She had been caught in many a raid in her time, but this one, one she hadn't even been a part of, had been the worst. The floors creaked beneath her, and she whipped around, flicking the house lights on, trying to see if there was anyone behind her. She was the only one there. She was alone, and she knew it.

The air skittered over her exposed arms, raising the hair on the back of her neck. She bit her tongue, reaching into her purse to grab her gun. To distract herself, she pictured her first night in the Zodiac. She had just left her father's home and had nowhere to go. She had overheard some bright young things gossiping about it, and she had decided to see it for herself. She leaned down, dragging her fingers through the dust, picturing the noise from the club, the band, the singer, the dancers moving as fast as they could. It was easier to do it in the low light, when she could barely see the stage and the bar.

She hadn't known how a club would change her life. She hadn't known what she had been capable of until she had stepped foot into the Zodiac.

Right near her fingers, a cockroach slid across the floor, leaving tracks on the dust. She moved her hand away, shaking it as if the bug had touched her.

Louise and Martin had a plan. This was the last part of it. Martin wouldn't let Louise confront the detective alone.

The silence rang in her ears, nearly deafening her. Every sound was exaggerated, booming off the walls, making her jump every time she stepped on a creaky floorboard, or a car drove past the abandoned building. She was being irrational. She was making things up.

She turned on her heel, moving from the dance floor back to the front door. As she started up the low steps, the lights flickered on above her. "You beat me here." Detective Gilbert was leaning on the doorjamb.

"You scared me."

"Are you alone? You shouldn't be here alone." The detective closed the door behind him.

"I know what you did," she said.

The detective took one step toward her, forcing her back. "You know, you all act like this place was some big secret. It's not even subtle." He was talking so softly that she could barely hear him.

He was still walking toward her, a steady, controlled pace.

"You people. Out here, every night, like you don't have a care in the world. And this . . . this place was the worst. This place made you think that people like you were, well, people." The last two syllables fell from his mouth to her feet. A cruel, cold smile had stretched over his face. A shiver ran down her spine and she took a step back.

"Oh, no, sweetheart. You're not going anywhere. It's just you and me, darling."

58

HER HEART WAS pounding in her ears. She could feel the blood rushing through her body. His gaze on her was clear and filled with hatred.

"You were the one I wanted. You must know that. You couldn't possibly be that stupid, could you?"

Her skin froze as she reached into her purse. Above them, the lights flickered.

"I thought it was . . ."

"I know what you thought."

Gilbert pulled out a rather long knife. "I know what's in there. Drop it." If she had thought a little quicker, that would have been the moment she shot him.

But she did as she was told. The purse dropped from her hand, clattering to the floor. "Good girl. You were always good at doing what you were told."

"Why me? Why this?"

He played with the knife for a moment. The blade shone in the flickering lights. He laughed again. "I worked so hard, and you are an ungrateful little bitch."

He swung at her and she ducked, his fist making contact with the wall behind her. His eyes were large in his face, crazed with anger. Her palms were sweating. She remembered sizing him up in that tiny office the night they had met. The panic that had coursed through her then was nothing compared with now.

She flung her right fist into his side, hoping she could knock the knife from his hand. His grip on it was tight, but he stumbled back. "You have caused me too much trouble. You have been a pain in my ass since we met. I was going to help you. That's what you don't realize."

"You were going to *kill* me." Her fear was paralyzing. She was small and quick, but she faltered and he grabbed her by the neck, slamming her against the wall. He was stronger than she was, holding her in place. Fury bloomed in red roses on his cheeks.

"I was going to *save* you." The argument didn't matter. She didn't care about the minutiae of it all.

"You killed all of those girls. You killed my sister. You . . . you . . ."

"They were all whores. Just like you, Louise Lloyd. And just like that bitch Laura who left me." His breath was hot against her ear. She tried to recoil, but the blade of the knife was angrily shining and so close to her neck. One quick swipe and it would be over for her.

"What about Annie?" That was one thing she really needed to know.

"I can admit when things don't go to plan."

"What about Bernard Thomas?"

He paused for a moment. His eyes were locked on hers. "He was a stupid bastard. Did whatever I told him to."

"How'd he die?"

"There was arsenic in the tea. I thought you would have figured that out by now."

The lights flickered off. Using all her strength, she pushed him hard, sending him stumbling, and she reached for her gun. It was lying where she'd dropped it, a few paces away. By the time the lights turned on again, she had her pistol aimed on his heart. He dropped the knife and pulled out his own sidearm. "Why don't we make this a fair fight? I always liked that you were clever."

"You liked that I was willing to submit. You were trying to control me." She relaxed, keeping her gun straight. "What was your plan?"

"Thomas was just a red herring—he'll take the fall for the others. But your sister. She was the wild card I didn't expect. I'm going to pin it on you. You're going to kill yourself in the place you loved, filled with remorse."

"No one is going to believe I killed my own sister." She was trying to keep him talking, but for what? Martin hadn't come and no one knew she was here. No one was going to help her.

She'd have to save herself.

"It's all here in your suicide note. Typed, of course. You couldn't stand that your sister was younger, prettier, full of life, full of things you never got to enjoy. It's quite good, really. A masterpiece, if you ask me. Now, Louise, you have to let me do this. Then it'll be all over."

"You watched those girls die." Louise had no intention of letting him get away with any of this.

He shot first, impatient and angry. He wanted to make his vision come true but narrowly missed her. Louise shot second, hitting him directly in the heart.

EPILOGUE

⟁

T HE FOLLOWING HOURS blend together. She's escorted by Martin not to her own home but to Rafael's apartment. He and Rosa Maria have been awake, waiting all night, with Annie and Josie.

She still has blood on her clothes. She may have a streak of it on her face, on her cheek. When she closes her eyes, she can see Gilbert's deranged glare in her mind. Her hands are still shaking, unsteady. In the car, she allows herself to close her eyes for one moment, to really believe it's all over.

When they open the door, Rosa Maria is clearly several drinks in, as is Rafael. It's Josie she goes to first, wrapping her arms around her sister until the younger one protests she can't breathe.

When she pulls away, both sisters are crying, heaving sobs of relief and liberation. A drink is pushed into her hand and she drains it before she says anything.

The thoughts are odd to marry. She briefly thinks that she's technically now a murderer too.

Does it count if it's out of necessity? Does it count if she killed a killer?

If she had hesitated for a moment, it would have been her lying dead on that club floor. She can't think about that now.

Her heart is still thrumming in her chest. Her whole body is on high alert, as if there's someone waiting in the shadows to try to finish the job that wasn't done earlier. She takes a deep breath and is escorted to the piano bench. She sits with her back to the keys as she explains the last few hours: the dark of the club, the plot to pin the murder on her, the need to survive.

There's complete silence in the little apartment, and it's Annie who breaks it first. Her voice wavers on the verge of cracking. "It's over?"

Louise closes her eyes for a moment, letting the rush of the bootleg alcohol, the warmth of the candlelight, ground her. "It's over. It's all over."

Tomorrow, she'll have a new mountain to climb.

But they won. She won.

The news will break early, the dead body found in the former Zodiac. Her name will make headlines again, her photograph on the pages. The *Tribune* and Virginia Thomas will be vindicated.

Life will return to normal. Slowly but surely, the fear will ebb and the summer will remain as a horrible memory. The story will be passed from mother to daughter, repeated until the details are fuzzy. Her story, Harlem's Hero's story, will be passed over time too. People will want to talk to her. But one day, sooner rather than later, she'll be walking down the street and no one will notice her.

Or that's what she hopes.

The idea of being anonymous again is something to aspire to.

And, slowly, the group begins to relax. Rafael plays a tune on the piano, a standard that's much too happy for the current times. Annie is wrapped in the arms of Officer Martin, and for a few more hours, their secrets are kept. Louise averts her eyes. She doesn't know what Annie sees in him. Their romance is one that can never be, and he's not a good man.

Even now, there's a cool grip of guilt and fear on her heart that she knows will never go away. But she has won.

Josie sinks down next to her, curling up like she used to do when she was young. Louise wraps an arm around her sister. Across the living room, Officer Martin and Annie are in the same position. Rosa Maria sits next to Rafael at the piano.

After six dead girls, after a summer of torment, they can finally close this chapter and move on.

Louise extracts a cigarette from the pocket of her trousers, lights it, and exhales a plume of smoke.

There is one thing she is sure of.

Her life will never be the same again.

HISTORICAL NOTE

While it is true that the 1920s were an era of social change in the Western world, with the Eighteenth and Nineteenth Amendments to the Constitution of the United States of America, that change was for white women. The New Negro Movement was started in direct opposition to these inequalities, as a refusal to submit to laws outlined in the Jim Crow era, laws that were active until 1965.

The New Negro Movement was a template for the "respectable" Black man and woman. In "A Study of the Features of the New Negro Woman" by John Henry Adams, published in *The Voice of the New Negro*, one of the seven types of New Black Woman was outlined as "an admirer of Fine Art, a performer on the violin and the piano, a sweet singer, a writer mostly given to essays, a lover of good books, and a home making girl . . ."

Along with social change came the Harlem Renaissance and art by Black people for Black people. Poets like Langston Hughes, writers like Zora Neale Hurston, musical artists like Duke Ellington, and entertainers like Josephine Baker all flourished, as well as new styles of dance and jazz music that reflected the new world.

Every notable contribution to 1920s culture, especially in American cities such as New Orleans, Chicago, and *Dead Dead Girls'* setting, New York City, was made by Black people, then stolen and repackaged for white consumption.

With popular culture and today's media, it's easy to look upon the 1920s with rose-colored glasses and see the decade as nothing but raging Gatsby parties and people doing the Charleston in the street. I would love to subscribe to that notion as well, but it's just not true. After decades of inactivity, the Ku Klux Klan re-formed in 1915 following the release of the KKK-glorifying film *Birth of a Nation*, and minorities were simply not afforded the same freedoms and status as white people.

I could have set Louise's story in modern times, with the continuous and excessive murders of Black and Brown bodies by white people, and almost nothing in the story would have changed; however, this period of creativity, change, and growth is one I'm fascinated with. Louise's story helped me feel closer to my own history and culture.

ACKNOWLEDGMENTS

First, I'd like to thank myself for choosing a dream early and never wavering from my goal. We did it!

Writing a book is a solitary act until it isn't. My deepest thanks and gratitude go to:

Travis Pennington, for finding me in the pile and being the best agent a girl can ask for.

My entire Berkley team, starting with my editor, Michelle Vega, for loving Lou just as much as I do. My marketing team, Natalie Sellars and Jessica Plummer; my publicity team, Dache Rogers and Stephanie Felty; my copy editors; Alison Cnockaert for beautiful book design; and Emily Leonard for flawless cover art.

My family for being my #1 champions, Lou's #1 fans, and my support through writing this novel, especially my mom, Joanne, for being an early reader and always making sure I know all her thoughts. I love you guys!

Sarah Strange for being my best friend and longest friend and for supporting me always.

Lora Maroney for Starbucks dates, making me eat and sleep, and always being there with calm and rational advice.

Meghan (July) Vorisek for reading maybe every iteration of this story that has ever existed and always giving perfect feedback. I love you so, so much.

My friend Vince for all the shitty dinosaurs. Your enthusiasm and gentle encouragement have been everything.

Allan Perkins for being enthusiastic, excited, always cheering me on, and always coming in clutch with a picture of a dog when I really need it.

Sarah Desabrais for watching musicals and going dancing and being the #1 distraction when I needed it.

Molly Clark for absolutely everything, from dissecting Hot Takes on Twitter to introducing me to *Six* to watching the Tony Awards with me. I am so grateful every day that I met you.

Chloé Maxwell. We met in an internet chat room when we were literal children, and you have been there for every step of my writing life.

Stephen Sondheim for creating the lyrics in every show I love. For showing me how. For being an inspiration. Couldn't have finished this hat without you, sir.

The 2018–19 Centennial College publishing class. Special thanks to Matt Doyle for literally holding my hand through the querying process, Cristina DaPonte for unknowingly loaning her name to a minor character, and Cecilia Lyra for overwhelming love and support.

My Toronto Lindy Hop friends for being there when I need to step away from the computer screen, then not being surprised when I spend the majority of a dance writing on my phone. Special thanks for Jasper Palfree for playing those two Ella Fitzgerald songs that time.

Fury Road. I know I'm breaking Rule #1, but you all have listened to me complain and whine and have been there through the good and bad from the inception of this story. Thank you so, so much to all of you and your pets.

The Fury Road Kids. Always, *always* reach for your dreams.

The Berkletes. I couldn't ask for a better group of writers to debut with, and I'm lucky to be one of you.

Black girls everywhere. I see you and I'm so proud of you. Tell your story.

And finally, you. Thank you so much for picking up my novel and taking a chance on a debut author. Thank you so, so much.

DEAD DEAD GIRLS

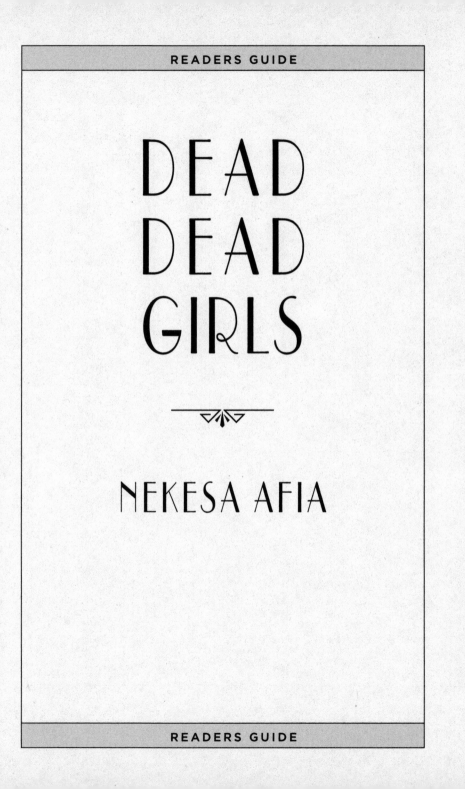

NEKESA AFIA

QUESTIONS FOR DISCUSSION

⏤⟋⋀⟍⏤

1. *Dead Dead Girls* is set in Harlem in 1926. How does the setting of the novel add to and define the story?

2. After Louise frees herself and the other captives from their kidnapper, she's given the name Harlem's Hero. Was this fair? How does society place expectations of heroism on the shoulders of Black women?

3. The Zodiac serves as a home of sorts for Louise, Rosa Maria, and Rafael. What does this say about the concept of "home"? Is it a place, a feeling, or something else?

4. Louise has to keep her relationship with Rosa Maria Moreno secret. What other relationships in the story are secret? What were the ramifications of being gay in the 1920s?

5. Louise's father "raised her and her sisters with the sternness of a military officer" (chapter. 4). How does Louise go above and beyond what is expected of her? What does that say about her place in society and the way she was raised?

6. In chapter 4, Louise realizes that the only reason she is given the unorthodox deal from the detective is because she is a Black Harlem native. What does this say about the police investigation? Was this a ruse?

7. In chapter 7, Louise notes that her twin sisters were always content with their world. What does this tell you about Josie and Celia? Does Louise have a biased opinion of them?

8. In chapter 7, Louise is given the "rules" of the job. How does she follow these rules? How does she disobey them?

9. Louise is given an impossible choice: either help the police solve the Girl Killer case or go to jail. How are the injustices that Black women face in the criminal justice system depicted through the novel? If you were in Louise's shoes, would you take the deal as she did? Why or why not?

10. Although Louise is the eldest of her sisters, she notes that second-born Minna is the daughter their father wanted. What are the differences between the sisters, and what are the similarities?

11. Louise becomes the voice for the girls who are victimized. How does she stand up for them? Why does she do it?

12. Frank Lister notes that girls like Louise will "only ever belong to men like me" (chapter 23). How does he, and, by extension, the Girl Killer, see Black girls and women such as Louise?

13. In chapter 24, Louise tells Annie Taylor, "You can't mistake kindness for someone who's good." What does this tell the reader about Louise's viewpoint? Does Louise trust people easily? Does Annie believe her?

14. Bernard Thomas' story describes Louise as an "ornery waitress" (chapter 48). Louise is outspoken and tries to do the right thing. Does Louise act like a woman "should" for her era? How does her behavior differ from that of a typical 1920s woman?

NEKESA (Nuh-kes-ah) AFIA (Ah-fee-ah) is a Canadian millennial who is doing her best. When she isn't writing, she is either sewing, swing dancing, or actively trying to pet every dog she sees. *Dead Dead Girls* is her debut novel.

CONNECT ONLINE

NekesaAfia.com
🐦 NekesaAfia
📷 NekesaAfia
📘 NekesaAfia

Ready to find
your next great read?

Let us help.

Visit prh.com/nextread